The Mistakes I've Made

A BY THE BAY NOVEL

USA TODAY BESTSELLING AUTHOR

J.L. BERG

ISBN-13: 979-8-9893204-5-5

ALSO BY J.L. BERG

THE WALLS SERIES

Within These Walls

Beyond These Walls

Behind Closed Doors

The Cavenaugh Brothers - A Box Set

THE LOST & FOUND SERIES

Forgetting August

Remembering Everly

BY THE BAY SERIES

The Choices I've Made

The Scars I Bare

The Lies I've Told

The Mistakes I've Made

The Secrets We Keep

By The Bay Series: A Box Set (Books 1-4)

STANDALONES

Fraud

The Tattered Gloves

The Affair

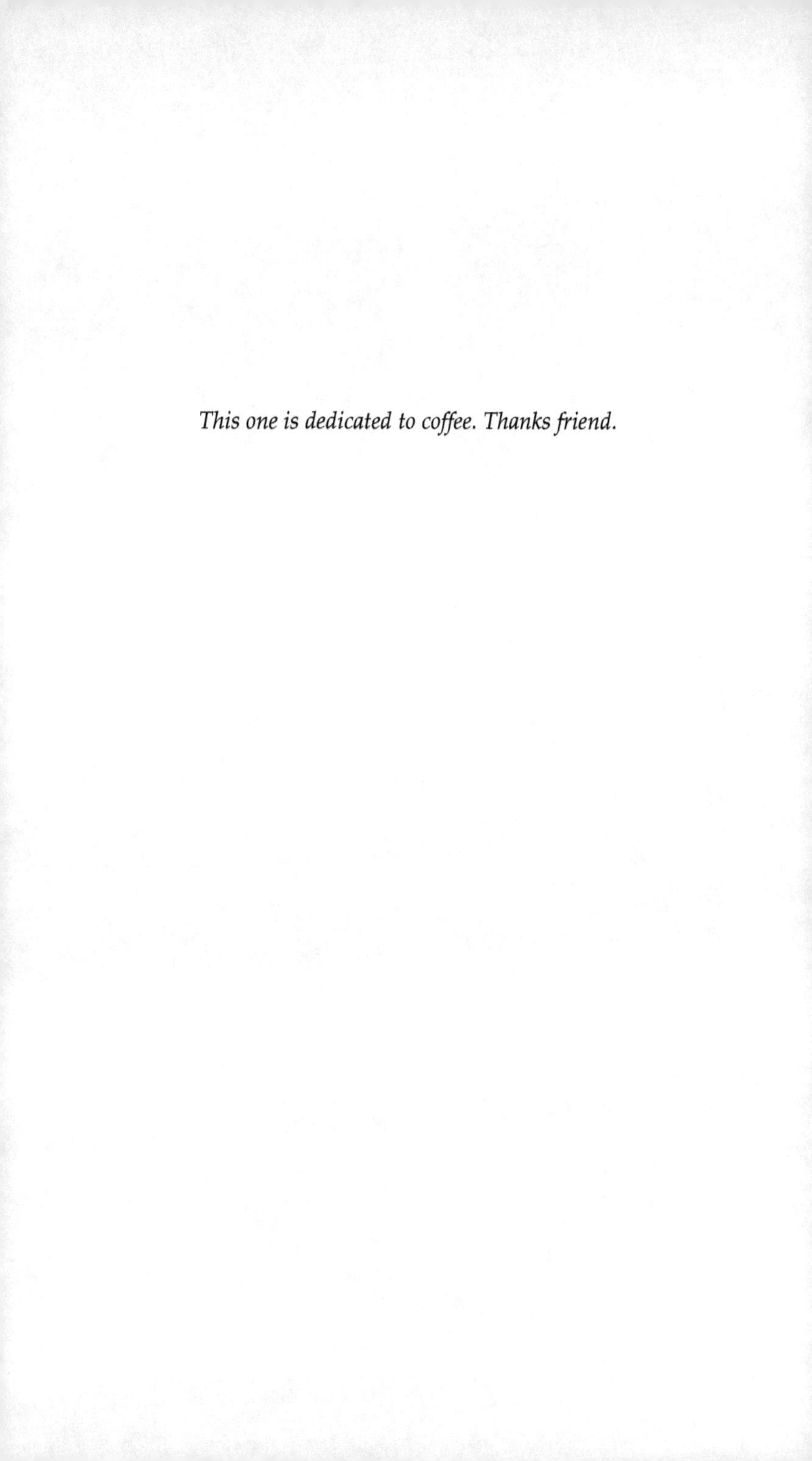

This one is dedicated to coffee. Thanks friend.

PROLOGUE

Taylor

TEN YEARS EARLIER

My eyes cracked open, the sun drifting in through the bedroom window as the weight of yesterday's events hit me full on.

I was a high school graduate.

The moment that rolled-up certificate had passed into my hands, it'd felt like a giant weight had been lifted from my chest.

Freedom.

From the town, from the dark shadow my brother had cast over me since birth.

From everything.

I could finally start anew.

Jumping out of bed, I ignored the slight ache from my head caused from too many late-night beers at the dunes last night, and I headed down the hall. I had only a handful of weeks before I headed off to early enrollment at The University of North Carolina in Greensboro.

I didn't want to waste a second of it.

June was the start of peak season in Ocracoke. Soon, this

island would be filled with pretty, young tourists stuck on family vacations, bored out of their minds, with nothing to do.

And I was just the one to liberate them from the monotony.

Nothing like having your own personal tour guide around the island, right? And I even offered my services for free.

Although tipping was strongly encouraged. Especially the physical kind.

Wearing only a pair of pajama pants, I took the stairs two at a time toward the kitchen in the large, old house where I'd spent my childhood. The hardwood floor creaked as I hit the bottom step with a thud.

No need to be quiet. It was almost noon after all.

Going straight for the cereal, I reached for the largest bowl I could find and poured an embarrassing amount of Apple Jacks into it, but I found myself disappointed when only a handful fell out.

"Hey Ma! Do we have any more Apple Jacks?" I called out.

No one answered.

It was a Saturday, which meant she should be home. She often left the family's fishing business to a few trusted employees over the weekend, choosing to spend her time with her boys and God. Although, now that we were older, she usually dedicated most of the weekend to the latter.

She still managed to pin us down every Sunday evening for supper though. Not that I minded too much. The woman was a wizard in the kitchen.

Abandoning my half-empty bowl of cereal on the kitchen counter, I wandered down the hall into the living room in search of her. But that proved fruitless as well, so I tried the dining room. No one was there either.

Finally, I heard the sound of chatter just outside on the patio.

Sticking my head around the corner, I caught a glimpse of my older brother, Dean, and the familiar brown curls of my mother as they huddled together over several notebooks spread out over the glass table we sometimes used for cookouts.

Why they were sitting out there in the hot weather was beyond me. It might only be early June, but we were experiencing record heat, and the temperature had probably already surpassed ninety outside. I could see the sweat dripping down my brother's temples as frown lines creased his forehead. And my mom? The look on her face was grim.

No, not grim. It was devastating.

The kid in me—the somewhat selfish teenager who didn't want to ruin his fun-filled day of flirting with tourists and sunbathing at the beach—decided to retreat.

Better leave this one to the grown-ups, I decided.

Just as I was about to tiptoe back to the kitchen and make do with my half a bowl of Apple Jacks, Dean noticed me playing Peeping Tom and immediately stood up.

"Damn it," I cursed under my breath.

There went my plans for the day. No doubt he was going to put me to work, doing one thing or another. Dean was only five years older, but it felt like ten. Without our dad around, he'd taken the older brother role to heart. He'd skipped college to help Mama with the family business, and he took it all really seriously.

Sometimes, I swore, he had been born with a fishing pole in his hands, ready to fill my dead father's shoes the first chance he got. Me? I didn't hate it, but I could probably find a dozen other things I'd rather be doing than discussing tides and cleaning fish guts off the decks of a dozen boats.

"What are you doing?" he whispered as he stepped inside, wiping his brow with the bottom of his T-shirt.

"I could ask you the same thing. It's hotter than the devil's armpit out there."

"Charming," he said, rolling his eyes as he held up his wrist at eye-level. A quick glance at his watch had judgment written all over his face. "You know it's almost noon?"

"Yeah. So?"

Letting out a disgruntled sigh, he motioned for me to follow him. I'd learned over the years to not mess with my big brother, so I gave into the inevitable and followed him. To do otherwise usually resulted in purple nurples or some other sort of uncomfortable situation.

The disapproving glare only worsened when he saw my cereal on the counter, but he chose not to comment on it. Instead, he went for the refrigerator and grabbed a bottle of water, and I watched as he drained it in seconds.

"Sit down," he commanded.

Looking longingly at my bowl, I begrudgingly did as I had been told, taking a seat at the kitchen table as he did the same.

"I was going to wait to tell you this," he said, his gaze shifting to the floor as he let out a huff of air. "Actually, you know what? Just eat your Apple Jacks and go do whatever it was you were going to do today."

He'd just given me my out. It was exactly what I wanted, but something in the way he said it grated on my nerves. Maybe it was the disparaging tone of his voice or the shake of his head as he cupped his forehead in his hand.

He looked lost.

My brother never looked lost.

"Tell me," I said. "I want to know what's going on. Does this have to do with what you were talking to Mom about, all secret-like, outside?"

He nodded.

"Well then, tell me. If it has to do with the family, it has to do with me."

His brows lifted, as if he finally agreed. "The business isn't doing so great. We're having serious financial difficulties."

"But I thought we were doing better since Abernathy's Fishing Company closed last year. More fish for us, right?"

His head tilted, and he began to rub his temple like I'd just said the stupidest thing in the world.

Maybe I had. I really didn't know shit about our business other than what they told me.

"They closed because they had to," he explained. "And, if we don't figure something out, we might need to as well."

"Oh."

Silence fell between us as I tried to sort all this out.

"Why didn't you tell me sooner? Abernathy's has been closed for a while. If we've been having problems for so long, how come you're just telling me now?"

He leaned forward in his chair, his gaze leveling with mine. "Because, up until yesterday, you were a kid Taylor. And you deserved to be a kid for as long as possible."

"But, now, I'm not," I said, filling in the rest of what I assumed he was thinking.

I'd woken up that morning, thinking of only one thing.

Freedom.

Adulthood equaled freedom, right? Freedom to wake up when I wanted—well, I'd already done that, I guessed. But what about the freedom to go where I wanted, when I wanted, and the freedom to choose my destiny…

In less than an hour, my brother managed to teach me that, no, adulthood means so much more. I had responsibilities now. My uncomplicated summer plans of picking up chicks at the marina and playing tour guide suddenly felt unimportant next to the possibility of our business collapsing.

How would we live? It wasn't like there were a lot of job opportunities around here.

"What can I do to help?" I asked, remembering the sad look on my mother's face as she'd sat outside with my brother in the heat, probably so I wouldn't overhear what they were saying.

Well, no more, I thought. *No more.*

It was time I stepped up and took my place.
At least until the summer ended.
Then I'd go fulfill my destiny in Greensboro.
Sorry, ladies. This summer belongs to my family.
Time to get us back on track.

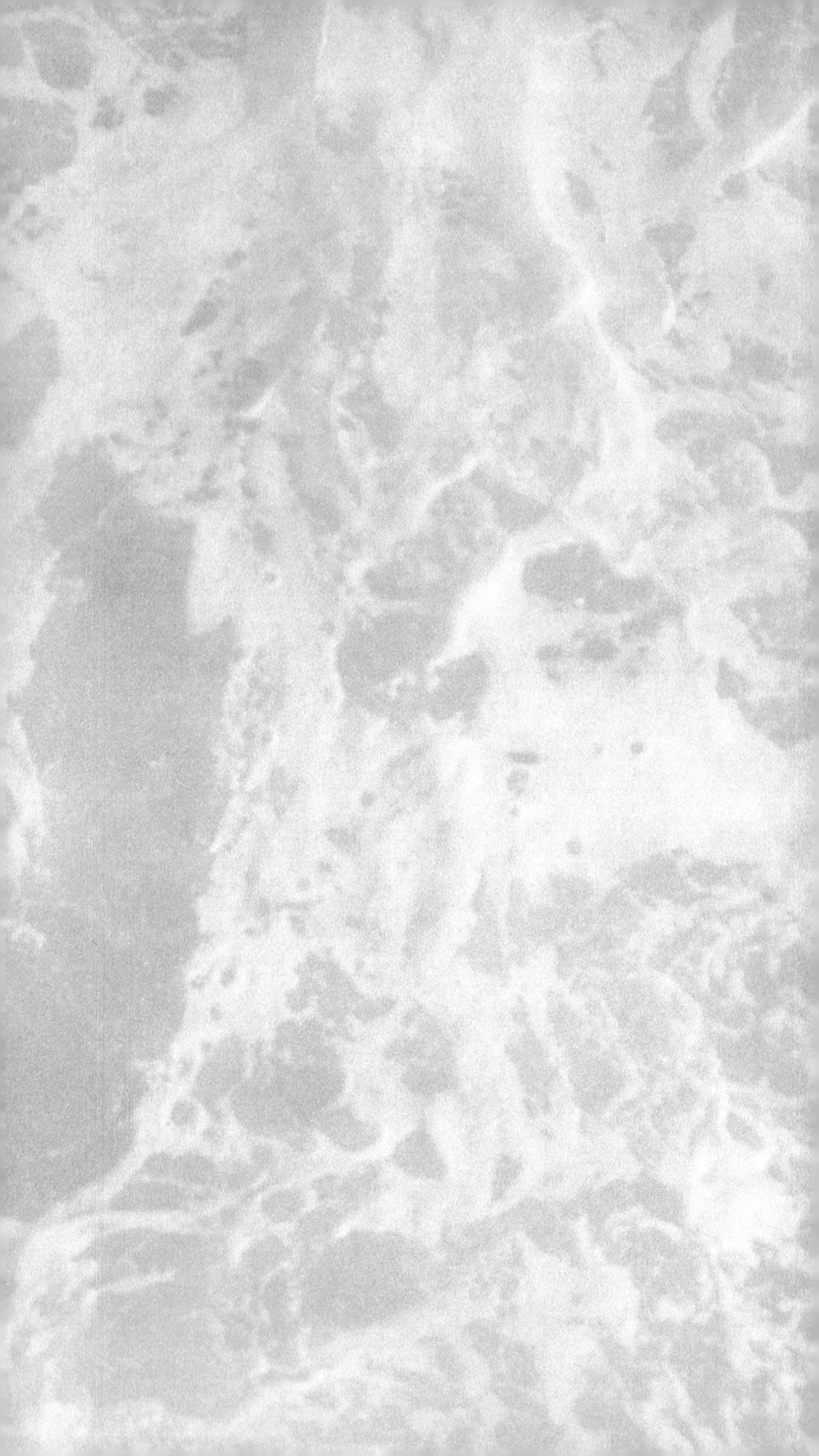

CHAPTER ONE

Taylor

My alarm woke me, as it did every day. The blaring sound of the radio made my eyes spring open, the sun barely breaking over the horizon on a new day.

"Jesus," Sierra cursed beside me. "What the hell is that?"

"It's called an alarm," I said, throwing the covers off me. The cool air hit my bare skin at once, and I immediately missed the warmth of my bed. "It's what responsible people use to wake up in the morning."

I heard her groan into the pillow. The sight of her naked body moving underneath those sheets did all sorts of things to me as I dragged myself out of bed.

"I'm responsible," she argued.

I listened as she rustled out of my bed, and by the time I managed to pick up a shirt and shorts for my morning run, she had found her own set of clothes.

"You're a fifth-year college student, taking a semester off to spend time with your grandparents on a nearly deserted island."

She finished pulling her shirt over her head, just in time to give me a hard stare. "I am a double major. That takes longer, and I happen to like my grandparents and this island, even in the low season."

My brow lifted. I didn't believe her for a second.

The truth was, she'd broken up with her boyfriend last semester and taken it hard, and she was using Ocracoke—this little blip of an island town where her grandparents had chosen to retire—as a place to hide out while she tried to get over her heartbreak.

I was just someone she used to pass the time, and I was more than okay with our arrangement because, as a guy who didn't do more than casual dating, *low season*, as she'd called it, was also a dry season for me—at least in the ladies department.

"Now, what does a girl need to do to get breakfast around here?" she asked, giving me a pouty look that made me all sorts of uncomfortable.

And not in the *there's a naked girl in my bed* sort of way.

"Creep back to your Grandpop's place and make some there?" I suggested. I watched as her pout only deepened. "Come on, Sierra. You know I don't do breakfast. Hell, I'm already a dead man if Jimmy finds out you've been sleeping over at my place. You know he flew me and my mom to the hospital when my brother was nearly killed on that ferry? He's a good guy, your grandpop."

"Yeah"—she nodded, her hands going to the pockets of her jeans—"he is."

"Look, if this is getting to be too much for you, maybe we should just call it quits before anyone gets—"

"No," she said a bit too quickly. "I'm fine. Really." A fake smile pulled at her cheeks. "Just hungry. I'll grab something when I get home, and you're right. We wouldn't want Grandpoppy finding out about this. God knows he doesn't need the spike in his blood pressure. Go ahead and grab your run, I'll let myself out."

"Okay," I replied, knowing full well this wouldn't be the last time we saw each other—the town was too small for that

—but it would definitely be the last time we saw each other like this.

Because, if there was one thing I didn't do, it was complicated.

<hr>

My morning jog did nothing to help clear my head, and after I came home to an empty house, I noticed how Sierra had tidied up after herself. The twinge of guilt I felt for even allowing this thing between us to move past drunken flirting only grew as I drove into work.

"Dude, you look like shit, little brother," Dean said the moment I stepped into the office.

"Thanks," I replied. "That's real kind of you. I'd say the same, but…well, you always look like shit."

He chuckled, shaking his head, as I took a seat at my desk. I looked out over the marina. The sun beat down onto the water which scattered tiny, glistening diamond lights across the bay.

I shook my head.

Damn, it was early.

Too damn early.

"Did you make coffee?" I asked, stretching my back against the old leather chair.

I'd managed to pull this business out of the brink of bankruptcy twice—most recently when my brother's medical bills from the ferry explosion had nearly crippled us—yet, somehow, we still had these piece-of-shit office chairs that probably predated both of us.

No one could argue that the Sutherlands were excessive with money; that was for sure.

"Of course," he said. "I have a child who refuses to sleep at night because it's precious hours she could be learning. How do you think I survive? I'm already two cups in."

I chuckled, loving that my brother had laid such a fierce

claim on his stepdaughter. Honestly, I had too. Lizzie was a keeper for sure.

"Good," I said.

Wasting no time, I made a beeline toward the counter in the back we had set up for break times. There was a mini fridge and one of those fancy new coffeepots with the individual pods for customers during the slow, winter months when they waited indoors for scenic tours. But, for the two of us, we still relied on the regular drip machine.

"Is there a particular reason you look like shit today, or is it a new look you're going for?"

Only my big brother could hassle me like this without getting a beat-down.

I let out a sigh, pouring my coffee as he waited for an answer.

"Sierra," I finally said.

"Jimmy's granddaughter? That Sierra?"

I nodded, having just added an ample amount of flavored creamer to my giant cup of coffee.

"Man, I thought you were done with that?"

I merely shrugged.

"You know he'll kill you if he finds out. Like *drag your ass onto that puddle jumper of a plane of his and drop you in the middle of the ocean* kill you."

I took a long sip of coffee. It was like liquid fuel to my brain cells, and I instantly felt better.

God, I loved coffee.

"It's not a big deal."

"Really?" he said, his brow rising in disbelief as both arms folded in front of him.

I had to force myself not to glance in the direction of his prosthetic arm.

Even to this day, I couldn't help but look.

Up until the night Dean had lost his arm in that ferry accident, I'd always told myself that staying here in Ocracoke was temporary. That one day, I'd finally get out of here and fulfill all those dreams I'd had in high school. I'd go to college, do something other than this. But, the moment I had seen him in that hospital bed—so lost and helpless, my super-hero of a big brother—I'd known.

I wasn't going anywhere.

Ever.

"If it's no big deal, then why are you chugging down caffeine like it's whiskey?"

I looked down at my mostly empty coffee cup, realizing he was right. I was already in need of a refill.

"She wanted breakfast this morning."

A smug smirk tugged at the corner of my brother's stupid face before it quickly disappeared. He knew breakfast was the kiss of death in my book.

"Have you ever thought about maybe, one of these times, saying yes to breakfast? Obviously not with Sierra because of the whole *her Grandpops will kill you* thing, but maybe someone else? It is just a meal after all."

"No," I answered immediately, finishing off my coffee.

"Jesus, Taylor. At least think it through."

I shrugged and headed back to the coffeepot for a refill. "I don't need to think it through. I'm perfectly happy with my current arrangement."

He waited as I did my usual routine of copious amounts of creamer to coffee before speaking again, "You mean, you're perfectly happy with banging every single tourist you meet and the occasional grandchild of a family friend even if it means possible dismemberment on your part."

"Jimmy won't hurt me," I scoffed. "He's the most lovable—"

"That guy was a fighter pilot in Vietnam. I'm pretty sure he got a medal for how many enemy planes he shot down. He's a beast."

"Really? Well, that's…unsettling."

"So, stop fucking his granddaughter then!"

"I am! I did, I mean. Remember, breakfast?"

He let out a huff. "Don't you want to have something real with someone?"

"Like you and Cora?"

His smile softened at the mere mention of his wife. They'd been married less than a year, and they still had that glow about them. It was disgusting.

"Yeah," he said.

Running my hands through my light-brown hair, I let his question sink in, giving it a few seconds of my time; he was my big brother after all.

"Not really," I finally answered. "Honestly, I'm good, Dean. Stop trying to save me. I know, now that you're all in love or whatever, you feel it's your mission to make sure everyone else around you is just as happy as you are, but I'm really good. Promise."

He eyed me warily.

"Besides, I seem to remember that not too long ago, the name on every young tourist's lips was a different Sutherland brother entirely."

"That was a long time ago," he argued. "And let me tell you something; it got tiresome. The chase, the same boring conversation, the awkward morning after."

"So, you thought it'd be a better idea to marry your best friend?"

His eyes narrowed as I mentally high-fived myself for that jab.

"It wasn't my best decision, but thankfully, Molly and I came to our senses."

Oh no, I wasn't letting him off that easy.

"You mean, Jake came back to town and took what was rightfully his. Man, have you ever noticed how much drama this little town has going on? It's like there's a mini soap opera going on every time I turn around."

"Yeah, weird," he answered, clearly annoyed. "Anyway, what I'm trying to say is—"

"What you're trying to say is that your way—love and

commitment and all that—is the best and, obviously, the only way. But here's the thing, Dean. I've been handling things on my own for a while now. While you were recovering from your accident, I was busting my ass off, rebuilding this company like I had done time and time before that. So, don't come in here and act all big brother on me like you did when we were kids. I love you; I do. But we're past the age for love advice, okay?"

He looked a bit taken aback, and I felt bad for the harshness of my tone, but I wouldn't apologize for my lifestyle.

Not when he'd traveled the same path only a few years earlier.

"Okay," he finally agreed.

"Good. Now, if you'll excuse me, I've got to prep for an early morning tour—"

I was cut off by the bell on the office door.

Turning around, I saw our mother flying through it, her eyes wide and full of panic like she was being chased here by a wild animal.

It wasn't an impossibility, I guessed, given the town we lived in.

"You'll never guess what I just heard!"

Oh great, town gossip.

Just what I needed to hear at the ass crack of dawn on Thursday morning.

"I'd better put on another pot of coffee," Dean groaned.

"Make it a strong one."

As a rule, news of any kind spread like wildfire in our small town.

You could get in an argument with your spouse in the morning on one side of the island, and by noon, it was old news, having already reached the other side and back again by the time everyone finished their second cup of coffee.

So, it was no surprise that something as big as this had caused a flurry of activity; so much so that an emergency meeting had been called that very night to try to help calm everyone's nerves.

Mine included.

Being low season, we met at By the Bay, a popular inn owned by none other than Molly Jameson, one of Dean's best friends and ex-fiancée. They were both married now—to other people. Molly was married to her high school sweetheart, Jake, the town doctor, and Dean had just recently married Cora, the town nurse.

Honestly, it kind of made me ill, how well-adjusted and happy they all were.

I watched as they all took seats next to each other, the girls complimenting each other on outfit choices while crooning over baby Ruby as the guys joked.

Not a single bit of animosity or latent jealousy floating about.

Talk about weird.

"Hey."

I looked up to see Millie McIntyre, Molly's younger sister and my former classmate from high school, although now she was Millie Fisher, since she'd recently been married herself.

"Hey yourself," I said as she helped guide her husband, Aiden, to a seat beside her.

Although I didn't know the British artist well, I did know Millie, having gotten the chance to reacquaint myself with my good friend since her move back home just over a year ago. She'd come back to help out Molly during her maternity leave and ended up falling in love with Aiden, who was internationally recognized for his stone sculptures and the fact that he did them almost completely blind.

"Do you know what's going on?" she asked. "All I know is that something was sold and it's a big freaking deal because my mom said, 'Get your ass to that meeting, Millie. All the other business owners will be there, and you'll look stupid if you're not.' So, here I am."

I laughed. "There's no way your mom said the word *ass*."

She shrugged as Aiden chuckled. The dark glasses he wore to help enhance what little sight he had left made it hard to see his full expression.

"Okay, so I might be paraphrasing, but she did say it was important."

"You know that dive of a hotel along the marina?" I asked.

"Of course. Is that what sold? I told my sister to buy it months ago."

I let out a sigh. "Well, it's too bad she didn't. Maybe then we wouldn't be in this shithole of a mess."

"Why? Who did buy it?"

"Hart International."

"Oh fuck," Aiden said under his breath, causing his wife to turn abruptly toward him and then back to me, her eyes wide with alarm.

"Okay! Hello!" my mother said loudly at the front of the room. "We're going to get started. I've been asked to lead, as the seller of the hotel in question, The Cozy Hotel, prefers to not participate."

I bet she doesn't, I thought to myself. *Selfish bitch. I bet the old hag took all that money they'd given her and hopped the first ferry out of here.*

"Hart International? Like the resorts?" Millie whispered into my ear. "What do they want with us?"

I let out a sigh as my mother began, "We're just going to do this casual-style, so does anyone have any questions?"

A million hands shot up in the air.

"Nothing good," I answered back. "Nothing damn good."

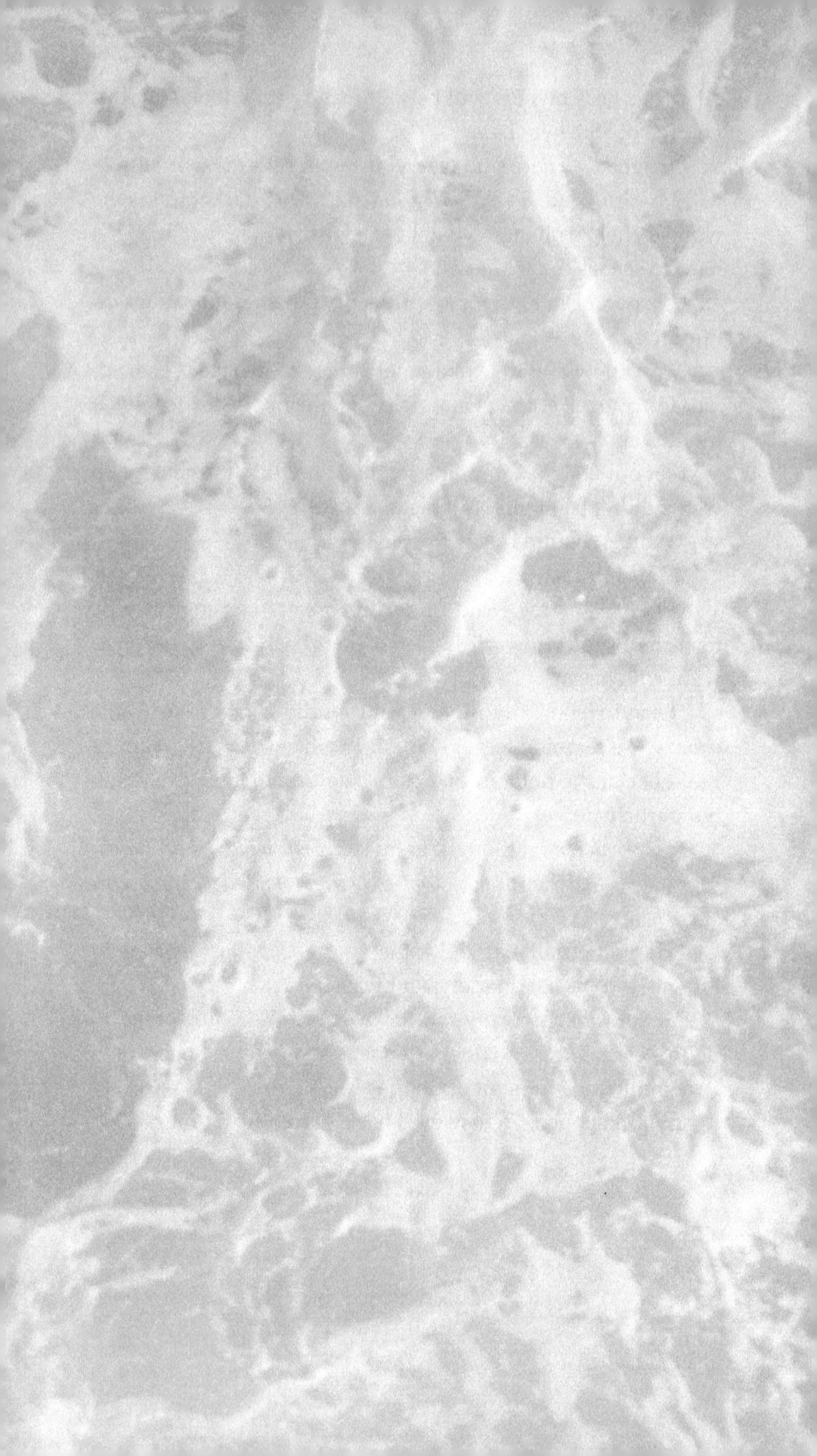

CHAPTER TWO

Leilani

"Just set the canapés down right there," I instructed, nervously buzzing around the conference table, making sure every little detail was taken care of.

"Like this?" my coworker and best friend, Piper, asked, adjusting the large platter just so.

I surveyed the lunch spread, feeling pretty proud of myself.

"Yes." I nodded. "I think that's perfect."

We both stepped back to appreciate our hard work. I'd planned this menu weeks ago, ordering food from my father's favorite restaurants—the main course from a little place he'd loved to take me and my mother to when I was little, which was famous for their authentic Polynesian fare, and then dessert was straight-up Italian, like his Nonna used to make.

"You do realize that there is enough food here to feed the entire floor, right?" Piper joked. Her hand reached toward the perfect Italian desserts I'd plated on delicate china I'd brought from my own apartment.

"Don't you dare," I said, slapping it away. "And, yes, I realize that, but this is special. It's not every day that my father comes home, and I want to make it special."

"You mean you want to woo him with your superior skills so that he'll finally promote you."

I defensively folded my arms across my chest, the polka-dot blouse I'd chosen just for this occasion wrinkling beneath my tight embrace. "Would it kill him? I mean, would it really?"

"He doesn't show favoritism, that's for sure. That man is making you earn your keep."

"No! He's making me work ten times harder; that's what he's doing. Do you know Becky Knowles?"

Piper's blonde eyebrows rose, but she went with it. She was used to my abrupt change of topics. We'd been friends since college, both attending the University of Hawaii, here in Honolulu. We'd become fast friends one night at a freshman mixer when I, who was well on my way to blending perfectly into the wall, overheard her discussing Hogwarts houses with a guy so desperate to get in her pants, he was willing to try to play along.

His deadly mistake? Saying he'd laughed when that "old dude died."

I'd stepped in before she committed murder or tried to off him with an unforgivable curse.

The fact that she, too, was majoring in interior design had just sealed the deal.

We'd been inseparable ever since.

"Of course I know Becky Knowles. Although I'm not sure she goes by Becky anymore. Not since college."

I let out an annoyed huff.

"Okay, okay," she said, holding out her hands in defeat. "Yes, I know Becky. What about her?"

"She was just given the Chicago project."

Piper's eyes widened. "You mean, that big one? The old historic hotel right on the water? Damn."

And the way she'd said the last word said it all. *Day-um.*

"Exactly."

"Didn't she just start here—"

"A year ago," I confirmed, looking over my ridiculous attempt to wrangle my dad into a promotion that should have been mine by birthright alone. "She's about to temporarily relocate halfway across the country to head up a major remodel worth millions while we sit here, at the top of this high-rise, gathering dust."

"Ew, I'm not dusty," she argued, her pert little nose pointed sky-high in defiance.

"Really? What was the last project you worked on? The last viable thing you did for this company?"

That confidence she wore suddenly slipped, and a strong pout formed on her porcelain skin. "Fine, but when you present this amazing meal to your daddy, you'd better make sure you mention my name. Otherwise—"

"I know, I know. You'll go to The Wizarding World of Harry Potter without me."

"And?" she pressed.

"And…you'll drink all the Butterbeer without me."

"You bet your ass I will. And I'll send you selfies the whole time, too."

I shook my head. "Well, that's just evil."

She shrugged. "I'm a Slytherin. What do you expect?" Making a last-minute adjustment to the salad bowl, she patted my shoulder and took my hand. "Okay, you've got this. Remember what we talked about?"

"Stick to the talking points—my strengths as a team player and a leader and the fact that I've committed myself to this company for six long-ass years."

"Might be good to leave off the word *ass*."

"Right," I agreed.

"And what are we avoiding?"

I let out a sigh. "That I'm entitled to it and that I deserve the promotion because he's my father."

"Good." She smiled. "I think you're ready."

"Great, because"—I looked at the time on my phone—"I think he's just about to step out of his meeting."

Her hand squeezed mine before she pulled me into one last hug. "Good luck, and remember, talk me up!"

I laughed, before she stepped back and turned toward the door.

"You're going to be fabulous."

I nodded, knowing she was right.

This was my time to shine.

My father had always wanted me to earn my success, hating the title *hotel heiress* and terrified that his daughter would somehow become the next Paris Hilton. He'd put strict rules on me while I was growing up. No extravagances, no access to my trust fund until a certain age, and everything had to be earned. After four years of college and six years of working in the trenches, I was finally going to show him all the hard work I'd accomplished.

Look out, Becky Knowles. I'm right behind you.

Checking my phone again, I made a mental note of the time. It was a few minutes past noon, but meetings were known to drag late around here, so I decided to open up my laptop while I waited and peruse the company database.

My father had made a name for himself decades ago when I was nothing more than a toddler. Back then, Hart Hotels had been just a small chain here in Hawaii, which had been started by my grandparents, who'd met during World War II.

My grandfather, who had been stationed at Pearl Harbor, had fallen in love with the island and then with my grandmother. After the war, they'd opened the first Hart hotel, a small bungalow-style inn that welcomed guests from all over the world. Over the years, my grandparents had been fortunate to open several more and lived a comfortable lifestyle.

But it was my father who had really taken it to a global level, creating Hart International—a company that, in only a matter of a couple of years, now rivaled even the biggest hotel chains.

Looking through the database, I pulled up the latest acquisitions, seeing what properties my father had purchased. This was something he was known for—scooping up less than desirable properties in glamorous locations and turning them into something no one had expected. At any time, we had about a dozen hotels in progress globally.

These would be the future of the company over the next few months, if not years, and I wanted in. I wanted in so badly that I could taste it. Clicking on several, I could see he'd bought a property in Paris, one in Bali, and several other island locations I didn't recognize, all varying in size and price.

Honestly, I'd take any of them as long as I wasn't stuck in this building anymore. I just wanted to make my mark. Hell, I'd even take Chicago with its arctic winters if it meant something different for a change.

I really hated that I was jealous of Becky.

I'd written her a letter of recommendation for this job as a favor since we'd been friends in college, and now, she was off living my dream.

I checked the clock again.

Thirty minutes past twelve.

I started to get antsy.

My father was a talker and a known perfectionist. This could take a while. Thankfully, the food could keep awhile longer.

Fifteen minutes and two games of solitaire later, a knock came at the door. I jumped to my feet and tried to smooth the wrinkles in my blouse as the handle turned. My heart pounded, and I wondered if that was a normal reaction to a daughter seeing her father.

I also tried to remember the last time I'd seen him.

Six months?

Nine maybe?

Had we spent Christmas together? No, he'd canceled.

Letting go of my nerves, I plastered on a confident smile,

only to feel it shatter when my father's assistant walked through the door.

I already knew what that meant.

"Hi Leilani," he said, a careful tone he'd used with me on more than one occasion. In fact, I recalled the same formal cadence in his voice when he'd called only hours before my father was to arrive for Christmas dinner, telling me he'd had a change of plans. "I'm so sorry, but your father—"

"Isn't coming," I said, finishing his sentence for him. "What's his excuse this time?"

Troy, who wasn't much older than myself, gave me a sort of nod. His head tilted to the side, and his lips pursed.

I got it.

He couldn't say.

Or wouldn't.

"Well, thanks for doing his dirty work," I said. "You want a canapé? They're the best in the city."

His eyebrows lifted as I motioned to the pretty platter of desserts. It was the most emotion I'd seen. Well, the truest emotion, I guessed, considering my dad had basically turned him into a walking, talking robot.

"Uh, no, but thank you."

"Of course," I said, my lip quivering as I fought off tears.

If there was one thing that could stop a man in his tracks, even a half-cyborg like Troy, it was tears. He stood frozen in place, staring at me, unsure of what to do as I sniffled into the palm of my hand.

Finally, his cyborg programming must have kicked back in because he turned toward the door to leave.

"Troy?" I said meekly, completely hating myself for the tears currently trailing down my cheeks.

"Yes, Miss Hart?"

"Do you think you could do me a favor and not tell my father about the crying?"

He didn't say a word, but I saw a brief nod in my direction before he grabbed the door handle and exited.

Well, at least the tin man of an assistant still had a sliver of a heart left. There was some hope left for him after all.

Unfortunately though, there wasn't even a scrap left for me.

"You sure you want to drink that?" Piper asked, pointing to the double shot that had just magically appeared at our table.

And by magically, I meant, I'd waved my finger, and the cute bartender I'd massively tipped to keep the alcohol flowing in my direction had walked his adorable butt over here and placed it in front of me.

He might have also dropped a note with his phone number too, but party-pooper Piper had snatched that out of my hands before I could get any ideas.

Something about making enough bad decisions for one night.

Whatever.

The night was just getting started, and the bar was filled with tons of people just waiting to make poor choices. To our right was a rambunctious bachelor party, and to our left was some sort of girls' night out. Their shrill laughs made my eardrums hurt, but I kind of dug eavesdropping on their conversations.

"Why would you even ask that question?" I gave her a wide-eyed look that caused her to roll her own set of peepers.

"Why? Because this isn't you, Lani! Flirting with the bartender, drinking shots... You're acting out, and you know it."

I gave her a look that said she was seriously destroying my buzz.

"Fine," she relented. "But don't call me in the morning, complaining about your massive headache."

I made a sound from my lips that reminded me a lot of the

noise Piper's little niece made when she was spitting out baby food.

"Please. Like I'd ever do that."

We both knew I would. It was how this whole friendship thing worked. She took care of me, and I took care of her. It was symbiotic…well, mostly. I thought Piper gave more than her fair share of motivational speeches.

Especially when it came to my dad.

That was exactly why we were in a bar and why I was currently ordering shots like I was a college freshman on spring break in Cozumel.

Or at least, I thought I was.

I really had no idea the frequency of shots ordered on a spring break in college. Piper and I'd spent our spring breaks ordering room service in my high-rise penthouse while binge-watching all the TV shows we'd missed during the year.

"Why didn't we ever do anything fun for spring break?" I blurted out, deciding to sip my latest round of shots. My lips were starting to feel sort of tingly, and I had a nice buzz going. No use in ruining it.

"Because you were always hopeful that your father would show," she said. "Every year, you'd send him the dates of every break we had, from fall break to Christmas and right through to spring. And every year, he'd miss every last one of them."

Grabbing my shot, I downed it.

So much for sipping, I thought.

The bachelor party nearby cheered me on, causing me to blush as I held up my empty shot glass in their direction. The girls next to us laughed. I couldn't help but overhear one of them talking about a recent vacation. I was in the hotel busi-ness; it was kind of my whole life. And wasn't that just a little sad?

"The hotel was horrible. Absolutely horrible. I don't know what my husband was thinking when he booked it. Thank

God it's for sale. Maybe someone decent will buy it or, better yet, bulldoze the thing!"

Everyone laughed.

"But the town was as cute as a button. Like small-town Americana meets island life."

"Why do you do this to yourself?" Piper asked, pulling me back, front and center.

"Do what?"

"Torture yourself over your father," she said.

"I don't know, honestly. I mean, I can't even remember the last time I saw him."

"We saw him at the Christmas party," she said with an ounce of hope.

"That was a company party, and he said a few awkward words to me, just like he did to everyone else."

"He hasn't been the same since—"

"My mom died. Well, you know what? That was thirteen years ago. The rest of us learned how to move on. Why can't he?"

Silence fell between us, and it was times like this when I knew Piper really deserved something close to sainthood. In seconds I'd gone from a playful drunk, flirting with the bartender, to a woeful heiress, complaining about her daddy issues, and my best friend had barely batted an eyelash.

"You deserve better," she said, taking my hand in her own. "And one day, your father's going to wake up from that coma he's put himself in and see the amazing woman you've become while he's been too busy to notice."

"And then will he give me a job?"

"Is that all you're after? A job?"

I shrugged.

"You have a job, remember?" she reminded me. "And your dad will promote you. Eventually. We might just need to get a little creative on how we get his attention next time."

For some reason, her words settled at just the right moment.

Maybe it was the alcohol.

Maybe it was the girls laughing in the booth next to me or the fact that, in a couple of weeks, another year would pass without my mother around.

"Creative you say?"

"Oh no." Piper's eyes went wide with the look of panic she got whenever she knew I was getting a wild but genius idea.

It was the same look she'd had on her face the night I talked her into matching lightning bolt tattoos on our ankles. She'd been scared out of her mind when we walked into that tattoo parlor, but she'd walked out, grinning like a damn fool after that burly biker dude tatted up her ankle.

"What are you going to do?" she asked, her voice already rising an octave.

"Shut up. I'm thinking," I said before turning my chair toward the cackling girls next to us.

"Oh God, what are you doing?" she said as I waved my hand behind me in an attempt to get her to shut up.

"Hey," I said in my most uppity, girlie-girl voice possible. "I'm sorry to butt in, but I heard you speaking about a hotel—"

"Oh my God, yes!" one of the women answered. She didn't seem fazed at all that I'd been eavesdropping or the fact that I was a total stranger.

The group of women was probably our age, maybe a bit older. Young mothers out for a night on the town. Most of them had rocks the size of my fist on their left ring fingers and were dressed head to toe in designer clothing.

Honestly, I was surprised I didn't know any of them.

High society in Honolulu was a tight-knit community, full of backstabbing, gossip, and climbing your way to the top. I'd done a good job of keeping out of the way, but I would always be the daughter of Stephen Hart, hotel tycoon. It was a hard title to run away from.

"My bestie and I are planning a little vacay for spring break next year, and I overheard you talking about that cute little town…" I literally hated myself right now. I sounded like a sorority girl from the movie *Legally Blonde*, but I had a feeling this was what these particular women identified with, and I was right.

Their fake blonde heads bobbed up and down as they gave me the lowdown.

"And you said it's where?"

"Ocracoke. North Carolina. It's just darling. But don't stay at the hotel there," she warned. "It's awful."

"Oh, I don't plan on staying there," I said with a mischievous grin as I turned back to a worried-looking Piper. "I'm going to buy it."

As it turned out, my dear old daddy was one step ahead of me and had actually bought the property in question only days earlier.

Seemed my father and I had similar taste.

That, or fate just had a wicked sense of humor.

Either way, it made this quest-for-independence thing a whole lot easier in a way. I'd planned on just buying the property myself with the trust fund he'd set up for me years ago—the one I hadn't touched once in my entire adult life in a desperate attempt to prove to him just how responsible I was.

In my drunken haze, this plan had all seemed pretty cut-and-dried. Buy hotel, make it amazing, and finally prove to my father just how worthy I was of his adoration.

The fact that he'd bought it first?

Well, it definitely made things a bit more interesting.

And by interesting, I meant terrifying. Because, now, if I failed, it wouldn't be just my money I was wasting.

It would be my father's.

Of course, I had to get to it first.

All that required was a couple of white lies.

Okay, a few giant lies.

But the building did have my name on the side of it, and damn it, I deserved this chance. And I was going to take it. No more waiting around in empty conference rooms while my father slipped out the back to avoid seeing me.

There was no way he'd be able to ignore this.

Piper, being the strict rule-follower that she was, wanted nothing to do with my evil scheme, and I didn't blame her. If and when I got caught by my father, I had a number of things to fall back on—my stellar personality, guilt over the fact that he'd basically checked out after my mom died, followed by tears, and then finally, the fact that I was an only child and if he sacked me, who else would he pass this company on to?

Piper, on the other hand, basically had her good work ethic and talent, which would continue to be wasted if I didn't get us out of this office and knee deep into a project of our own.

So, for now, I was solo.

No one deserved to be on the brunt end of my father's wrath for pulling a stunt like this, except for me.

So, after a bit of hacking, thanks to a few tricks I'd learned from a brief interlude with a certain IT guy, I was on a company jet, headed for North Carolina, ready to check out my first solo project.

It didn't take long for Piper to track me down. A mere fifteen minutes in the air, and my cell phone started blowing up, her distinctive ringtone filling the small space with a smooth R&B jam that reminded me of her quirky sense of humor.

"Where the hell are you?" she demanded.

"Well, hello to you, too!"

"Please tell me you didn't do what I think you did."

I looked out the window of the jet. There was nothing but

water for hundreds of miles, the Pacific Ocean sparkling below like a blue sequined blanket.

"It depends," I said. "What do you think I did?"

I heard a heavy sigh on the other end. Well, not quite a sigh. It was more of an exaggerated huff. "What I think you did is hacked into the company's database—although I have no idea how—and put your name down as the lead designer for that tiny hotel in North Carolina."

My lips pressed together as I tried not to smile. Even though we weren't physically together, she'd be able to sense it.

And she wouldn't be happy about it.

"Okay, so, yeah…that I did."

"What the hell, Lani?" Her voice was low, her words hushed, but they carried an intensity that spoke volumes. "You could be fired for this. Worse, you could be arrested. That's a crime!"

I made that noise again, the one that reminded me of Piper's niece. "Arrested? Please. Do you really think my father is going to arrest me?"

Silence followed my question until she finally groaned. "No, but seriously, what were you thinking? This isn't you! The Leilani I know doesn't do this."

She'd said something similar last night while I was knocking back those shots from the bartender. It hadn't bothered me so much then, but it did now.

"Exactly!" I said. "The Leilani you know just sits idly by while her father promotes everyone but her. The Leilani you know continually gets hurt time and time again when that same father constantly bails on her. I'm sick of being that Leilani. I want to be better than that Leilani." With every word, I'd let my emotions build until tears welled beneath my eyelids, and my chest grew heavy.

"Okay," she said. "I get it."

My lips quivered. "I can't wait any longer. I have to show him what I can be, if he just lets me."

"Then go show him."
I could hear the smile in her voice.
Like I'd said, even miles away, I could sense it.
"I will."
"And, Lani?"
"Yeah?" I smiled back.
"Make sure you show him good. For the both of us."

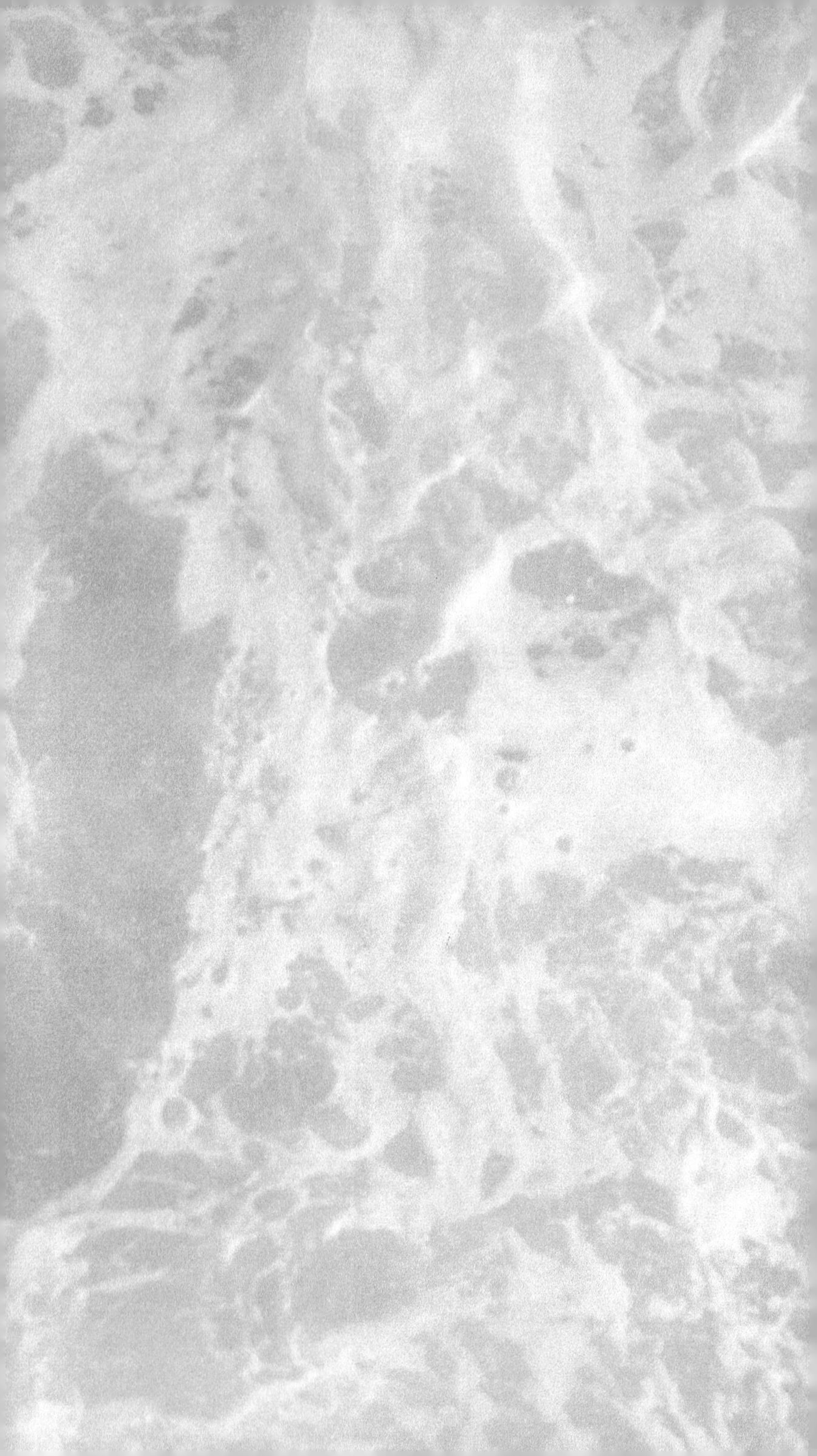

CHAPTER THREE

Taylor

It had been three days.

Three days since the announcement of the sale that had rocked the small community of Ocracoke.

Three days of endless chatter revolving around a single word—*Hart*.

It was all anyone could talk about.

"How will this affect my restaurant business?"

"What about the view from my house?"

"Do you think they'll tear the whole building down?"

Every single conversation circled around that damn hotel, and in those three days, I hadn't had a decent night's sleep.

With everyone in an uproar over this hotel tycoon coming to town, my brother had taken it upon himself to try to calm their fears, once again leaving me to man the family business.

Ever since Cora had shown up and my brother had finally started to give a damn about the world around him, pulling himself out of the rut he'd found himself in after his accident, the town had begun to see him as a sort of leader.

He headed several committees and led town meetings.

I guessed it was a good thing we didn't have a mayor; otherwise, I'd probably be sitting in this office by myself —permanently.

Feeling my foul mood growing by the second, I decided it was time for a break. Pulling out my cell, I called the only person I knew who could pull me out of this horrible funk I was in.

"You know, you could just walk across the street," Millie greeted me, not even bothering to say hello.

I smiled, thankful for her friendship. We'd been buddies in high school, but we had grown apart after she went on to college, and I stayed here. It had been a mutual distancing, but honestly, I had been grateful for it at the time. I had been bitter back then. Bitter and angry over the life I'd given up, and hearing about hers just starting out? Well, it hadn't helped.

"Yeah, but what would be the fun in that?" I goaded.

"I could try to sell you one of these fancy soaps I just got in. I've got one that smells like lavender and another that smells exactly like vanilla ice cream. It's divine."

"Why in the world would I ever want to smell like ice cream?" I asked, leaning back in the old leather chair. I propped my feet up on the desk and allowed myself a moment to relax. It'd already been a long day, having been out on the sound twice with tourists already and it was barely noon. And my day wasn't close to being over yet.

"Well, I'm sure Sierra wouldn't mind."

My feet dropped to the floor with a thud. "Who told you?"

She laughed, a lyrical laugh that sent my nerves into panic mode, my eyes darting around for any sign of Sierra's crazy grandfather.

"Seriously, Millie, who?"

"Relax," she said. "Dean told me about it, and I said I'd rile you up a little just to make sure you were done and past it. Because, really, Taylor? She's, like, twenty-two. Tops."

"So?"

"She's in college. Do you even remember college?" Her

voice held a certain amount of judgment mixed with a healthy dose of amusement.

"Hey! We're not that old. You talk like we're a candle or two away from retirement. And, to answer your question, no, I don't remember college. Remember, not all of us got to go."

I heard her suck in a breath.

"Sorry. I forget how much I missed while I was—"

"Gone? Well, at least you came to your senses and came home."

"I did," she confirmed. "It only took ten years and one hell of a sexy Brit to get me back here. Now, how about I make up for some of that lost time by taking you out for lunch? I'll swing by and pick you up in a few minutes."

"Sure," I said, feeling my stomach grumble in agreement.

We hung up, and I used what little time I had to look at my schedule for the afternoon and pick up around the office. While there wasn't much in here for the customers, we did have a small rack by the door of products and a mini fridge of drinks and snacks, all of which got thoroughly ransacked with each tour.

Just as I was rearranging the small box of Airheads, I heard the door chime, signaling the arrival of my lunch date.

"You'd better be taking me to Billy's because I have a hankering for shrimp, and you know no one on this godforsaken island does shrimp better than that man."

"I don't believe I'm familiar with the word *hankering* or a man named Billy." The voice that replied was smooth as silk and immediately made my boy down under come to attention.

Definitely not Millie. I'd trained myself to ignore the fact that she was a smokin'-hot female a long time ago. She'd always been the kind of friend I wanted to keep, which meant I'd basically been treating her like a dude since puberty.

My head popped up, and I nearly slammed into the female with the sexy voice.

"Sorry," I said, holding my hands out to steady us both. "I, uh, thought you were someone else."

"Clearly," she replied, a sort of smirk tugging at the corner of her mouth.

And what a beautiful mouth it was. Pretty and pink with just the right amount of pout. A man could kiss those lips for days and never get bored.

But the gorgeous view didn't stop there.

No, it spread from head to toe.

With golden skin and long, wavy brown hair, she had legs for days and damn, if I wouldn't mind spending some time with those wrapped around my—

"I'm Taylor Sutherland, and you are?" I managed to choke out.

"Curious," she simply said.

I watched as she strolled around, looking at the product rack at the front with an appraising eye. Her fingers grazed the assortment of candy as I took another moment to check out her long, flowing dress and all the ways it hugged her luscious curves.

And then I thought about all the ways I'd like to tear it off of her.

"Are you the owner of this establishment?" she asked.

"I am," I boasted, giving her a wicked grin that was sure to earn me a dinner date. It had a smashing success rate with tourists.

And I doubted she'd be an exception.

"And you're the only company like this on the island?"

My grin slipped a little. That was an odd sort of a question for a tourist, but maybe she was thrifty, shopping around for the best bargain.

"There are a few others. Used to be more, but listen, I'm the best, hands down. And if you let me take you out to dinner tonight, I'd be happy to show you."

Her eyebrows rose in surprise. Thankfully, it was a playful surprise and not an *I'm gonna slap you* surprise.

"Dinner, huh?"

"Why not? I don't see a ring on that pretty little finger of yours."

She glanced down at her left hand and smiled. "Okay. I'm staying at By the Bay. Do you know where that is?"

I let out a chuckle. She did know you could drive from one end of this town to the other in less time than it took to play a single song on the radio? "This island is about as big as a minute," I said. "Yeah, I know where it is. I'll pick you up at seven."

I watched as she headed toward the door, but she turned back before exiting.

"You know, you still don't know my name."

I shrugged. "I guess we'll have something to talk about later then."

Her smile widened. "Oh, I'm sure we'll have plenty to discuss Mr. Sutherland."

And with that bold statement, she stepped into the warm September day and disappeared.

By the time Millie finally showed up, my bad mood had all but dissipated after my mystery date's appearance.

"What took you so long?" I asked after she peeked her head through the door and waved me out.

"Sorry!" she apologized, watching me lock up. "I'd all but closed up when Cora called and started spilling the latest Hart gossip."

"Please don't tell me you've fallen down this rabbit hole, too."

"No. Well, not until just now."

We began walking toward Billy's, our favorite restaurant in town. He was a townie like us and was known for his dynamite seafood and casual atmosphere. The killer views of the bay didn't hurt either.

"Why? What happened?"

"A private jet landed at the airport about an hour ago."

Even that got me interested.

"Really? So, old man Hart has arrived."

"No!" she said, her eyes wide with excitement. "That's the interesting part. It wasn't Stephen Hart. It was his daughter. Or at least, that's what people are saying."

"He has a daughter?"

Millie shrugged, her long skirt swaying against the pavement as we walked. "I know, right? Who knew the devil had a daughter?"

We'd begun calling Stephen Hart the devil because of what his company could possibly do to our small town. His resorts were big, bold, and high class—everything Ocracoke was not. They brought in the sort of clientele that wouldn't appreciate the low-key lifestyle this island was revered for.

"Yeah, and apparently she's gorgeous. She's Hawaiian. I had no idea the Hart family was from there."

I began to feel a twinge of unease settling in my gut. "Oh?"

"My mom said their Polynesian roots went way back on the island. She's been all over the internet, stalking Hart International since the hotel was sold. She and my sister are worried sick about how it will impact the inn."

"Right. Sure," I said, trying to appear as the concerned friend, but really, my mind was swirling with thoughts of the mysterious woman I'd met only minutes earlier.

The very Hawaiian looking woman I'd met.

"And what about By the Bay?" I asked, remembering my date that evening. "Molly's inn would be the place to stay if a Hart had arrived on the island."

Millie's eyes widened. "Oh, you're right!" She immediately pulled out her phone and began texting Molly, asking for details.

With each stroke of her fingers, I began to feel my nerves piling up. We made it to the restaurant and were seated before I managed to say another word, my gut now churning as I tried not to think of the implications of what I might have just done.

"Do you happen to have a picture of her?" I asked Millie, trying to sound as nonchalant as possible, but I couldn't wait another second for the text to come in. I had to know.

"Of who?"

"Hart's daughter."

"Why? You want to date her?" she said with an abrupt laugh attached to the end.

"What? No! I just want to know what she looks like. You know I can't resist a nice piece of ass. So, if this one shows up in my office, I want to make sure I can spot the enemy."

"Oh," she said, dragging out the syllable like she'd finally landed on the same page as me. "Good call. That would be horribly uncomfortable. Wouldn't want you to pull another Sierra, would we?"

"No," I said, tugging at the collar of my shirt. "Definitely not."

I watched as she pulled up an internet browser. Within seconds, the woman in my shop was staring back at me.

Shit.

Fuck.

Damn.

"Great," I said, my voice cracking a little as I tried to force a smile. "Now, I know."

She smiled back, not a care in the world, as Billy came to take our orders. "Yep. Now, you know."

"Oh, and here is a text from Molly," she said, as if the information was relevant to me anymore. I'd already confirmed I was a louse. A horrible person.

A traitor to my town.

"Molly wasn't there," she said, scanning over the text. "But, it seems my mom checked in Miss Hart over an hour ago. I guess it's true, then. The daughter of the devil is officially in Ocracoke. Let the madness begin."

Truer words had never been spoken.

———

The internal berating and name-calling in my head continued long into the afternoon as I tried to put my best foot forward and do my damn job for the rest of the day, taking the last touring group out for an afternoon on the sound.

What a heaping pile of shit I'd managed to dig myself into.

Barely twenty minutes of her being on the island, and I'd not only hit on the hotel heiress, but also ask her out to dinner. This woman could destroy our town with the type of resort her family built, and here I was, trying to get into her pants.

She wasn't wearing pants, I reminded myself.

My thoughts drifted back to her long dress and just how much I'd wanted to get up under it.

Damn it.

Perhaps Leilani was the daughter of the devil because, even now, after discovering who she really was, I still wanted her.

Maybe a little more.

And, if that wasn't pure evil, I didn't know what was.

But what made it truly sinful was the fact that, at seven o'clock, my ass was not firmly planted on the cushions of my sofa at home in protest of the date I'd planned with the devil's daughter.

No, my ass was walking up to the door of By the Bay Inn, about to make a dozen mistakes I'd probably regret in the morning.

I shook my head as I held my hand out to twist the handle.

Not mistakes. There would be no mistakes.

I was here on official town business.

Dean isn't the only Sutherland who can be a leader, I tried to convince myself.

I might have acted rashly and asked a complete stranger out for dinner. It hadn't been the first time. It certainly wouldn't be the last. But it didn't mean I had to waste this opportunity with Ms. Hart.

I could use it to my advantage—the town's advantage.

Right, good talk.

I let out a breath as I stepped into the foyer of the familiar inn. This place was almost like a second home to me, the fresh smell of lavender and pine bringing back a slew of childhood memories. Even before my brother and Molly had been engaged, I'd spent a great deal of time here when I was growing up.

I might have been Dean's annoying younger brother to him and his group of friends, but, growing up, he'd always done a good job of including me, and many events had been spent within these walls. Birthday parties, holidays, and summer cookouts. It wasn't just an inn. It had been the family home for the McIntyres, and they'd made it their mission to treat every guest who entered as an extended member of that family. Growing up without a father, Dean and I had always appreciated the sentiment.

"You clean up nice, Mr. Sutherland."

That voice. It was like melted butter, and it made my chest tighten and my balls ache. Never in my life had a woman's voice done such a number on me.

And, just like the first time, I hadn't even seen her face.

Turning around, I finally got a glimpse of her, and damn if that didn't make that little pep talk I'd given myself just seconds ago seem almost laughable.

If looks could kill…well, let's just say I'd be the happiest dead man on the planet.

No longer wearing the long dress, she'd traded it in for something shorter.

Much shorter.

The red dress, although casual with a bright floral pattern, had an incredibly striking appearance on her, and I found myself almost out of breath as I took her all in.

"You, too," I said, trying to sound confident rather than bewildered.

Remember who you're talking to, my common sense reminded me.

Right. Hotel heiress here to ruin my life.

I straightened a little, my hands finding my pockets as I took a cursory glance around the foyer. I tried not to concentrate too much of my attention on the beautiful woman at the bottom of the steps, her legs so long that they could wrap around my waist without difficulty.

Nope. Not the thing to be thinking about.

Definitely not.

"I am actually surprised you showed," she said, her sandals echoing against the old wooden floor as she stepped off the last step. It brought attention to her height.

Or lack thereof.

At six foot four, I dwarfed just about everyone, but Leilani was at least a foot shorter than me, barely coming up to my shoulders. For a brief moment, I wondered what it'd be like to have her in my arms, her head buried in my chest.

Would her hair smell as good as I imagined?

"Oh?" I asked, dismissing the thought with a shake of my head. "Why wouldn't I have shown? Do I look like a guy who stands up his dates?"

She walked a sort of semicircle around me, like she was circling her prey. That, or she was checking me out. I preferred the latter.

"No," she said with a knowing grin. "You definitely look like the type who always shows."

What the hell does that mean?

"But I figured that once you found out who I was, you'd pass judgment like the rest of the town has, and bail."

My eyes widened. Oh, so the gossip had spread long, far, and fast.

So much so that even Leilani had heard.

She gave me an amused expression, her eyebrows raised

as she looked up at me. "Your town thinks I'm the devil, huh?"

"Well, no," I said. "More like the daughter of the devil."

She threw her arms up in disbelief, the icy demeanor she wore beginning to slip. "That's great! That's just freaking great. And you came here to what? Exorcise me?"

"What?"

"You know, like *The Exorcist*, the movie?"

"Oh." I grinned. "No. Well, I mean…would that work?"

She didn't find my brand of funny amusing, but I found her frustration delightful.

"No," she growled.

"I'm here, hoping that maybe you'll reconsider."

Her eyes met mine, and it was the first time I noticed their color—deep brown, with tiny flecks of gold. "Reconsider what?"

"Whatever it is that you're about to do, because I can tell you right now; this town isn't your cup of tea. We're not into glitz and glam. We're simple."

Those mesmerizing brown eyes seemed to darken right before me as the words I'd spoken settled. "Does the town own The Cozy Hotel?"

"No," I said. "But they feel—"

"Who owns The Cozy Hotel?"

"That's not the point, Leilani—Miss Hart, I mean. You see—"

She pressed, "Who owns The Cozy Hotel, Taylor?"

Hearing her say my name nearly made me stumble. It was like hearing it for the first time.

"We're just asking for input."

"Who owns—"

"You do, okay? Are you happy?" I blurted out, my chest heaving with anger.

It was then that I realized how close we'd gotten in our heated exchange. Our bodies were nearly touching as our eyes locked together, but before I could do anything about it, she pulled back, a satisfied smile on her face.

"Yes, quite happy actually. Now, I expect any actual town concerns will be voiced through the proper channels, yes? Or is this how Ocracoke conducts business? Shall I plan on more disappointing dinner dates with you?"

I felt a growl rumble deep inside inside my chest.

Damn, she'd gotten me good.

"Oh, don't worry; I don't make the same mistake twice. You won't be seeing me again."

"I guess that's good for me then."

I stalked toward the door. "You have no idea."

I heard feminine laughter follow me as I left.

Great comeback, douche bag.

Just great.

At least I had one thing going for me. There had been no one from town to witness my epic fail with Leilani, which meant there was no one to spread the gossip.

Thank God for small miracles.

Or so I thought.

I woke up to the sound of my front door being slammed shut.

"Wake up, asshat! We've got to talk!"

"Shit," I moaned.

Hearing the angry shouts of my big brother in the wee hours of the morning was never a good thing.

Throwing on a pair of flannel pajama pants and an old T-shirt from high school, I made my way down the steep stairs toward the tiny kitchen of my one-bedroom bungalow to find Dean helping himself to my fridge.

"Don't you have food in your own house?"

"Yeah," he said. "But you make a damn good omelet, and we have some words to exchange. So, get to cooking. That is, if you think I'm worthy of breakfast." He waggled his eyebrow as he handed over a carton of eggs.

"Now, who's being an asshat?" I muttered, taking the eggs and getting to work.

"It is kind of frustrating that you have a fast and firm rule against breakfast with female companions, yet you are a wizard in the kitchen."

I shrugged. "I learned a lot from Mom when I didn't go away to college."

"You took that manning-up thing pretty damn seriously."

"Not seriously enough, according to my older brother who believes I should have a wife, kids, and a minivan by now."

"Hey!" he argued. "I never said anything about a minivan."

We both chuckled as I got the burners going, and I pulled out a block of cheddar cheese and some bacon.

"So, why the shrill wake-up call?"

"I heard you paid a visit to the inn last night."

I let out a giant huff of frustration. "Seriously? Can nothing in this town go unnoticed? A bunch of fucking peeping Toms, that's what this place is."

"So, it's true?" He shook his head in disbelief. "Fuck, Taylor. Did you sleep with her? Because the whole town is going to hear about it by noon, and considering your reputation—"

"I didn't sleep with her. Give me some credit."

His brow lifted.

"Okay, so maybe I asked her out."

He began to groan.

"Before I knew who she was! But you know how I am— see a pretty woman, and ask her out! I can't help myself."

"So, why go then? If you knew who she was, why show up at the inn at all?"

"Because I thought I could talk some sense into her."

His disbelief grew. "You thought you could talk sense into

a woman who's set to inherit a billion-dollar company? What did you think would happen? You'd just lay out your simple point of view, and suddenly, she'd just agree with you? She'd pack her things and go hop back on that fancy plane of hers, and go head to Hawaii?"

"Well, I—"

"Oh my God, you did."

"I just thought she might listen to my—our concerns."

"And did she?" he asked, clearly not amused by my attempt at leadership in the least.

"No," I said, my head hanging low in shame. "She actually requested that all town concerns be sent through the proper channels. Whatever that means."

Dean began to pace the length of my kitchen floor. "Jesus, Taylor."

"I know," I said, feeling exactly like the idiot kid brother I used to be.

"Do you? Because what we're facing is massive, and it needs to be handled delicately. We needed a plan—a goddamn formal plan. And you blazing into that inn, pissing off the one woman who stands between us and possible disaster wasn't it!"

His words stung, but they weren't wrong.

I'd fucked up.

Royally.

I'd let my emotions and my dick get the better of me, and it could have cost us all majorly.

"What do you need me to do?" I asked, swallowing my pride, breakfast momentarily forgotten.

"Stay away from her," he said. "And let the powers that be figure this out."

I nodded, taking his instructions to heart.

I was to stand down.

Dean was the town leader. I was just the business owner, ready to be led.

"And one more thing," he said, looking up at me for the first time in what seemed like ages.

"Anything," I answered.

"Make me the biggest damn omelet you can fit in the pan. I'm starving."

I let out a laugh, grateful for the break in tension. "Sure thing, brother. Happy to help."

And I was.

I was always happy to help.

Because this was my home and the life that went with it.

CHAPTER FOUR

Leilani

"Piper, I was literally shaking the entire time," I said as I paced my room after recounting the dinner that never happened with Taylor Sutherland.

"Man, one day away, and I already don't recognize you. Are you sure you didn't inherit more than your daddy's dark brown eyes? After hearing how you made that townie your bitch, I'd almost believe you got his mean streak, too."

I let out a laugh, remembering how angry Taylor had been when I finally got him to admit who owned that miserable excuse for a hotel. I'd watched as his chest heaved and his eyes hardened in response to my demand. Just recalling it now, I found myself biting my lip to keep from giggling like a besotted schoolgirl.

It had all been a little terrifying. And incredibly thrilling.

Who knew I could be such a ballbuster?

It was too bad he was strictly off-limits because that man was hot.

Like *send out the fire trucks because we've got a scorcher* kind of hot. And it wasn't the typical gym-rat hot I was used to, growing up on the beaches of Waikiki. No, his toned physique was thanks to years of hard labor, and it showed.

Yes, it was a damn shame he was on the opposite side of the line that seemed to have been created by the townspeople.

"So, it wasn't the welcome you were hoping for, huh?" Piper asked as I stood by the window of my beautifully decorated room.

It was sort of a shabby chic with buttery-yellow walls and a soft quilt adorning the bed. It made me feel at home even though I knew I was anything but.

"No, not exactly. But it's just a minor hitch in the road."

"You call the entire town bickering about you behind your back a minor hitch?"

I shrugged, taking in the picturesque view of the bay. "They can voice their opinions, but what I do to my property is really my choice, isn't it?"

"I guess, but don't you care about what they think at all? It is, after all, their town."

I let out a solid breath. "Of course I care; I'm not made of stone."

"Okay, good. Just checking to make sure you didn't change completely since I last saw you. I've just been a little concerned, you know, since you basically committed a felony to get this gig."

I shook my head. "Hacking into the company system—my company, by the way—is hardly a felony."

"Let's see how your dad feels about it."

My stomach did that little flip-flop thing that it tended to do whenever I'd done something wrong. Like when I'd cheated on my spelling test back in second grade by glancing at Sarah Smith's paper for the correct spelling of the word *pineapple*. Afterward, I could never look at that particular fruit without feeling a little guilty.

"How long do you think I have?" I asked. "Until shit hits the fan?"

"I don't know, Lani," she said, a note of hesitation in her voice. "But you'd better be ready when it does."

I let out a deep breath before entering the kitchen. "You can do this, Lani. You are a strong, independent businesswoman. And, besides, it's just breakfast. There's nothing scary about breakfast."

I shook my head, hoping no one inside heard me.

Smoothing out my skirt, I took the all-important first step and headed into the inn's kitchen for their world-famous breakfast, expecting to be treated like the piranha everyone thought I was.

Instead, I was welcomed with open arms.

"You must be Leilani!" a happy, very attractive blonde woman greeted me the second I stepped into the bright space. "I'm Molly. I believe we spoke on the phone."

"Um, yes," I said, mirroring her movements as I reached out to shake her hand.

"It's so nice to meet you. Did you sleep okay? The yellow room is one of my favorites. It has such a wonderful view of the bay. Of course, your place has some great views as well, doesn't it?"

"Um, yes." It was all I could manage to get out because I was completely bewildered by this woman.

Her words seemed genuine and sincere as she offered me a cup of coffee without even asking, chatting with me like we'd been friends for years.

"Now, today is scone day. Do you like scones? If you don't, I can whip up something else for you. I know you West Coasters often like to eat a bit healthier than we do."

"Scones?" I looked to the table, and sure enough, there was a pile of pastries. The second my eyes landed on them, my stomach growled in agreement. "Scones sound great."

"Well, excellent! I won't keep you," she said, placing a warm hand on my shoulder. "I know you probably have a million things to do today. But, if you ever need an extra hand or just a friend to talk to in town, you know where to find me."

Again, every word she spoke felt totally sincere, and I was left speechless.

"Thank you," I answered, my brows furrowing, before I found my words, "But can I ask you something real quick?"

"Of course."

"Why are you being so nice to me? I heard the chatter coming into town yesterday. I know my presence here isn't well received, and with you being an innkeeper—"

She pressed her lips together, a knowing smile showing through. "Don't let the gossip drag you down. People talk, but they don't bite around here. Having been the fuel for several gossip wildfires in this town, I've learned to just ignore it mostly. They'll get used to you, believe me. And, as for being an innkeeper"—she simply shrugged—"I'd be lying if I said I wasn't worried, but I have a good feeling about you. Besides, I'd rather be your friend than your enemy."

Her words made me want to burst into tears. Maybe the gossip had gotten to me a little more than I'd realized.

"Thank you," I answered. "I'd like that, too."

She left me to my scones, and as I sat there at the long farmhouse table, nibbling on my breakfast and sipping coffee, I wondered, *Is this what my father's life is like? Gossip mills and emotions all over the place?*

Because I seriously doubted it.

What exactly had I gotten myself into with this town?

With my belly full of homemade scones and a second cup of freshly brewed coffee in my hand, I headed off to The Cozy Hotel with a new outlook on Ocracoke and its inhabitants, thanks to my new friend, Molly Jameson.

Maybe we could all work in harmony.

I mean, I didn't envision us all sitting around, singing

"Kumbaya" or anything, but perhaps, when all of this was over, I could create a place we were all proud of.

Including my father.

Especially my father, I stressed.

With a pep in my step, I headed out into the town, ready to conquer the world.

Unfortunately, my journey took me straight to Taylor Sutherland, and then I almost died.

Literally.

The sight of him, shirtless, as he hosed down one of his boats in the marina nearly caused me to stumble into oncoming traffic. The water streaming from the hose seemed to catch the early morning light perfectly, creating a spotlight on his flawlessly chiseled abs.

"Dear God in heaven," I mumbled as I tried not to stare.

I tried and failed miserably.

Did I mention the damn halo around him?

It was then I noticed just how close The Cozy Hotel was to Sutherland Fishing Company. We were literally next-door neighbors. I guess I noticed the proximity yesterday when walking the property, but that was before—before I met the overbearing, super hot owner who nearly caused my death a few minutes earlier with his abs.

This was going to be all sorts of awkward, wasn't it?

All the more reason to scurry along before he noticed me staring.

Of course, he chose that moment to look up, and like a tractor beam, our eyes met. The heated intensity that had existed between us ignited once more, and I felt something stir deep inside my belly.

Look away, Lani. Look away.

I swallowed deeply and jutted my chin forward, forcing my feet to do the same. I could feel his eyes on me the entire rest of the way to the hotel.

It felt like a small victory the moment my hand touched the door handle.

I'd done it again.

I'd conquered Taylor Sutherland.

It felt like a win for all womankind.

Until I pulled out the key and couldn't get the damn door to unlock. I jiggled the thing, twisted it ten different ways, and even briefly considered using a Harry Potter spell to spring the damn thing loose, but no matter how hard I tried, I could not get it to open.

"Need a hand?"

It didn't take a genius to recognize the deep, masculine voice behind me.

This is why I should have checked out the inside of the hotel yesterday, instead of sticking my nose in the stupid fishing company next door. But, I'd taken one look inside that window and I'd been like a moth to a flame—unable to stop myself.

I'd told myself I was going to check out the neighborhood, a friendly walk to see what businesses were nearby. But that was a total lie. I'd made a beeline into that fishing company like a parched man looking for water in the dessert when I saw Taylor standing just inside.

And look where it'd gotten me.

Here I was, wiggling a key in a lock, with a half naked wet man behind me and all I could think about was jumping his bones.

Feeling my little win fall firmly to my feet, I let out a huff of air from my lungs as I tried to gather my composure. Turning on my heels, I found myself face-to-face with a very wet and shirtless Taylor Sutherland.

Damn, he was even sexier close up.

I wondered if I could just lean forward and lick that tiny little droplet of water before it fell down his chest…

"So, do you? Need a hand, I mean?" he asked, clearly amused with my delayed response.

"No, I've got everything handled. I am a professional, remember?" I answered, folding my arms across my chest.

In doing so, my skin made just the briefest contact with his, brushing across the tight planes of his stomach, which only made that wicked smile plastered across his face grow even wider.

"No? Okay. Well then, you won't mind if I hang out while you handle everything? 'Cause I'd really love to see how a professional does it, seeing as I'm just a nobody from the sticks."

I let out another huff of frustration, the air vacating my lungs in one fluid motion. "I didn't mean it like that."

"Really?" he said, taking a step back to lean his wide body against one of the many weathered columns that adorned the front entrance of the shabby hotel—an eyesore I planned on rectifying quickly. "Because it sounded like you were implying that I—a prominent business owner in this town—had no clue what I was doing."

"It's not—no. Would you just let me do my thing?" I asked, resisting the urge to stomp my foot.

This man frustrated me like no other.

He also set my loins on fire.

I wasn't even sure I had been aware I had loins up until I walked into that office yesterday afternoon to check out the businesses surrounding the hotel. But, now that I was aware of their presence in my world, they were raging—wild and hot and uncontrolled for the man standing in front of me.

And I had no idea where the off switch was.

"By all means," he said, raising his eyebrow as his eyes met mine, "go do your thing."

My stomach flip-flopped again, and before I did anything stupid, like step forward and try to catch one of those lucky droplets of water slowly cascading down his sculpted chest, I forced myself to turn back toward the door.

And away from Taylor Sutherland.

I thought he'd walk away, that our conversation had come to an end, but as I began to fiddle with the door again, I heard his distinct voice sound off behind me once more.

"These columns are still nice and stable," he said. "Structurally, I mean. They could use some patching and fresh paint, but I doubt they need anything more."

His words seemed genuine, and the sincere tone was almost jarring compared to the sarcastic, brooding man I'd met just a day earlier.

"Actually, I'm thinking of having them completely removed, along with much of the original structure."

I could feel the air change the moment the last word left my lips. Like Thor gathering energy from the sky to power his hammer, that was how it felt, waiting for a reply from Taylor. If I could take it back, I would. I'd told him myself, just last night, that these things needed to go through the proper channels, and here I was, dropping bombs like they were nothing, onto ordinary townsfolk.

I let out a breath.

Don't lie to yourself. There is nothing ordinary about Taylor.

Turning around, I prepared myself for the onslaught of his wrath, the anger, and the speech that was sure to follow.

But nothing could have prepared me for what I found.

"You really are going to destroy this town, aren't you?" he said, his words soft and defeated.

"What?"

"This building," he began. "I know it doesn't look like much with its run-down interior and outdated architecture, but it's a part of us, and you'd know that if you spent even a moment getting to know the people who lived here. Like Terri, who lives next door to the town doctor. She spent her wedding night here. And, every year after, she and her husband come to this shabby hotel to celebrate."

"There will still be a place for them to do that," I urged, feeling uncomfortable by the raw look of desperation written across his face.

"But it won't be ours anymore. Don't you see?"

"It's never been yours," I argued, my arms firmly crossing

over my chest as I looked up at the worn and weathered column. "It's a hotel. It's for the visitors."

He shook his head, his eyes briefly closing as he turned away. "Spoken like a woman who grew up in a hotel."

My chin jutted out as I swallowed down a whole lifetime of pain. "And what is that supposed to mean?"

"It means, heiress," he said, "that you wouldn't know the first thing about the meaning of home, seeing as you've never had one."

Now, it was my turn to look away, mostly because he was right.

A hotel was no place to call a home.

But inside that big skyscraper, up at the very top floor, I'd had one for a brief time. But, now, all I had was one negligent father, a crappy hotel, and an extremely hot townie standing in my way.

"Who owns this hotel, Mr. Sutherland?" I asked, standing a bit straighter.

His nostrils flared almost instantly, but he refused to acknowledge my words, pushing off the column to rise to his full height.

Damn, he was tall.

But, this time, I wasn't intimidated.

"I'll ask one more time, and then I'm going to ask you to get off my property. Who owns this hotel?"

"I'm not going to let you get away with—"

"Taylor!"

We both turned to see a man standing on the docks of the marina, outside the Sutherland office. He mirrored Taylor in almost every way, and the way he was eyeing him, I was guessing there was a family relation there.

"Fuck," he grumbled.

"Oh no, is someone in trouble?" I feigned concern as he gave me a look of disdain.

"This isn't over," he promised.

Oh, I hope it isn't, I replied silently to myself, hating myself for even thinking it.

But, as much as I hated to admit it, I liked warring with Taylor Sutherland.

I liked it a little too much.

It took a bit of effort, but I finally managed to get through the door and into The Cozy Hotel for the first time.

Holy shit, what a dump.

That was my first thought as I took my grand tour.

What had my dad been thinking?

What was I thinking?

It was small, much smaller than any of our other properties, only serving about twenty rooms, tops. And, with a barely functioning kitchen, the most we could offer in its current state would be a light breakfast.

But, as I stood in one of the rooms, trying to avoid the horribly thin, wacky-patterned bedspreads or the Formica countertops in the bathrooms, I couldn't help but be awestruck by the view. Each room was like this, equipped with its own balcony and water view of the bay.

And what a view it was, going on for miles in every direction.

This was the reason my father had bought it.

Probably the only reason really.

I could already picture guests sitting out here, drinking a glass of wine while the day drifted by.

So serene and peaceful.

It was exactly the theme I was going for. The ultimate hideaway.

I mean, wasn't that kind of what Ocracoke was? A little hidden gem off the coast of North Carolina. Now, it would be a hidden oasis where people could come to relax and unwind.

I was so filled with ideas, with images of crisp white

linens and chic spa decor filling my brain, that I was nearly giddy.

Until my phone began buzzing, and my father's name appeared on the screen.

"Shit. Reckoning day is upon me," I grumbled, deciding I needed to be seated for this particular conversation. Not trusting the scary looking bedspread or the stained oversized chair in the corner, I decided the only relatively safe and clean spot in the room was outside on the balcony.

At least I'd have a nice view while my father tore into me for my behavior.

"Hi, Daddy," I answered, placing my phone on speaker in hopes that perhaps the soothing sound of the bay would calm his uptight nature. It was a long shot, but I was willing to take whatever small chances I could.

"Where are you?" he asked, getting straight to business.

My father wasn't known for warm and fuzzies. It was why he was able to turn an adorable chain of Hawaiian hotels into an international conglomerate that was worth billions.

"On a balcony, overlooking the water," I answered inno-cently as I took a seat in one of the plastic chairs. *Plastic? Seriously?* At least they were clean. "Can't you hear it?"

"Leilani," he said, a distinct warning in his tone.

"North Carolina," I sighed.

"When this was brought to my attention today, I hoped it was a mistake. I hoped that my own daughter wouldn't have done such a thing. Please tell me you have a reason for this, that there is some logical explanation for this."

"I want to prove myself to you," I said, feeling more and more like a child with every word that fell from my lips.

My father was also known for that, too—making everyone around him feel small and insignificant.

I was no exception.

"You do that by hard work and determination, not by taking something that isn't rightfully yours."

"How is it not rightfully mine, Dad?" I asked. "How did I

not work for it? I've been at that company for six years, and not once have you promoted me or even thrown my name into the ring for a project. How long will it take for you to see that I have talent and drive and commitment to this company? A company that will be mine one day, I might add."

"Not if you keep acting like this!" he roared.

"Let me buy it from you," I blurted out.

"What?"

"I haven't spent a cent of my trust fund. I can afford it."

"You want to buy something from me with money that I gave you?"

Suddenly, the idea seemed ludicrous. This was the real reason I'd never spent any of the money. It wasn't really mine to begin with. Not really.

Silence fell between us as I stared out onto the crystal-blue water of Silver Lake Harbor and waited for him to calm down.

Finally, I heard him release a breath on the other end as his mind worked to fix the problem I'd created in his life.

God forbid, he had to deal with his daughter from time to time.

If it wasn't for this little event, he probably wouldn't have thought of me at all.

Well, until the next time he canceled on me, that was.

"Here's what we're going to do," he began, a distinct note of authority to his voice. It was the tone he used whenever he was in business meetings or giving a speech. It was also the tone he used when disciplining me. "You will have plans to me in six weeks."

"Six weeks!" I immediately protested.

"Let me finish," he demanded, an air of finality in the way he spoke. It was as if God himself was proclaiming the Ten Commandments to Moses.

There was no room for negotiation.

There would be no appeals process.

It was either his way or the highway, and if I wanted my hotel and my big break with my father, I needed to shut up and listen.

"You will have six weeks to produce design plans that are both on budget and generally cohesive with our brand as a company. However, you know we don't do cookie-cutter hotels, so give it its own distinct flavor that speaks to the location."

I rolled my eyes.

Keep it the same, but make it different.

Sure, Dad. That makes sense.

"I want names of everyone you plan to hire as well as a list of all materials and where you plan on purchasing. Impress me, Leilani," he stressed.

I nodded even though I knew he couldn't see me. My father was nothing if not meticulous. This part I'd expected.

"And, lastly, you must show me that you have the blessing of the town."

"What?" I said, nearly choking on my own saliva as I remembered my latest conversation with Taylor. "Why?"

"Why? Town approval is crucial to any project—something you've obviously never learned."

No, because you've never let me out of the office.

"Without it, they'll stop you at every corner. They'll put up a barrier, a wall, an injunction to stop not only your plans, but also your work. It's a nightmare. So, make nice with the locals, or this project will be shut down before it begins."

My heart sank. "You'll shut me down?"

"You have six weeks to wow me, but if I'm not impressed when you present your plans to me at the corporate office, if they aren't up to par with our incredibly high standards, or if those locals aren't singing your praises, yes, Leilani, I will shut down this project."

I was stunned.

I'd thought I'd get a slap on the wrist, a stern talking-to, and that would be the end of it.

Even when he'd said six weeks, I'd figured he meant, *you have six weeks to get me design plans.*

Not, *you have six weeks, and that's it.*

Six weeks to prove yourself.

Six weeks to show you're worthy of my approval.

"I understand," I found myself saying.

Because I did understand.

I understood perfectly.

I was just part of the job.

Something to manage, and that was exactly what he'd just done.

"Good. I'll have Troy send over the particulars, including your budget and everything we just discussed. Good luck."

And, with that, he hung up.

I was just another problem on his long to-do list, and I'd just been checked off.

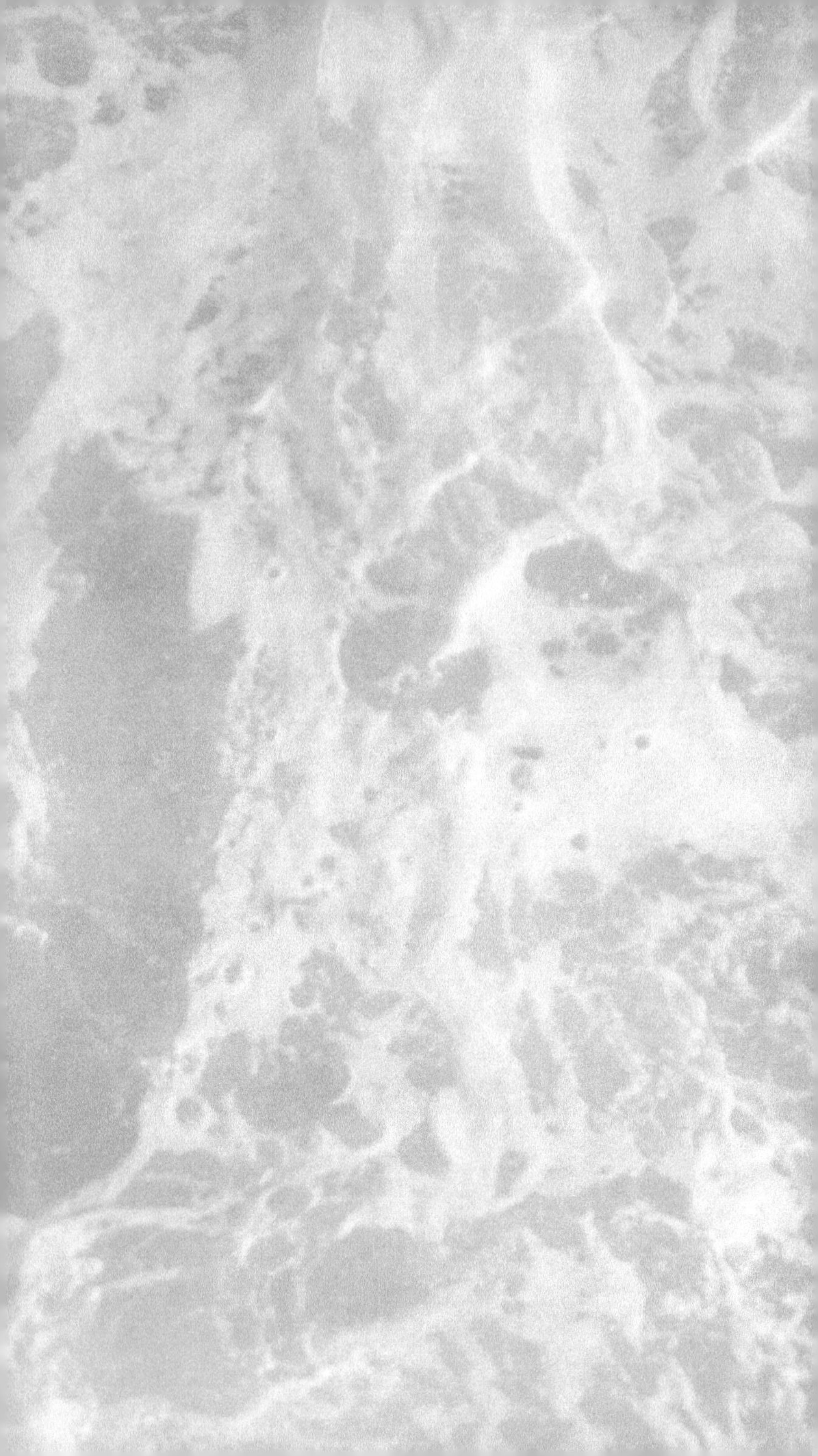

CHAPTER FIVE

Taylor

"Six weeks," I whispered.

Six weeks, and I could be rid of Leilani and this whole damn problem.

I smiled widely and thanked my impeccable timing and the nature of the wind and how it managed to carry conversations so crisp and clear right over the bay.

Just five minutes ago, I'd been minding my own business, going through my checklist of chores for my afternoon fishing tour when I heard it.

That voice.

It'd crawled up my spine and sent electricity straight to my gut. My back had straightened, and I'd immediately looked around, wondering what I'd done to deserve this kind of punishment twice in one day.

Oh, come on, Taylor. You know you like it, my brain argued.

And that was the root of the problem.

I did like it. I liked her.

Too damn much.

But, as I'd turned around to face my sexy nemesis, I'd found nothing but air. I'd thought for a split second that maybe I was going crazy, that this hot brunette from the

Pacific had done such a number on me that I was now imagining her.

But then I'd heard it again.

That sultry voice. But, this time, it hadn't been so sultry. It had been angry.

No, not angry.

Pissed.

"Six weeks!" I'd heard her shout.

So, like I'd learned in kindergarten, I'd put my listening ears on, and that was when I'd gotten all the sordid details I needed to destroy her. And, now, all I had to do was deliver the good news to my brother.

"You overheard?" Dean said, a bit taken aback. "So, you're stalking her now? I thought I told you to stay away from this woman!"

I let out a frustrated breath.

I'd breezed into our office with the good news not three minutes earlier, and rather than hugging me with delight and words of thanks, my brother was staring at me like I was a raving lunatic.

"I wasn't stalking her!" I replied, throwing my hands up in the air. "It's not my fault she's a loud talker. Or that she put her father on speaker for important calls."

His eyebrow rose in suspicion as he leaned back in his chair. "All right, I'll give you that. But I fail to see how this is going to help us."

Now, the pacing began. "What? How can you not see this as a victory, Dean? She is on shaky ground with her dad. He gave her six weeks to prove herself. That gives us a month and a half to demolish her."

Still not convinced, he pressed me further. "And how do we do that?"

"She's trying to tear down the building, so we have it

declared as a historical building. She wants to use a local construction company; we talk them out of it."

"You're going to try to talk hard-working people out of a job? A job that could be huge for not only their families, but also their careers?"

I groaned. "You're not seeing the big picture here. What she does to this hotel, it could affect all of us."

"No," he said, rising to his full height. "That part I get. What I don't think you get is this, Taylor. This monster you're trying to slay is far bigger than you realize. You cut off one head, and four more grow back."

"What the fuck are you talking about?"

"I'm talking about the fact that, if you manage to do what you're saying—you talk construction crews out of working with her, you have the building declared historical—fighting her every step along the way, and her father shakes his head at her little project at the end of that six weeks, it doesn't mean this is over. Hart International still owns the building. Do you think they're just going to let it sit around until the end of time?"

"No," I answered. "But it's a start."

"It's a Band-Aid," he replied sadly.

"Even her father said they'd have a hell of a time getting shit done without town approval."

"But did he say it was impossible?"

I didn't have a comeback for that.

He shook his head, disappointment showing in every creased line on his face. "They'll just send someone else to finish the job. Maybe Mr. Hart himself. You saw what they did to that hotel up in Corolla? It's massive now!"

"So, that's it? You're just gonna roll over and play dead? Wave your white flag of surrender and let her do whatever the fuck she wants to that hotel and our town?"

He looked over at me, the wheels spinning in his head. "No. I'm going to use you."

I let out a breath of relief. "Thank you, Dean. You won't

regret this. Seriously. When I have her out of this town, you'll see—"

He shook his head. "I think you misunderstood me. I don't want you to sabotage her. I want you to work with her —on behalf of the town. You said you overheard her father say that she needed the town's approval."

"Right," I said, my voice wary.

"Then, I'm appointing you as the official go-between to make that happen. I'll need to run it past the other members of the building and planning committee, but when I let them know how well you two have already hit it off, well, I don't think anyone will mind."

"What?!" I was dumbfounded.

"We won't solve this problem with backhanded tactics or lies. We will solve it by joining forces and compromising."

"Compromising?" I hissed. "You want us to compromise?"

"If it means the difference between middle ground or completely losing control, then yes, I'm all for compromise. This town has always been welcoming of newcomers. I don't see why we can't do the same for Leilani Hart."

"But she's not a newcomer looking for a house to rent, Dean. She's a multimillionaire, hoping to take over a huge chunk of the marina."

"So, let's make her one of our own," he suggested. "Make her understand why we are the way we are, why we love this place, and why we protect it."

"And is this a demand or a request?" I asked through gritted teeth.

"We're not kids anymore, Taylor. I can't demand anything of you—unless it is business-related, and in that regard, it's always been the other way around. You've always had a handle on this business, more so than me."

"Damn straight," I muttered.

"It's a request," he clarified. "But one I think you should take."

"And why is that?"

"That woman has been in Ocracoke for twenty-four hours. She's spoken to no one, yet you've managed to run into her on numerous occasions. You can't seem to stay away."

I swallowed hard.

"Don't you want to find out why?"

"So, let me get this straight," Millie began while waving a large cutting knife in the air. "You overheard this woman—a woman who, by the way, you were supposed to avoid but didn't—and now, you've got some evil plot to overthrow her?"

I shrugged, wincing a little when I smelled something possibly burning in the oven. After being told very sternly by my brother just how this all was going to go, I'd sought out the only voice of reason on this blasted island.

Millie.

She'd, of course, immediately invited me over for dinner. It was a kind gesture, and it gave me the opportunity to get to know Aiden better, but the idea of Millie in the kitchen…

I still remembered By the Bay overflowing with smoke after several of her cooking incidents years ago. She definitely did not inherit that particular gift from her mother, like her sister had, but I appreciated the effort.

And, after the day I'd had, I could use a friend's good nature.

Even if it involved Millie and a kitchen full of hazards.

"Basically," I answered. "But I'm doing Dean and everyone else a favor, and once she's out of here, he'll see just how right I was."

Aiden, who had been observing our conversation but had yet to participate, finally decided to chime in. "But he does have a point, doesn't he? Your brother? Even if you run her out, which I'm all for—I didn't move out of one big city to watch another spring up in its place—but say you do—drive her out, I mean—how do you know someone else won't show up days later, ready to take her place? She's just one of a thousand staff members. Hart International is huge. Their resources are vast, limitless even. They have lawyers to back up their lawyers. How can we compete?"

"I don't know," I answered honestly. "But it would give us a little time to figure it out. And isn't time better than lying down in the middle of the street and giving up?"

A slow, meticulous grin spread across Aiden's face. "I like your friend, Millie. He's tenacious."

Millie rolled her eyes. "He's impetuous at best. And possibly crazy."

I eyed the stove one more time. "I'm definitely crazy if I let you continue in the kitchen like this," I said, hopping off the stool I'd been sitting on for far too long. "Let's trade places."

"What?" she exclaimed. "I was the one who invited you over for dinner. You can't cook it!"

Aiden laughed. "Please cook, Taylor. It would be a nice break from the charcoal diet I've been consuming."

Millie's eyes jerked over to her husband. "You said you liked my cooking!"

"What else am I supposed to say? I can't cook anymore! Unless you'd like to eat nothing but Lucky Charms and Cheerios for the rest of your life."

Her face warmed, and I watched as she cozied herself into his embrace.

"I'd eat your Lucky Charms every day."

His hand snaked around her rear. "That just might be the sexiest thing you've ever said to me, love."

I turned away before I felt like a Peeping Tom. I heard Millie giggle, and it was one of those ridiculous, high-pitched squeaky laughs that women made when men were doing something highly inappropriate to them in public.

I knew because I'd perfected the move that caused that laugh by my junior year.

"Feeling kind of uncomfortable here!" I called out, my back still facing them.

"Sorry!" Millie blurted out, a couple of more squeals escaping her lips as she jogged back into the kitchen to join me. "Newlyweds, you know? Can't help it."

I shook my head, unable to fight returning the infectious grin plastered across her face. "I have a feeling you two will always be newlyweds. You'll be like that old couple, The McKennons. Remember them from way back?"

"Who are the McKennons? I don't know that name, and I thought I'd met everyone by now," Aiden said.

I handed Millie a couple of vegetables to chop for a salad while I tried to recover the chicken she'd tried to char in the oven.

"The McKennons were the cute old couple— we used to make fun of when we were kids," Millie explained.

"They'd walk hand in hand and kiss on every corner. After a million years together, they couldn't seem to keep their hands off each other, and as kids, we naturally found it beyond disgusting," I added.

"I wonder what happened to them," Millie said wistfully, making nice, neat piles of carrots for the salad. "I only remember, as a college student, I'd come home and not see them around anymore. But being the busy, self-involved person I was, I never bothered to ask anyone."

"The husband got cancer," I explained. "And, about two weeks after he passed, she did, too."

"Did she have cancer, too?" Aiden asked.

"No," I replied. "My mom said she died of a broken heart."

A sad sort of smile took over Millie's features. "Your mom would know."

"Yeah," I agreed, thinking of my father for the first time in a while. "I guess she would."

"I want to be like that dirty old couple when we grow old," Millie said, returning to Aiden.

This time, instead of heat and passion, there was a quiet stillness between them. He pulled her onto his lap, both of them perched on the kitchen stool like a single unit.

"You want to die of a broken heart?" I asked, making the final touches on the chicken salad I'd thrown together.

"No," she explained. "No one wants that. I want a love that endures the test of time. A love that lasts forever."

"You have it," Aiden vowed.

And I turned away once again.

Not because I was jealous or hateful or even embarrassed.

No, I turned away so they wouldn't see the doubt in my eyes.

Nothing lasted forever. Especially love.

I had a dead father to prove it.

After leaving Millie and Aiden's house, I went home and spent the majority of the night planning the next day.

My brother might have asked me to reach out to Leilani on behalf of the town, but it didn't mean I had to do it his way.

On the outside, I'd be cordial and a fucking bishop for change, but on the inside, I'd be figuring out any way possible to thwart her and her plans for that hotel.

Before I left Millie's, she had asked me why I felt so impassioned to take on this mission myself. I'd asked what she meant because, as far as I could see, the fate of our town should impassion all of us.

"I agree," she said. "But it seems to affect you more than anyone else."

"That hotel is right next door to me," I explained.

"Yes, but I'm not that far away either, and honestly, it affects me just the same. You don't think she hasn't considered having an upscale gift shop in that fancy hotel?"

My mouth searched for the words.

"We're all passionate about this, but you're"—she shrugged for a moment—"something else. Do you think it's maybe not a why but a who?"

"What?" I exclaimed, completely taken aback. "You think I have the hots for her?"

Her eyebrow simply rose, as if that was enough of an answer.

"You're insane," I said, shaking my head. "You're all fucking insane."

But part of me knew they weren't. As much as I was looking forward to besting Leilani, a small part of me—which seemed to double every time I saw her—was just glad I had a reason to seek her out.

To be around her.

And that part of my obsession had nothing to do with this town or the people in it. She was a risk I couldn't afford, and I needed to keep my head in the game. I needed to stay focused.

So, I did the only thing I could think of.

It was stupid.

It was crazy.

And possibly life-threatening.

But it was necessary.

"Good morning," Sierra yawned, stretching out next to me on the living room sofa.

I'd been awake for a while, staring up at the ceiling, berating myself for this latest mistake.

It wasn't a mistake, I reminded myself.

It could have been a mistake.

I'd called her up late last night, knowing she'd come if I asked.

And sure enough, she did.

She'd barely made it through the door before we were hot and heavy on the couch. Her hands had found my belt buckle and that's when I'd frozen.

Like a damn statue.

I'd thought that if I could keep my body was occupied elsewhere, my mind would be free to do what was necessary. And what was necessary was getting rid of Leilani.

But it turned out my mind and body were much more aligned than I realized.

"Hey," I said, rising from the couch to put some much needed distance between us. After putting the breaks on heavy last night, I'd offered up an all night movie marathon, hoping to keep us occupied, and although she'd given me a suspicious gaze, she'd agreed.

And she kept her distance.

"Thanks for hanging out with me," I said lamely. "But I need to head into work—"

Her eyes perked up, a glimmer of hope. "How about you go hop in the shower, and I'll whip us up some—"

"No breakfast," I said, stepping towards the stairs. Her face fell instantly. "The rules haven't changed, Sierra."

She studied the floor before searching for her purse. "No, I guess they haven't."

"I shouldn't have called you last night," I said softly.

"No," she protested, turning away. "I was stupid to assume. Just, please keep calling, Taylor." There was a distinct note of desperation in her tone.

"Why, Sierra? I can't give you what you need. And I can't keep seeing that haunted look of hurt in your eyes."

She smiled, but it was a ghost of a smile, as if she were practicing something that had once been so natural. "You're not the one who put the hurt in my eyes," she answered. "But you help soothe it, even for a moment or two."

I stepped forward and pulled her into my arms, her tears already falling onto my chest.

Nothing ever lasted.

Love always hurt.

For Sierra, it was a cheating boyfriend. My mother, a widow too young. Mrs. McKennon, a broken heart.

No, calling Sierra wasn't a mistake. If anything, she was the best kind of medicine.

Because, if Millie and Dean were correct and I was indeed falling for Leilani Hart, seeing the pain and feeling Sierra's tears stain my t-shirt were exactly what I needed.

If falling in love was a sickness, I'd just been immunized.

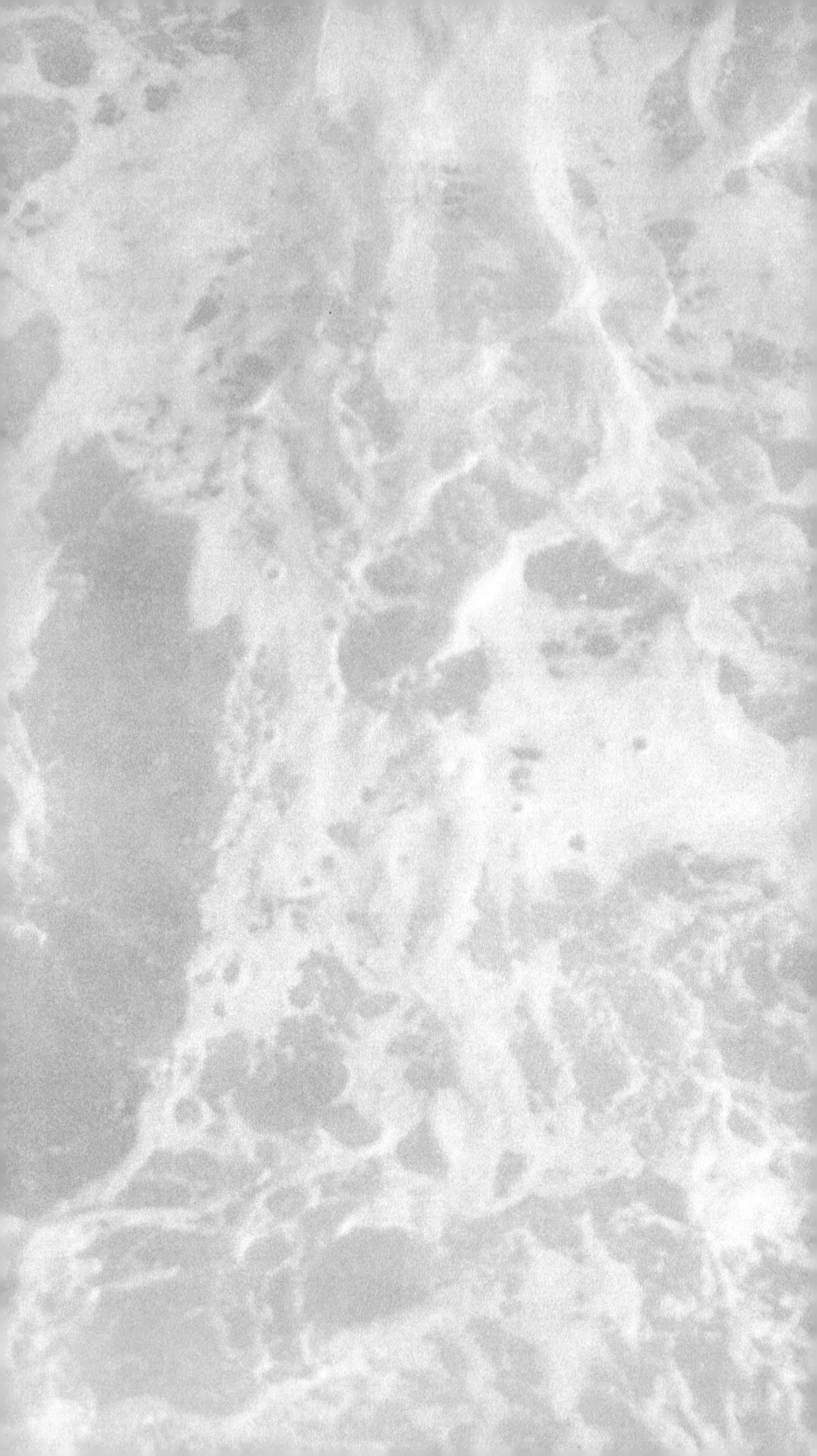

CHAPTER SIX

Leilani

etting off to a much later start than I liked, thanks to a few very chatty guests at breakfast this morning, my pace to the hotel was much quicker than normal.

And, today, I kept my eyes straight ahead.

With my six-week deadline, I did not have time for shirtless men on the marina.

No matter how hot they were.

It was a particularly hot day in September, the weather in this town fluctuating so much that I wasn't sure what to wear at any given time, so by the time I made it to the hotel, I was sweating.

A lot.

I mentally gave myself a pat on the back for flipping on the air-conditioning units and thanked whoever had been genius enough in the past to actually install them.

Considering the state of the rest of the hotel, it was a small miracle.

As I closed the short distance to the door, my hand reaching out for the handle, all I could think about was cool air and having something cold to drink.

"You have mail, you know."

The masculine voice stopped me in my tracks.

I didn't even need to look to know who it belonged to.

I spun on my heels and looked to my left, and leaning on the same column with the same sexy smirk was Taylor Sutherland.

At least today, he'd bothered with a shirt.

A small part of me was actually a little miffed about that last part.

Okay, a large part.

If he was going to be here, back on my property, badgering me, I might as well have something nice to look at.

"What do you want, Taylor?" I asked, so hot that I felt like I might melt into a puddle right before his very eyes.

"You have mail," he said once more, gesturing toward the big, worn mailbox at the corner of my parking lot.

"No, I don't," I replied. "I checked it yesterday. I might be new around here, but I know mail doesn't come at"—I checked my watch on my right arm—"eight thirty in the morning."

My words didn't seem to faze him at all.

"Check it again," he demanded.

The wicked smile on his face caused my belly to flip-flop. Why, I wasn't sure. Maybe because I remembered how he'd looked without that T-shirt covering his torso. Or maybe because he seemed to know something I didn't.

And that, I didn't like.

So, I found myself marching toward the parking lot—not because he'd told me to, but because I couldn't wait to wipe that smug, stupid smile right off his face.

That was, until I reached the mailbox.

And found a letter.

"Told you," he whispered into my ear, sending chills down my spine.

I hadn't even realized he'd followed me.

Or that he'd been standing so close.

I swallowed hard and stepped back, the smell of his

woodsy aftershave still lingering around me like a warm cocoon.

Jesus, Lani, get it together.

Clearing my throat, I looked down at the envelope, a very official-looking address at the top.

"Business and Planning Committee?" I said out loud.

"Mmhmm."

"Is this your doing?" I asked him as I began walking the short distance back toward the hotel. If there was bad news in here, I wanted to read it in the comfort of air-conditioning.

"No," he answered. "Definitely not. But it does involve me. Would you just open it? Some of us have successful businesses to run."

I stopped once we reached the door and gave him a pointed look. "Some of us?"

He looked up at the peeling paint and cobwebs that adorned the front entrance of mine. "Yeah." He grinned. "Some."

I didn't bother hiding my frustration, a loud huff bubbling up from my lungs as I pried the door open and stormed inside.

Of course, he followed.

The instant temperature difference felt a little jarring but deliciously wonderful at the same time. I couldn't help but let out a sigh.

"I thought you were from Hawaii," he said.

"Yeah, so?"

"So, isn't it just as hot and humid there? Isn't hanging out at the beach like a profession out there?"

I shrugged. "Yeah, but I'm not really a beach person. Or an outdoorsy person for that matter."

His eyes widened, complete shock written across that handsome face of his. "You live in one of the most beautiful places in the world, and you don't go outside?"

"I'm an interior designer," I explained. "Since college, my

world has been all about the inside. I guess I just lost interest."

"So, you did love the outdoors then? At one time?"

I swallowed hard, remembering the smell of the ocean, the feel of the sand, and the sound of my mother's laughter as she'd danced along the shoreline.

"Yeah," I said. "At one time."

A moment passed between us. Our eyes locked, and I felt something.

Something beyond heat and want.

Something more.

But, before it could become more, before I could identify it, he turned away.

"Are you going to open that letter or not?"

"Oh," I said, feeling rather embarrassed. "Right. Of course."

Without wasting another moment, I ripped open the envelope and pulled out the letter waiting inside.

> *Dear Ms. Hart,*
>
> *The people of Ocracoke welcome you to our town. We are a small community with big hearts and a long line of traditions and values. We hope that as you move forward with your renovation of The Cozy Hotel, you'll take into consideration those traditions and values, but we know that compromises will have to be made.*
>
> *Like our town, our committee is a modest one with many busy individuals. Gathering us all together is a cumbersome task, and we want you to have a reliable source to contact when you have concerns and questions when it comes to the town and its inhabitants without having to go through an entire committee.*

Well, that's nice of them, I thought.

But then I remembered the man standing in my hotel, and the nerves woke back up.

My eyes jerked up to find the man in question staring at me.

"This says you're some sort of town liaison to me. That we're supposed to—"

"Work together," he said, finishing my sentence.

"No," I said.

"I'm afraid so." He simply shrugged.

My eyes narrowed as I watched him take an appraising look around the lobby. "Did they blackmail you or something?"

"What?" He turned to me, looking incredulous. "Why would you say that?"

"Well, in case you haven't noticed, we don't exactly get along, and this letter is all about making peace and crap."

"Peace and crap?" His lip twitched.

"You know what I mean!"

"I don't think I do." He grinned. "Can you explain? 'Cause I want to make sure I get this down correctly for my official report."

I groaned. "See? This! This is what I'm talking about. You infuriate me. I infuriate you. This is not how working relationships are formed. And I only have—"

"You only have what?"

I stopped short, unwilling to show my hand to the enemy. Because, no matter what they said, no matter how peaceful this town said they wanted to be, they would always be the enemy. I was the daughter of the devil after all.

"I don't have time for this."

"Well"—he raised his shoulder—"seems like you're going to have to make time. You wouldn't want the town officials thinking you're not being agreeable, would you? I mean, that could be seen as an act of war...and that could definitely slow you down if we were to do something to cause a roadblock in your plans."

Our eyes met with that struggle for power again, and finally, I gave in. "Fine," I agreed. "But try to keep up."

His brow rose, as if a challenge had been issued. "You first."

I realized very quickly that Taylor was going to be a hands-on type of partner.

After several days, he'd managed to make his presence both known and heard, all while running his own business quite successfully. I knew the latter because I had a rather good view of it from pretty much every window in the hotel. And, no matter how hard I tried, I couldn't seem to stop myself from looking out each and every one of them whenever I got close, just to see if I could spot him.

I'd already memorized his weekly schedule, which basically consisted of office work, tours, and a lot of manual labor. Of course, he'd also squeezed in plenty of time for chatting it up with a few beautiful, young tourists.

Not that I cared.

On one particularly long day, I'd even snapped a photo of him and sent it to Piper just to prove that men in North Carolina were just as hot as the guys back home.

My eyes ventured to the window one more time.

Hotter even.

Thankfully, today, Taylor seemed to have a busy afternoon of eager tourists to entertain, which meant I was free to work. I had a pile of fabrics and tile samples that had just arrived, plus a few DIY projects I wanted to accomplish in one of the suites, and having someone looking over my shoulder would seriously delay my progress. My town go-between had been so involved and full of questions that I was seriously starting to wonder if I'd get anything done with him around.

That, of course, had me wondering.

What were Taylor Sutherland's motives?

I might be new to this town and fresh out of the office, but even I knew, that no one did a one-eighty on their feelings that quickly. He'd hated me and my reasons for being here when I arrived. Why the sudden interest now?

Was he trying to impress someone—either the town committee or perhaps that older relative I had seen—or was he here to sabotage me?

Either way, I knew one thing was for certain.

Taylor Sutherland was not to be trusted.

<hr>

I felt completely overwhelmed.

Staring at everything I'd put together over the last two hours, I realized my father had set me up.

There was no way I could do this.

No possible way.

Sure, TV shows made interior design look incredibly easy. Those hot *Property Brothers* would swoop in every episode and totally renovate a house in weeks.

Without batting an eyelash.

But I wasn't renovating an adorable house in an up-and-coming neighborhood for a couple of newlyweds. I was completely rebuilding an entire hotel from the ground up, which meant designing over two dozen rooms and getting more permits than I could count, and I hadn't even gotten to the part where I had to find a suitable architect to redesign this eyesore for me.

Were there any architects in this part of North Carolina? I guessed I'd find out.

My head fell to my lap as I sat on one of the tattered, old pleather sofas in the lobby.

"Looks like you could use a drink."

My head shot up as my back straightened.

"Did you just sneak in here?" I asked, turning to see Taylor making his final approach.

He was dressed in jeans today, thanks to the cooler temperature.

And, damn, didn't they look good on him.

That denim hugged and squeezed all the right places, and it took every ounce of willpower I had to look away.

"No. I knocked actually, but when you didn't answer, I peeked my head in and found you with your forehead all scrunched together like that. Hard day?"

"No," I replied quickly. "Just a long one. Don't you have tourists to flirt with?" I hadn't meant to say that or to inject such venom, but I couldn't help it. The window-watching had gotten to me.

Did he have to speak to every hot blonde who walked his way?

"Nope," he answered with a sly smile. "All done for the day. You're not still planning on tearing this thing down, are you?" His eyes fell to my notes.

"You know I can't leave it like this, Taylor. It's hideous and absolutely nothing like I envisioned."

His gaze looked out over the small lobby. It had seen better days, that was for sure. Layers of wallpaper—and not the trendy kind people were buying these days—covered the walls, the check-in counter was chipped and stained from years of use, and the floors were so damaged and worn that you couldn't take a step without hearing a creak or a moan.

"It just needs some TLC," he said, motioning his head towards the door. "Come on. Let me show you something."

"What? Where?"

He was already headed for the front door but turned his head. "Don't trust me, huh? Good. Let's go."

He kept going, so confident that I would follow. I looked down at my unfinished work and back toward him and finally let out a huff.

"Fine, but if they find my body two days from now—"

He pulled the door open for me and smiled. "Like I'd make it so easy."

"I hate you."

His hand brushed the small of my back, and he followed me out. "Hmm, I don't think you do." he said. "We're going for a walk."

"A walk? Now?" I sounded incredulous, but it didn't stop me from following him down the street.

"Yeah. Why? Do people not walk in Honolulu? Or is it just you? Too outdoorsy? Don't think I haven't seen you walking past my office every morning this week."

My arms folded across my chest. I grumbled. "I just—I have a lot to do."

"I know," he replied. "And I thought a walk might help you, especially when you see where we're going. Besides to and from the inn, have you gone anywhere else in the town?"

"Does the corner market for coffee count?"

"If you can tell me the name of the owner, it does," he said hopefully.

My lips pressed together as I tried to remember what he even looked like. *It had been a he, hadn't it?*

"You don't remember, do you?"

I shook my head as he let out a frustrated breath.

"What?" I finally said. "What did I do wrong this time?"

"This is all part of it," he said, raising his hands out in a wide gesture. "Don't you get it?"

"What is all part of it?"

"Us," he said. "Here. Ocracoke. Jesus, I sound just like my brother."

"It's just a hotel, Taylor."

His chest fell. "To you maybe. But, to the people staying in it, it's an adventure, a world away from home. And shouldn't that adventure be an extension of its surroundings?"

I looked around. Local kids rode their bikes past us, happy to be done with another day of school. They all waved and giggled hellos to Taylor, calling out to him by name. Several restaurant owners were setting up for dinner while tourists zipped down the street in golf carts.

"And you think The Cozy Hotel fits this better than anything I could create?"

"No," he pressed. "But I don't think tearing it down is the answer."

"Clearly, we're not seeing the same building."

He smiled, staring down the tree-lined street. "Clearly."

"So, where are you taking me anyway?"

He smiled, his hands shoved into the pockets of those worn jeans of his. "You really don't like not being in control, do you?"

"No," I answered frankly. "But it seems like you don't much like it either."

His eyes met mine, and I found myself nearly stumbling.

"No, I guess I don't."

Somehow, I didn't think we were talking about work anymore.

"It must be something you get from your dad," he said as we continued down the street.

It seemed flirting time was over.

"Why would you say that? You don't even know him."

He shrugged. "No, but it doesn't take more than a Google search to learn about the guy. Nor does it take a genius to figure out the type of man it would require to support a company of that magnitude."

"Well then," I said, feeling defeated, "I guess you have him pegged."

He must have noticed the change in my voice because his next words were softer, less direct. "Has he always been like that?"

"You mean, always Stephen Hart, super CEO?"

"Yeah."

I tried to think back, tried to remember a time when he was a father first.

"When I was little," I said. "Before there was a Hart

International. When it was just Hart Hotels. There were only a few of them back then. Quaint little island hotels my grandma and grandpa had opened right after World War II. My grandmother was a native of Oahu, and my grandpa was stationed there. Back then, he was more of a normal dad. Chill, you know?"

"Wait, your grandfather was stationed at Pearl Harbor during World War II?" This bit of information piqued his interest.

I nodded. "He rarely talked about it, but I know he was trained as a medic, but after everything he saw and went through during the attack, he never wanted to work in a hospital again. So, after he married my grandmother, they purchased a small inn and then another one years later. I think they had maybe four or five when my father took over the business, and he kept it going that way for years."

"What changed? Why your father's sudden thirst for power?"

"The threat of failure, I think," I answered. "I don't remember it well, but I know from public record that the hotels weren't doing well, and the company was facing bankruptcy. My father must have been racked with guilt over the idea of losing the legacy he'd been given."

"Mmm," Taylor agreed. "I know that feeling. The fishing business has been near ruin more times than I can count."

"Yeah?" I found myself saying. "And what did you do?"

"We fought back," he answered. "We changed gears, thought up new strategies. Adapted."

I nodded in agreement, becoming more impressed with this man with each passing minute. "And that's exactly what Stephen Hart did. He took my grandparents' cozy island hotels and turned them into billions."

It had been a gamble, but it'd paid off big time.

"So, why didn't he stop there? He'd obviously reclaimed your family's legacy and secured your future. What drove him to go on to dominate the world?"

"I don't know," I answered truthfully, remembering all the times I'd wished for a father and seen an empty seat at my ballet recital. Or a voice mail instead of a hug. "I guess he wanted more."

"We're here," Taylor said softly as we came to a full stop.

I looked around, seeing a small house to my right. But it was the bright white fence that captured my immediate attention. My eyes followed it down a long path until it reached the end.

"Wow," I said.

"She's a beauty, isn't she?"

I simply nodded, my feet already moving forward toward the massive white lighthouse in front of me.

"I saw it from the sky when I flew in, but honestly, I kind of forgot about it."

"I figured. Come on. Let me give you a history lesson."

He took my hand, something I hadn't expected but didn't mind. His fingers wove between mine, so warm and sure as he pulled me down the wooden path toward our destination. Every step only made the lighthouse bigger and more impressive in my eyes.

My expertise might lie in the interiors, but it didn't stop me from appreciating the beauty of this old lady.

When we got to the base of the lighthouse, Taylor let go of my hand. I couldn't help but feel a little disappointment coil around my heart and then a quick shot of annoyance that I'd even felt anything at all.

"Now," he said quite formally, "what you see before you isn't the prettiest lighthouse in the Outer Banks or the biggest, but she is the longest running, and she happens to be the second oldest to still stand."

"That's incredible."

He smiled. "I'm glad you think so."

I looked up at the mammoth white tower and groaned. "You're going to lecture me now, aren't you?"

He didn't respond. He just dived right into it. "There were

many times in the last almost two hundred years of this lighthouse's life when it's fallen into disrepair. The government could have chosen to tear it down and replace it with something better. I mean, why bother with something so old when there are better, newer designs out there that would work just as well? Better in fact?"

"Oh my God," I simply said.

"But they didn't," he went on. "And do you know why, Leilani?"

Hearing my name on his tongue sent a flutter down to my belly. "Because, Taylor," I answered, "it was part of the island?"

His grin widened. "Why, yes, you are exactly right."

My arms folded across my chest, a gesture that didn't go unnoticed by his captivating green eyes. "I get what you're saying; I really do. But the government was dealing with a beautiful structure. And not just one beautiful structure. They have, like, a dozen of them. That's like built-in tourism right there."

"Seven," he said.

"What?"

"We have seven lighthouses in North Carolina, not a dozen. You really need to get outside more."

My hands flew up in the air. "Whatever! It's still the same issue. They have beautiful, tourist-magnet lighthouses that people love to photograph and put on their walls. I have a fleabag hotel that looks like it time-traveled here from the 1970s."

"Actually, 1950s." He didn't wait for me to respond this time. "Have you even done any research on the building you bought?" he asked, those hands deep in his pockets again as he took several steps around the open area in front of the base of the lighthouse. It was roped off to prevent people from trying to enter, but there were several plaques where you could read about the history and background as well as a scale model that was perfect for pictures.

"I…" I honestly had no answer. I'd been so eager to change it into the vision I had in my head that I hadn't really cared what it'd been in the past. It wasn't like the historical hotel Becky had gotten in Chicago. It was just an unimpressive, boring building in North Carolina.

"I didn't think so. The building was constructed in the early fifties, and although the bulk of what you see inside is, yes, sadly leftover from a tragic renovation done in the late seventies, I've seen pictures of what it used to look like when it first opened. It was stunning."

"Stunning how?" I asked, not trusting his taste at all.

Fifties architecture and design usually meant mid-century modern, and I didn't see how that fit into his island lifestyle any more than my upscale, modern spa retreat.

"I think the term is art deco."

My eyes widened at just hearing him speak my language. It was kind of sexy.

"I don't know," he went on. "I had to look it up. But it was a far cry from what it is today. The lobby had these shiny, patterned floors, and there were big, tropical plants. It looked like a destination. Special, you know?"

It was the first time he'd said something that had me excited, and I suddenly wanted to rush out of there and look up everything I could about the hotel I owned.

That, of course, had me halting in my tracks.

"Why are you helping me?" I asked.

His eyes met mine.

Vulnerable, cautious eyes.

"Honestly, I don't know, Leilani. I really don't. Every bone in my body right now is telling me to just shut up and let you fail."

"Lani," I said in response. "You can call me Lani. Everyone else does."

A smile crept up the corners of his lips. "Maybe I don't want to be like everyone else."

"Oh, believe me, Taylor Sutherland, you aren't. You are definitely one of a kind."

He laughed. "I'm not sure if that's a good thing or a bad thing."

I could only join him because the truth was, neither was I.

Neither was I.

CHAPTER SEVEN

Taylor

"What are you doing?" a tiny voice asked, making me nearly jump out of my skin.

"Jesus!" I cursed, leaping back from the window.

I turned to find my niece, Lizzie, standing in the doorway of our office, looking at me with an inquisitive stare.

"Nothing," I quickly said, feeling embarrassed. "Shouldn't you be at school or something?"

She suspiciously eyed me. "It's Saturday."

"Right. Of course. Well, shouldn't you be with your tutor or doing something other than lurking around my place of business?"

"I was looking for my daddy—I mean, Dean."

I smiled. I liked hearing her call Dean her father. She'd had a rough go with her own dad over the past few years after he'd admitted himself into rehab for alcoholism and anger management. Since then, his visits had been spotty at best as he tried to work through his issues. Dean, however, had been there for her every step of the way.

"I'm pretty sure he's okay with you calling him Daddy," I said. "And I haven't seen him this morning. Are you sure he isn't at home?"

She nodded as I watched her take a cursory look around before she picked up a candy bar from the display at the front. She didn't eye it like most children, the look of pure sugar lust taking over the second their hands made contact with the plastic wrapper.

No, Lizzie was different. She always had been.

She flipped over the chocolate bar and began reading. I could see her absorbing the information like a sponge.

"Did you know there are at least twenty different kinds of chemicals in here?"

"Uh, no."

"And chocolate is actually known to trigger migraines in some people."

"I did not know that either," I said, always flabbergasted by the things this kid said.

Lizzie was beyond gifted and had already skipped several grades. She required additional classes and tutoring to challenge her accelerated pace of learning.

But, even knowing all of that, I still was taken aback by some of the things that came out of her mouth.

Like, how in the world did she know about migraines at seven years old?

But I guessed for a girl who was already doing high school math, a migraine was common knowledge. By the time she was my age, she'd probably have a cure for the damn thing.

"You never answered my question. What were you doing over there by the window? Were you spying on that lady everyone keeps talking about? Leilani Hart? Did you know her dad is one of the richest people in the world?"

My stomach tightened, the knot that had formed since the arrival of the woman in question growing stronger at the mere mention of her name.

"No," I answered before adding, "And I wasn't spying on her. Why would you think that?"

"Well," she began, her voice sounding far too grown-up for her little body, "I overheard Mommy and Dean talking about you last night. Dean said he thinks you have a crush on her."

"I do not!" I exclaimed, the sheer force of my denial making a mockery of my claim.

"And then there's the fact that you were staring out the window that happens to face the hotel she owns."

"So?" I said, not caring in the least that I was arguing like a child…with a child. "Doesn't mean she was out there."

"I saw her standing out in front on my way here."

Busted.

"Okay, fine," I conceded "But it doesn't mean I have a crush on her. I'm not in the fifth grade."

Her face scrunched up. "Of course you're not."

Sometimes, humor was lost on Lizzie.

"Anyway," I went on, "I was just looking out the window because it's my job to keep an eye out on her. The town needs to be informed of her progress, and they've appointed me to report on it."

"Well, it looks like she's planning on taking down the building. I saw the truck pulling up just as I was walking in." Shrugging, she ripped open the candy bar she'd just maligned and promptly shoved the whole thing in her mouth as she gestured toward the window I'd just been staring out of.

"What?" My eyes went wide as I glued my face to the glass.

She followed—albeit a bit slower but followed all the same.

Sure enough, the little genius appeared to be correct. The moment I got back to my perch, the spot I'd been frequenting more than my desk lately, I found her outside, next to a truck that said *Halladay Architecture.*

"Son of a bitch," I breathed out.

"I'm going to go get ice cream now," Lizzie said, clearly bored with me. "If you see Dean, can you tell him where I went?"

I didn't utter a good-bye, just waved her off. I was too committed to the scene set out in front of me. It was like a knife to my gut as I watched an incredibly tall, tan, and good-looking guy step out of the truck and offer a hand to Leilani.

The smile she gave him was dazzling.

The only kind of responses I got from her were usually eye rolls and frustrated huffs as she stormed away.

Never a smile. And never one as bright and beautiful as that.

She had a giant folder with her and didn't waste any time in opening it, planting it on the hood of his truck to show him whatever was inside—most likely her precious plans.

Plans I'd thought I'd changed.

I'd taken a risk, bringing her to the lighthouse yesterday. I'd gone into this hotel project with guns blazing, ready to fight her until the bloody end, but the moment I'd stepped into that hotel, I couldn't help but wonder what it could be if only put into the right hands.

I hadn't been lying. I'd done the research. I'd looked up pictures of The Cozy Hotel back in its glory days. It had been a destination, a place people would pay to stay.

A place Leilani would be proud to call her own.

Or at least, I'd thought she would have been.

When I'd walked her back to the hotel last night, I'd thought we were on the same page. I'd thought I'd finally seen what my brother was talking about.

Compromise and all that shit.

But then I saw this—a freaking architect showing up less than twenty-four hours later.

My words hadn't meant a damn thing to her.

Just like this town.

I continued to watch as they spoke. She gestured toward the hotel, and he nodded. My jaw clenched as his hand grazed her arm. She didn't seem to notice, but I sure as hell did. The two shared a brief laugh. His teeth were so damn white that I could see them glowing from here. He gestured toward the walkway that led to the road, and they both headed off in the same direction.

Where are they going?

Not into the hotel…

That was kind of a relief.

Too many closed doors and cramped spaces.

"Focus, idiot," I mumbled as I strained to catch my last glimpse of them from the window before they disappeared from my view.

Racing to the other side of the office, I realized I probably looked like a ridiculous moron, running from one side of my office to the other, but I didn't care.

I needed to know where they were headed.

I tried to tell myself it was for the sake of the town.

This was my duty after all.

But, as my feet carried me toward the front door and my eyes peered out the glass toward the unsuspecting couple walking past, I knew this had nothing to do with the town or the people in it.

Nobody, except for one.

Her.

It didn't take me long to figure out where Leilani and her architect were headed. After only a few minutes of spying, I deduced that they were off to Billy's for lunch.

I might have had to creep out onto one of the boats, climb up to the top deck, and use a spyglass to gather that information, but now that I knew where they were, I felt a little better.

No, I don't.

At this very moment, she was sitting across from the guy with the pearly whites, probably about to share a bottle of wine, laughing it up, while I was pacing the length of this boat, doing nothing.

Well, fuck that.

I'd gone into this, prepared to fight for the town I loved.

Pulling out my phone, I made a quick call, adding this to

the list of many idiotic mistakes I'd made since this woman arrived in town.

"Hello?" the familiar female voice answered.

"Hey, Sierra," I said. "You up for lunch?"

Oh, yes, it was time for battle, and I was playing dirty.

Seeing Sierra's brilliant smile as she walked up to me just outside of Billy's should have been my first clue.

Not only was I making a huge mistake, but I was also a giant asshole.

"This is a nice surprise," she said, cozying up to me as we headed toward the back deck.

"Just didn't want to eat alone," I said, desperately trying to downplay our date.

Because it wasn't a date.

Definitely not a date.

I looked into her eyes, so eager and full of hope.

Jesus, she thinks this is a date.

When am I ever going to stop screwing over this girl?

"Well, whatever the reason, I'm happy to join you."

I gave her an uneasy smile, although it faltered the moment my eyes stumbled upon Leilani's. She and Halladay, the architect, were already diving into an appetizer of shrimp while laughing over drinks, although I was happy to notice how her conversation seemed to stop, mid-sentence when she saw me saunter in.

And I definitely didn't miss the way her eyes had jerked toward Sierra and then back to me as she tried to quickly recover her conversation with Halladay.

That dazzling gleam of a smile she'd had was no longer there though. No, now there was something else.

Something that had me smiling—for real this time.

Jealousy.

Pure, unadulterated jealousy passed across Leilani's face

for a brief moment before she realized her error, her words stumbling over one another before she picked up her drink as a distraction.

But I'd seen it all the same.

Score one point for Taylor.

But that point was quickly lost when, just a moment later, I almost ran into a nearby table, all of my attention still focused on the dark haired beauty who was threatening to ruin my life.

"Shit!" I cursed, instantly regretting my word choice when I looked down to find one of the local ministers and his wife.

"Hello, Taylor," he said, an amused grin spread across his worn face.

"Hello, Pastor Reid," I said, feeling like that misbehaving kid in the church pew, who was constantly being scolded for fidgeting during prayers.

"I haven't seen you around on Sundays lately."

My hand reached to the back of my neck, as I felt like the air temperature around me had spiked to the mid-nineties. Sweat dripped down my back.

"I've been working," I said.

"Hmm," he replied, a disapproving tone in his voice as he looked up at me through his black-rimmed glasses.

Everyone on the island knew there were no fishing tours given during church time.

"Well, if you ever find you're not too busy, you know where to find us."

I swallowed hard. "Will do. Absolutely."

I caught Leilani's cheeky grin out of the corner of my eye as Sierra and I scurried off to our table, far away from the reverend and his wife.

She thought she'd gotten the best of me, seeing me stumble just now, but she must have forgotten the look of absolute torment that had swept across her face when she saw me walk in with another woman.

I wasn't the only one in over my head.

"Who is she?" Sierra's quiet voice brought my head back to face hers.

"What? Who?" I casually tried to play it off.

She wasn't buying it. Her left eyebrow rose in an entertained sort of way. "You think I haven't noticed the way your attention keeps being pulled in her direction?"

I let out a defeated huff of air from my lungs. "Leilani Hart," I said. "She's the heiress from Hawaii who bought The Cozy Hotel."

She seemed to force a smile. "Oh."

"I've been asked to keep an eye on her progress," I said. "For the town…to make sure we keep the lines of communication open. I'm her town liaison, I guess."

An amused chuckle fell from her lips. "Well, you are doing your job very well. If you need confirmation or a formal review, just let me know. I'll back you up." Every word she said was laced with sarcasm and pain.

Leaning forward, I took her hand—not because I wanted to make the woman several tables down jealous, but because I wanted the woman in front of me to know I was being genuine—something I wasn't normally good at when it came to the opposite sex.

"I'm sorry, Sierra. I shouldn't have asked you to lunch. I know it gave you false hope—"

A smile stretched across her beautiful face. "Taylor, I've never once thought there was a chance between you and me," she explained.

"You didn't?"

Her eyes met the table and then found mine again. "No," she said. "All I've ever wanted from you is friendship."

This time, it was me whose eyebrows were raised in disbelief.

"Okay, maybe a little more than friendship at times. But you've got to understand that breaking up with Robbie was the hardest thing I'd ever done."

"He cheated on you—"

"I know, but unfortunately, my heart hasn't exactly caught up to the news yet. So, even though I want to hate him, I can't. It might look like I'm hiding away at my grandparents', but I'm just trying to find a way to heal. And it's not always black and white."

"So, if we're just friends—with a few added benefits," I said with a smirk, "then why did you get upset over Leilani? Not that I'm into her."

She rolled her eyes, seeing through the lie I was trying to tell myself. "You know when you go on a diet?"

My brows furrowed. "Uh, no. Not really."

She gave me a blank stare. "Really? Not ever?"

"I run every morning for the most part, and my job is incredibly physical. I've never needed to diet."

Her eyes scanned my muscular physique, her teeth digging into her bottom lip. "Fair enough. Anyway," she went on, "when I go on a diet, I always give up certain things. Like chocolate because of the sugar. There are a few days of withdrawal where you literally hate the world."

"That sounds awful. Why would you do that?"

"Have you seen me naked?"

"Go on," I said.

She grinned. "But, after the withdrawals, you begin to think that it's not so bad. Until you sit down to a dinner out with friends, and one of those skinny bitches orders dessert. Then, you find yourself willing to fork your bestie to death just for a single bite."

"Wow, I, um—"

She laughed, and I joined in.

"Anyway, love is a bit like that. You think you've gotten over the worst of it, then one day, you see that single glance, that perfect beginning of something real, and you find yourself—"

"Willing to fork someone to have it?"

She smiled. "Exactly."

"Well, I hate to burst your bubble, but what you see happening between the heiress and me? It's just business."

Her brow lifted. "Really? Because she's looked over here half a dozen times, and she looks pretty damn put out about it."

"Seriously?" My eyes lit up, making Sierra laugh.

"Not interested, my ass," she muttered, leaning forward, giving me a flirty smile. "Now, let's see if we can really make her jealous."

"You, my friend, are an evil genius."

"And you, Taylor Sutherland, are so screwed."

"What? Why?" I exclaimed as one of Billy's waitresses came by to take our drink orders.

"Because," she explained, "take it from someone who's been there. Love is a gamble, and you have no idea what you're about to get yourself into."

I reached up to tuck back a piece of her blonde hair. "See, that's where you're wrong. This isn't love. It's just a game."

"And that's where you're wrong," she insisted. "Love, life…it's all a game. Sometimes, you win, and sometimes… well, sometimes, you lose. Hard."

Lunch with Sierra had done more than lift my spirits.

It had put things right between us.

Although I doubted we'd ever be more than just friends from now on, I was more than okay with the outcome and glad to know I hadn't completely screwed her over in my quest to ruin Leilani.

Speaking of, Sierra had done a good job of giving me a leg up on that front as well. By the time we'd finished our meal, Leilani had seemed to be more than a little distracted, her attention focused more on me and my lunch date than her toothy architect.

The ball was firmly back in my court.

Since Dean had taken this afternoon's tour, I found myself alone in the office, humming along to no song in particular as I dived into a mountain of paperwork.

That was, until the door slammed wide open.

"What the hell was that?"

That damn voice. It got me every single time.

Standing up, I turned and was struck once again by Leilani's raw beauty. Even today, dressed in a simple pair of jeans and a long-sleeved blouse to combat the chillier autumn temperatures, she looked stunning.

"Guess I could ask the same question," I said, trying to play it cool as I shoved my hands in my pockets and casually leaned against my desk.

"What?"

"Well, you see, I thought we had an understanding, you and me."

"An understanding?" Her shocked face was kind of adorable.

Not that I'd ever tell her that.

Pushing off from the desk, I sauntered toward her, and boy, did she notice. Her gaze worked all the way down my body and back up again as she took a step back and then decided against it, standing tall and defiant.

My grin widened.

"At the lighthouse, I thought we'd reached a compromise. That is what we're supposed to do, isn't it? Reach common ground for the sake of the town?"

"That's not—"

"That's not what? What you had in mind at all? I noticed."

She opened her mouth to deny it, but I beat her to it. "How long did you wait to call your hotshot architect after I dropped you off last night? An hour? A couple of minutes? Or did you already have him lined up before I took a chance on you?"

Her face was a mixture of emotions; a tangled web of hurt, followed by confusion and finally, anger.

Oh, yeah. I definitely recognized the anger.

"You know what, Taylor?" she said, taking a step closer.

I could feel the heat from her bronze-colored skin.

"What?" I grinned, matching her step with one of my own.

Our bodies were touching now. Chest-to-chest. Hip-to-hip. The feeling of it was electric, and I felt shock waves all the way down to my toes.

"You…" She struggled for the words as her chest heaved, so flustered and out of breath.

And it was then that I realized…

Now or never, Sutherland.

I couldn't go one second longer without—

So, I kissed her.

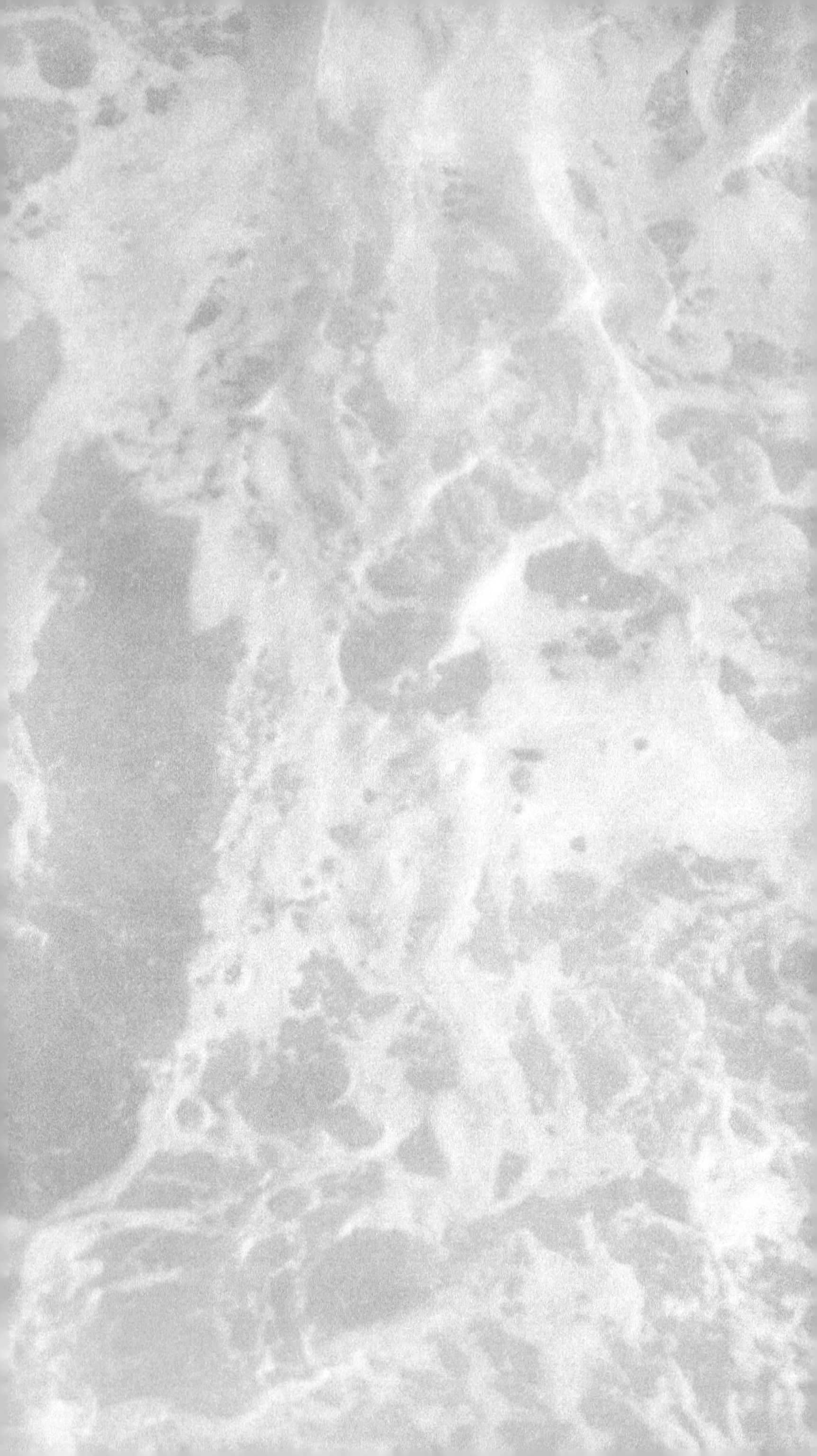

CHAPTER EIGHT

Leilani

aylor's mouth crashed into mine, and all the anger I'd had, all the rage I'd felt over his pompous behavior, suddenly fell to a mushy puddle at my feet.

Just this kiss.

That was all there was.

It filled my every thought. The way his hands seemed to have minds of their own—one so tender, gently cupping the curve of my cheek, while the other possessively pinned me so close to his chest.

And his lips.

Dear God, his lips.

They consumed and dominated. I'd never felt so utterly enthralled by a single kiss in my whole damn life.

I never wanted it to end, which was exactly why it had to.

I wasn't here for this, and as badly as I wanted it, as badly as I wanted him, the simple truth remained. I had six weeks to prove to my father that I was more than an heiress riding on his coattails.

So, as hard as it was, as much as it hurt, I placed my hand against his chest and pushed myself away.

Away from the heat and the spark.

Away from the need of something more.

Away from the possibility.

"I can't do this," I said, my lips still swollen and wet from his touch. "I don't have time for distractions."

My words hurt him, and I regretted them the moment I'd said them.

Wiping away my kiss like a dark stain from his mouth, Taylor snapped back in anger, "Seems like you had all the time in the world for Mr. Halladay."

My back stiffened slightly from the jab. "Yes…well, it seems like you have plenty to keep you occupied," I said, the visions of him flirting with the blonde at lunch still fresh in my mind.

It shouldn't have bothered me, but it had.

It really had.

An amused expression flashed across his handsome face as he traced his bottom lip with his pointer finger.

I tried not to watch.

"I think we need to set down some ground rules if we're going to continue working together," he suggested, taking a step back. He leaned against his desk once more, a stance that accentuated his long, lean body and reminded me of just how good it had felt to have him pressed up against me.

I swallowed hard and looked away. "I agree."

"Good," he answered. "First, this obviously shouldn't happen again. I wouldn't want you getting…distracted."

My stomach clenched as I noticed the way he'd said the last word like it was a foul taste upon his tongue.

I nodded in agreement.

"Also, I don't think we should date anyone else."

"What?"

He was amused with my shocked expression, but he simply leaned back, his arms firmly crossed over his broad chest, and chuckled.

"Well, it's apparent from today's lunch fiasco that we can't handle seeing each other with the opposite sex."

"That's not true," I protested, making his brow lift. "Okay, fine. But, just so you know, I had no interest in dating the architect anyway."

"Does he know that?"

"I don't know. Why?"

"That guy has it so bad for you; I wouldn't be surprised if he was calling out your name in the shower as we speak."

"What? Ew, gross."

He casually shrugged, pawning it off as no big deal, until our eyes met once more, and I found myself wondering if Taylor was speaking from experience.

Did he call out my name in the shower?

When he was thick and wet, did he think of me, moaning at the peak of his orgasm?

My breath caught, and I instantly flushed, just thinking of it. Turning away, I heard him clear his throat.

"So, you're good with not dating?"

"Um, yes," I answered. "Like I said, I don't have time for distractions anyway. The question is, are you? You'll have to give up the blonde."

"She's just a friend."

I made a sound of disbelief, not believing him for a second.

"Okay, great. Well, do you have anything to add?" he asked, becoming more detached by the second.

"No," I said, hating the wall that was being erected between us. I'd rather fight with him than this.

"Well, if you think of anything, you know where to find me. Otherwise, I guess I'll check in soon."

"Right," I said, feeling like I was being dismissed. "I'll let you get back to work."

And I did.

Turning, I walked out, feeling more confused about Taylor Sutherland than I ever had. Minutes ago, I'd been so wrapped up in him that I could feel the thunderous beating of his heart.

And, now, I was wondering if that kiss had really happened at all.

I'd been staring at the bay for far too long, lost in my thoughts, when my phone abruptly ended my daydream.

"Hello?"

"Leilani? It's Jack Halladay."

I was surprised to hear from him so soon. It had only been a handful of hours since our lunch meeting, especially since he'd ferried in all the way from Charlotte.

I didn't do a great job of hiding that shock in my voice when I replied, "Oh, hey, Jack."

He chuckled. "I know you're probably wondering why I'm calling, but I had some free time to look over what you want done for the hotel project, and I think I can make it happen in that time frame—that is, if you plan on hiring me."

Jack was a confident sort of guy, and I got the feeling he didn't hear the word *no* very often. And, if I were somewhere less rural where competent architects were plentiful and I had more time to interview and fully vet more than a few, I probably would have made him and his overinflated ego go through a few hoops before offering him this project that was so near and dear to my heart.

But I was on a time crunch, and he was more than qualified. Plus, he'd done amazing work on a Hart project up the coast already this year. It was a win-win.

"You can do both plans?"

"I can do both plans," he confirmed.

"Then, you're hired."

"Excellent. I look forward to working with you." I could almost hear the smile in his voice.

"Likewise."

Rather than wrapping up the call, there was some hesitation before he continued, "If you're up for celebrating, I could hop on a ferry back to Ocracoke and join you for dinner tonight. I'm staying at a friend's house in Hatteras for the evening."

I tried not to let out a frustrated huff.

Does Taylor have to be right about everything?

"I think it's best if we keep this relationship strictly professional, don't you?" I said, feeling all sorts of uncomfortable. This was not how I wanted to start out this working relationship.

"Of course," he answered quickly. "I didn't mean it like that. I just—"

"Good night, Jack," I said before he could say another word. "We'll talk again soon."

I ended the call, wondering just how I'd managed to miss all the telltale signs throughout the day that my architect had the hots for me.

Your attention wasn't exactly on him.

No, I'd been completely distracted by Taylor and his blonde lunch date to be bothered with Jack.

But all that was behind me now.

We had rules.

Rules that would keep our hands off each other.

Rules that would keep his lips from ever touching mine.

My eyes drifted to the nearest window, and soon, my body followed. There was a single light on in the Sutherland Fishing Company office.

With a single occupant.

From here, I could see Taylor hunched over that worn desk of his, staring at a laptop.

Checking the time on my phone, I found it was well past closing time.

I guessed I wasn't the only one who worked after hours.

My feet took a step toward the door.

Toward Taylor.

"What am I doing?" I said out loud.

I'd just turned down dinner with a man in order to keep it

professional, and now, I was running back to the one man I couldn't keep away from.

I stopped short of the door, feeling defeated.

Defeated and alone.

I'd always thought that moving to a new place would be adventurous.

Adventurous and fun.

For years, I'd been envious of every other project leader as they packed their bags and headed to a new destination. I'd lie awake at night, wondering what exciting things they were doing while I was stuck in the same, boring place.

But I had been okay with it because I knew I'd eventually have my chance.

Now that I was living it, now that I was here, the only thing I felt was trapped. Trapped inside this building with nowhere to go because everyone I knew was thousands of miles away.

My eyes traveled to the window once again.

Back to Taylor.

This time, when my feet stepped toward the door, I let them.

———

I'd almost lost my nerve half a dozen times by the time I walked through Taylor's door. My belly was a pile of nerves, and I had no idea why.

It wasn't like I'd never been here before.

Although the last time had been...

I swallowed hard, trying not to think of that dizzying kiss as Taylor's eyes met mine.

"Hi," I managed to say.

"Hi," he answered back, a note of surprise painting his handsome features.

An awkward silence followed as he waited for me to explain my reason for showing up after business hours.

"I saw your light on," I said. "And I thought you might want to grab a bite to eat."

His brow rose as his gaze gave me a once-over. "A bite to eat? Are you sure that's a good idea?"

"Why?" I asked, my arms crossing defensively in front of me.

"Well, I thought we were going to keep things professional."

"And we can't do that with food in front of us?"

His head cocked to the side. "Point taken. You have a place in mind?"

"Um…"

His smile was infectious, and I couldn't help but join him.

"Do you like beer?"

"I do," I answered proudly. "Well, as long as it's not too dark."

"Good enough for me. Let's go."

I followed him as he headed out the door, and I took a moment to appreciate the way his dark jeans clung to his backside. I'd never given much thought to jeans on a man, but seeing them on Taylor? Yeah, I was very thankful to whoever had created these denim marvels.

He made quick work of locking up the place, and soon we were side by side, walking down the road.

"So, where are we headed? Because I said food, right? And you asked me if I liked beer."

He chuckled. "A buddy of mine owns this tap-house in town. He makes great food, but what he's really known for is his beer. So, it seemed sort of lame to take you there if you weren't up to trying at least a few."

"A few?"

There was that smile again. "They come in flights—small cups," he explained, his thumb and pointer finger indicating the size for me.

"Oh, okay. Good. I was afraid you were trying to get me drunk."

"Now, why would I need to get you drunk, Leilani?" His voice was dark and full of promise, and when he said my name, I nearly tripped on the sidewalk.

Luckily, I didn't have time to answer his question because the restaurant he'd spoken of was closer than I'd realized.

Looking up as we walked through the doors, I discovered I actually passed by it daily on my way to the hotel.

I really need to explore the island more.

"Hey, Taylor!" a handsome-looking guy greeted us. He was wearing a gray T-shirt that boldly bore the restaurant's name, *Taps*, across the chest.

"Hey, Gavin," he said. "Got room for two more?"

The place was packed, which was impressive for a weekday in Ocracoke during the off-season.

"Of course," he answered, giving Taylor a goofy grin and sending me a flirty wink. "Saved you my best table."

I highly doubted that was true, but it was nice all the same. He handed us menus and made sure we were comfortable in our secluded booth before leaving us on our own.

"So, do you take all your conquests here?" I asked, giving him a knowing grin.

He gave it back tenfold as he peered at me over the top of his menu. "Only during happy hour," he answered. "Otherwise, it gets pretty expensive."

My mouth hung open as I tried to find a suitable response.

"I'm kidding!" He laughed. "Besides, you're not a conquest, remember?"

I shrugged, leaning forward. "I know. I just—"

"You're curious? Since you saw me with Sierra?"

Another shrug. "Is that her name?"

His grin widened. "Yes, that's her name, and like I said, she's just a friend."

I gave him a hard stare. *How dumb did he think I was?* I had seen the way she looked at him.

"Okay." He put his hands up in defeat. "She's just a friend

now. We've been a little more than friends, but that's in the past."

"And are you a little more than friends with a lot of women on the island?"

Now, it was him who leaned forward, his broad, muscled arms stretching wide along the table. "Is this how you conduct all your professional relationships?"

"That kiss this afternoon? Is that how you conduct yours?"

He laughed. "Touché."

Leaning back now, I couldn't help but notice the way his body seemed to go on for miles. And then I remembered how it'd felt when pressed up against me.

So hot and rigid.

"What's the real reason you asked me to dinner tonight, Leilani?"

Because I couldn't stay away…

Because I feel drawn to you…

"Because I don't know anyone else on this island," I answered. "And I guess I needed a friend."

"A friend?" He seemed amused by the word.

"Yes," I answered. "A friend."

"And you think we can be friends? We usually can't make it through five minutes without pissing each other off."

Or wanting to tackle one another to the ground…

"I really don't have a lot of other options."

That wasn't entirely true, and I knew it. Molly and I had chatted on several occasions. I could have easily called her tonight.

But I hadn't.

I'd come to Taylor.

"I thought you said you didn't have time for distractions."

My brows furrowed.

"Today, in my office," he said. "After we—"

"Oh." Heat rushed to my cheeks. "Friends aren't distractions," I said simply.

He looked doubtful as he eyed me, indecision written all over his face, until he finally said, "Well then, as your *friend*, can I tell you what an awful mistake you're making with Jake Halladay?"

I let out a laugh. "No, definitely not."

"What?" His laughter joined mine. "Why not?"

"Because you've had it out for him from the moment you saw him, and I don't think it has anything to do with friendship."

"He seems like a jerk."

"You're just jealous," I said.

He didn't reply, but the way he looked at me told me that, yes, he was very jealous indeed.

Soon, our waiter was at our table, taking drink orders, and my head was spinning from all the different beer options. Luckily, my new friend, Taylor, helped me out, picking out several North Carolina pale ales he thought I'd like.

After the waiter disappeared to go grab our drinks, we were once again alone, and I was left with the rare opportunity of a topic change.

One I took and ran with.

"Did you always know you wanted to be a fisherman? I mean, is that what you call yourself? I know you don't do, like, typical fisherman stuff. Is that the right title?" I was rambling, and the smile on Taylor's face told me he knew it as well.

"No to the first question," he said. "And yes, I still consider myself a fisherman, although not in the commercial sense of the word."

"I don't understand what that means."

His lip curled. "When my father ran the business, we were strictly a commercial fishing company and supplied most of the seafood for the restaurants and locals on the island. But we've since had to make changes to keep up with the times."

"Something to do with those financial difficulties you mentioned?"

He shrugged. "Adapt or die, right?"

"Bold words coming from a man so intent on keeping everything exactly the same."

His brow lifted. "Not exactly the same, no. But I do believe in honoring the past."

"Now, why do I have the feeling another history lesson is in my future?"

He grinned. "You know, I used to be an excellent tour guide back in the day."

I laughed, trying to picture a younger version of Taylor Sutherland wooing girls with his fun island facts. "I don't doubt it for a minute."

"Stick around long enough, and I might just win you over with that hotel redesign," he said with a wink.

I gave him an uneasy smile and attempted to change the subject again.

I could have told him that he almost had.

I could have told him that I'd spent all night after our trip to the lighthouse researching The Cozy Hotel, pulling up photo after grainy photo, trying to piece together in my mind what the hotel must have been like.

And then I'd done something insane.

I'd called up Jake Halladay and asked for not one, but two completely different plans for my hotel.

But I couldn't tell Taylor. Why?

I was scared.

Scared that if he knew his words had worked, that I'd already been won over by his love for his town, so much so that I'd nearly compromised my entire project to cram in another design plan, all this would end.

The daily visits.

The conversations.

The rules I so badly wanted to break.

If he found out his work was done, would all this disappear?

Would he?

As per usual, Taylor was correct, and Taps proved to be a spectacular place for both beer and food. But, by the time we got out of there, it was bordering on late.

"I should walk you home," he said, looking down the empty street.

"No," I said. "It's okay. I can manage."

He gave me a look that said there was no use in arguing with him.

"Okay, fine," I agreed. "But, if you're going to walk me home, I expect a history lesson."

"A history lesson? It's ten o'clock!"

"You said you were once the best tour guide on the island. Don't tell me you never gave private tours to cute, young tourists late at night."

"Of course I did, but usually, it was just to the beach to show them the wild ponies, and when none of them would show, we'd make out."

I let out a laugh. "And that worked?"

"Did you hear the part about the ponies? Of course it worked."

We'd already begun walking, the buzz from my beer working its way out of my body as the chilly air hit my skin.

"Are there really wild ponies?"

He grinned. "No. They've been penned since the fifties, but it's a good story, isn't it?"

"You're horrible!"

Hands firmly in his pockets, he shrugged. "I'm ingenious. And see? You almost fell for it, didn't you?"

"No."

"Yeah, you did. Everyone loves ponies. Especially girls. But, seriously, I'll take you to see them, if you want?"

I eyed him suspiciously, and his hands went up in front of him.

"Just for the ponies, I swear. You really should see them. They're stunning."

Another laugh fell from my lips. "Okay, deal. But that's tomorrow. Where are you taking me tonight?"

"Tonight?"

I could see that, even in the dim light from the moon, he was thinking it through.

"Oh, I have a good place, but we'll have to backtrack a few blocks. Come on." He abruptly grabbed my arm and pivoted around. "We're going to a cemetery."

"A what?" I exclaimed.

"It's just a small one, but that's not what makes it special."

"Okay, now I'm interested and a little creeped out. So, what makes it special?"

A knowing smile spread across his face. It was one I recognized well now. It was the smile he used whenever he was about to tell something epic.

"It's actually on British soil."

"Wait, what?"

He nodded. "Cool, right?"

"I don't understand."

"Back in World War II, several allied ships sank off the coast, and when the bodies washed ashore on the island, the locals buried them here. Great Britain leases the land where they are buried, hence the reason it is British soil."

"So, I could stand in the cemetery and say I'm in the UK?"

He looked a little dumbfounded. "I mean, I guess you could, but you'd also be standing on the poor soldiers' graves."

"Oh," I said. "Right. That's kind of horrible. Bad idea. Why do you know so much about history, Taylor?"

He shrugged. "You know how you asked if I always wanted to be a fisherman?"

I nodded.

"Well, back when I was younger and the business wasn't

tanking, I was supposed to go off to college and major in history. I guess that part of me never faded."

"That, and the die-hard tour guide." I laughed.

"Well, that's only for special people," he said, giving me a small side bump. It was a familiar and intimate gesture, one you did with someone you were close with, and I found a giddy smile spreading across my face.

And, to think, just twenty-four hours ago, this man had me so enraged; I thought flames might shoot from my ears.

What a difference a day made.

I opened my mouth to ask him more about the cemetery, but a loud noise stopped me in my tracks.

The piercing sound of a police siren seemed to go against everything I'd learned of the small town.

Quiet, peaceful, safe.

Taylor grabbed my hand and pulled me toward his chest as the flashing lights of a patrol car came toward us.

"What the hell?" I heard him whisper.

We both waited until it came to a stop, the deputy taking his time in getting out of the car, which seemed to be a bit of a struggle for him. I looked up toward Taylor, giving him a questioning look, and he seemed just as lost as I was.

Apparently, this wasn't a normal occurrence on the island. That gave me a little peace of mind.

"Evening, Macon," Taylor said the moment he stepped toward us. He was still holding my hand, still holding me close to his body, like he was protecting me.

From the deputy…

"You know it's late, Taylor."

"It's barely past ten," he answered calmly.

"You arguing with me?"

"No, Macon," he replied immediately. He squeezed my hand. "I was just walking Leilani back to her room at By the Bay."

We were pointed in the wrong direction, and for a moment, as the officer stood there, looking from one end of the street to the other, I thought he'd caught Taylor in the middle of a lie, but he just nodded.

"By the Bay?" he murmured.

Taylor nodded.

"That's Jake's place now, isn't it?"

Taylor seemed a bit taken aback by the comment but simply agreed. "Jake and Molly's, yes."

"Right," he said, a sort of sad, distant look on his face. "Well, carry on then."

Taylor's thumb brushed the skin over mine before he took a step forward, his voice low as he addressed the guy like a friend, "You okay, man?"

A flash of anger danced across Macon's face. "Of course I am. Now get out of here before I find a reason to be angry!"

Taylor and I made eye contact. There was a worried look on Taylor's face, but he knew better than to press his luck, and he did what Macon had asked.

"Have a good night," he said before he ushered us in the direction of the inn.

Neither of us said a word for several blocks until we were sure we were out of earshot, and the whole way, he never let go of my hand.

"Taylor, he didn't seem fine," I said.

"No," he agreed. "And the worst part? I think I caught a whiff of alcohol on his breath."

"What are you going to do?"

He shook his head as we headed for the inn. "I don't know, but I guess our trip to the cemetery has been postponed."

"That's an understatement."

"I could still take you to see the ponies tomorrow," he offered.

A smile flashed across my face. "That wasn't just a cheesy pick-up line?"

"Nope," he answered. "It's really a thing. Look it up."

"I believe you. And the answer is maybe, depending on how my day goes."

"I'll take a maybe."

I'd hoped he would, and the smile already stretched thin across my face grew even wider as we wandered down the street.

"So, tell me about Macon," I finally said, a cool breeze blowing through my hair. "It sounds like you know him. I mean, as more than just a local cop."

"It's actually my brother, Dean, who knows him best. They were in the same year in school."

"So, they're friends?"

He let out a small grunt of a laugh. "Not exactly."

"Oh." I got the feeling there was a plethora of stories to go along with that single sentence. "Is he normally so charming? Or did we catch him on an off day?

His head shook back and forth. "He's not exactly known for his stellar personality around here," Taylor explained. "The guy has been through a lot, though. His wife left him for his boss a few years ago."

"Ouch."

"I know," he said. "And then there was, of course, the ferry accident. He took a lot of the blame for it when the sheriff's department couldn't find a cause for the explosion—since he's the captain for Ocracoke."

My brows furrowed. "I don't know anything about it really-ly," I confessed. "I've heard about the beautiful memorial. Some of the other guests at the inn were talking about it the other day at breakfast and suggested I go take a look."

He agreed, "You really should. A friend of mine from school, Millie, her husband sculpted it. He's in a league of his own."

"Is it true that he's blind?" I asked, remembering that little tidbit from breakfast as well.

"Not completely. He can still see a bit when you get up close and personal, but for the most part, yes."

"Wow," I breathed out. "That's incredible."

"We're lucky to have him."

"Did you know anyone who was…" I stumbled over my words. "I mean, were you close with anyone who—"

"My brother," he answered, understanding my meaning.

My eyes widened. "Your brother? But he's—"

"He survived, yes," he answered. "But only because his best friend, Molly's husband, was there to save him. Jake saved a lot of lives that night."

"It must have been terrifying."

"It was. I've never felt so scared or so guilty in my life."

"Guilty?"

He nodded. "It was my day to run to the mainland for supplies, but Dean volunteered to take my place. He was antsy to get away for a while, and I was more than willing to give up the chore. Usually, we took one of the boats up the coast to gather supplies, but I guess, that night, Dean was in need of some extra alone time. That, or he just didn't feel like navigating the waters. Either way, he took the truck and ferried in."

"You couldn't have known," I said.

"I know that now, but that night, when I got the call that my big brother was in the hospital, at risk of losing his arm because of an explosion on a ferry that he wasn't even supposed to be on…"

"I get that."

"Do you? Because most people tell me it's ridiculous."

"Tragedy has a way of making you second-guess every decision you've ever made."

With his hand still encasing mine, the one he'd never let go of, he squeezed a bit tighter, sending butterflies down to my belly.

"That bit of wisdom sounds like it comes from experience."

"My mom died when I was a teenager. A car accident," I answered, not even sure why I was telling him this. "And for months, I analyzed nearly every single second of my life, trying to figure out every combination, every single scenario where I could have prevented that accident from happening."

"You must have driven yourself almost mad," he said.

"I'm pretty sure I nearly did. If it wasn't for some of the hotel staff, I'm fairly certain I would never have made it through that first year."

"Hotel staff? Where was your dad?"

I swallowed hard, the conversation growing a bit too heavy. "Oh, hey!" I said. "We're here."

He looked up to find the inn coming into view. "I guess we are."

I could see he was visibly let down by the abrupt change, but I just couldn't continue down that path.

Not when it would have led to conversations regarding my father. I'd already bared enough of my soul tonight.

"So, I guess I'll see you tomorrow?" he said hopefully.

I nodded, although I knew it'd be much sooner, for I'd see this man in my dreams, a place where there were no rules.

And where I could do whatever I wanted.

A small smile spread across my lips. "Goodnight, Taylor."

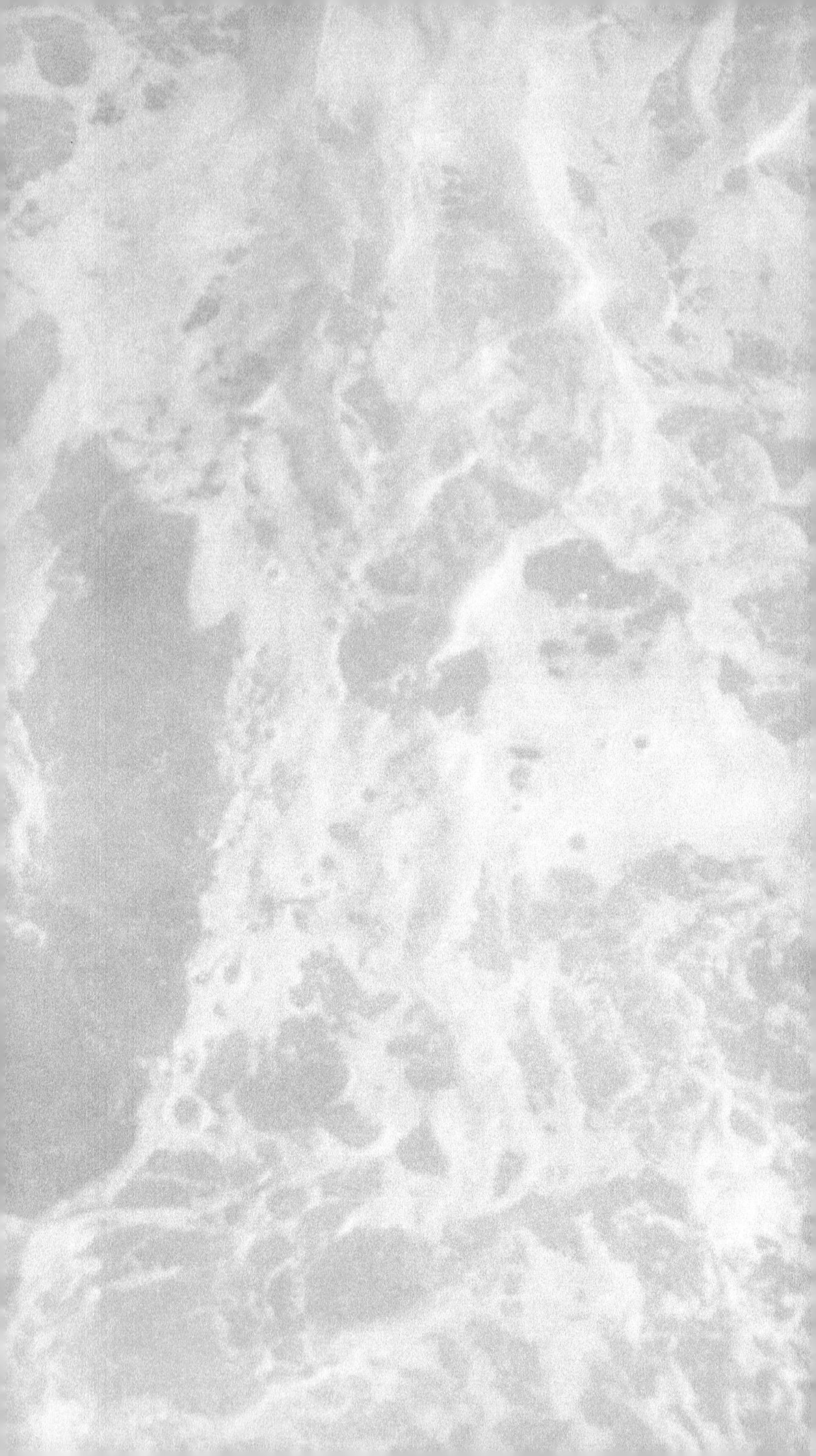

CHAPTER NINE

Taylor

"I think it's time for a report," Dean announced, not wasting any time.

I'd just finished telling him about my weird run-in with Macon Green the night before, and both of us had decided to keep an eye out on the troubled captain, despite the bad blood between us.

My brother, being the nosy son of a bitch that he was, couldn't let go of the fact that I'd been stopped by the deputy with the one woman I seemed to hate more than life itself.

So, here we were.

"A report?" I asked.

"How's the compromising going?" His lips twitched, and I could see it took him effort to keep from grinning.

Idiot.

I took a long sip from my cup, the hot, creamy liquid jump-starting my brain. "It's going good," I said before adding, "I think."

"You think?"

No, actually, I thought it was a complete disaster, but I wasn't going to tell him that.

My mind and eyes wandered to the very spot in the room where, less than twelve hours ago, I'd pulled Leilani close to my chest and finally taken exactly what I wanted. Closing my eyes, I could still remember every breath she had taken, every whimpered sound she'd made as her body melted into mine.

I'd never experienced a kiss quite like it in my life. It had felt like a live wire sizzling every nerve from my head, right down to the tips of my toes. And then, just like that, her hand had slipped to the center of my chest and pushed me away.

I was a distraction.

I'm a distraction?

Fuck that.

If anything, she was a distraction to me.

No, not a distraction. A damn nuclear bomb that had just detonated right in the center of my perfectly okay little world.

I didn't need this. I didn't need her.

But here she was all the same, all the time.

Right next door.

"Taylor?" Dean's voice slipped through my internal dialogue.

"What?"

There was that sly grin again, like he knew a secret I wasn't privy to.

"You were telling me about your progress."

"Oh, right," I answered. "She's hired an architect."

His brow lifted. "That doesn't sound like compromise at all."

My hands rose in an attempt to calm his nerves. "I know," I said. "But I think I've possibly chipped away at that rock-hard armor of hers."

His brow lifted further. "How so?"

"I'm trying to get her interested in the island," I explained, finishing off my cup of coffee and going for more. "She seems impressed with my historical trivia."

"Oh God, not that scheme again! How many poor tourists fell for that back in the day?"

"Hey!" I grinned. "This time, it's genuine. And for a good cause."

He chuckled. "You mean, other than chasing tail."

"Right," I halfheartedly agreed, hoping my brother wouldn't notice my hesitancy.

Because if there was one thing I wasn't sure about, it was my motives regarding Leilani Hart, and that kiss had made my indecisiveness even murkier.

Did I want her to destroy our town with her overly indulgent hotel? No.

But did I still want to run her out of town the first chance I got?

I wasn't so sure.

The thought of watching her walking away and never returning?

It made my chest tighten in a way I'd never thought I'd feel.

"Man, you've got it bad." Dean chuckled.

"What? Why do you say that?" I wrenched my head around to face him.

"Well, you can't keep a conversation going," he began. "And your eyes glaze over every time she's mentioned. And then there's the daydreaming."

"What the fuck?! I don't daydream!"

"The hell you don't." He laughed. "I just witnessed it. Twice."

I shook my head in disbelief but finally answered, "It's being handled."

My brother leaned casually against his desk. "It's being handled? What is that supposed to mean?"

Shrugging, I replied, "It means exactly what it sounds like. I'm handling it. Just because I have feelings for her doesn't mean I have to act on them."

His arms folded around his chest. A flash of metal from his prosthetic caught my eye and didn't go unnoticed by my brother's keen gaze. Like always, he ignored the extra attention and carried on. "Why wouldn't you act on it? You clearly like her."

Like her? Were we in grade school again?

"Well, I could think of several reasons," I said.

"Okay, shoot." My brother wasn't letting me off the hook quite so easily.

I let out an exaggerated sigh. "Well, there's the fact that we're working together. It creates a sort of a problem, don't you think?"

Dean shrugged. "I guess so, but this isn't an official job. You're not being paid, and honestly, I don't think anyone on the committee would care; especially if you have feelings for her."

I rolled my eyes. "Okay, fine. What about the fact that we can't stand one another?"

"I highly doubt that's true."

"Why do you say that?" I asked.

"Well, if it was true, we wouldn't even be having this conversation, now, would we?" His smug grin widened.

Sometimes, I hated my brother.

"Running out of excuses, Taylor," he said, his voice full of satisfaction.

But he was wrong.

I'd saved the best for last.

"She's leaving," I said, wiping that stupid smirk right off my brother's dumb face.

And mine as well.

"She's leaving. In less than six weeks. She'll return to her life in Hawaii, and my life is here. We're not destined to be together like you might think. We're just two ships docked at the same harbor, bound for different destinations. We're not meant to be."

Dean stared at me, those green eyes deep in thought. Finally, he opened his mouth and spoke, "You know, Jake once said something similar to me."

"Yeah, okay. So?"

"It was just after the ferryboat accident. I was still recovering in the hospital, and he'd just returned home to Ocracoke after a twelve-year absence."

"And he was busy stealing your fiancée," I added.

"I broke up with her, remember?"

"I know. And how long until she ended up in Jake's bed? Doesn't that piss you off?"

He let out a sigh. "No," he answered, "it doesn't. Molly was never mine to begin with. Stop interrupting me."

I couldn't help the sly grin that crept across my face.

"Anyway, one day, Jake came to visit me. He said things between Molly and him were hopeless. He had a life in Chicago, and she'd never leave Ocracoke."

"Yeah, but they had history. It's different."

"It's not different, Taylor. They found a way to be together and not because they'd been in love longer than the rest of us. It's not a long-distance race."

"So, you're saying if I give love a chance, love will find a way?" I gave him a dubious look, and each word was said with a serious dose of sarcasm.

"Yes," he said, completely straight-faced.

I merely shook my head, disregarding my brother's attempt at love advice. But as I made my way toward the coffeepot for my third cup of coffee, I couldn't help but hear my own words ringing in my head.

Love will find a way.

<hr>

Dean's talk had left me edgy all morning and well into the afternoon.

And, thanks to a slow day, I had no reason to cancel my plans to go to the beach with Leilani. Not that I wanted to cancel.

But the rational side of me knew I probably should.

She'd said she wanted a friend on the island, but I wasn't sure I could fulfill that particular request. What I wanted from her went far beyond the boundaries of friendship, and every second I spent with her only solidified that fact in my mind.

Dean wasn't wrong. I did indeed have it bad for this woman, but I could control it.

I had to control it.

Otherwise, I'd be lost when she left.

"Just remember how much you hated her when you first met," I said to myself, before remembering just how much of a lie that was. When we first met, I liked her.

A lot.

It wasn't until I discovered her name and the fact that I was supposed to hate her that my feelings changed.

No they didn't, a little voice in my head chided.

Feeling like I was already losing a hopeless battle, I headed over to the hotel, leaving the office to Dean for the rest of the day. We didn't have any tours scheduled, so he'd agreed to close up, so I could take a few hours to take Leilani out to where the Ocracoke ponies were kept. He'd agreed with a wide, knowing grin plastered on his stupid, dumb face, knowing this used to be a signature move of mine as a wild teen. I'd reminded him I hadn't actually taken anyone to see the real ponies. He'd just nodded and smiled wider.

I guessed he figured that meant something as well.

My brother, the love expert.

Walking up to her hotel, I could always feel my heartbeat hammering in my chest. I probably should have called or checked in with her before just dropping in and assuming she could take off at a moment's notice.

But I liked the idea of surprising her.

Maybe her heart would beat just as fast as mine.

With a quick knock on the door, I let myself in, knowing she probably hadn't heard me. In the vast space that was The Cozy Hotel, she could be anywhere.

As it turned out though, I found her in the lobby, hunched over a makeshift desk she'd erected out of an old card table.

Just as I'd thought, she hadn't heard my knock, which allowed me a few quiet moments to watch her.

The light from the large bay windows cast perfect rays, illuminating the beautiful way her hair seemed to flow down her back like a chocolate waterfall. It was long, so long it skimmed the edge of the seat. I wondered what it would feel like to be covered in it, her sitting high atop my body as she rode us both to ecstasy.

"Are you going to stand there watching me all day, Sutherland?"

Busted.

I grinned and took a casual lean against the check-in desk that had seen better days. "Just appreciating the view; that's all."

Her eyes met mine as a single brow lifted. "Now, that doesn't sound professional at all. I do believe that is a rule-breaking sentence, if I've ever heard one."

I couldn't help but notice a small smile tugging at the corner of her lips.

"How do you know I was talking about you?" I said, taking a cursory glance around the shabby lobby.

She let out a laugh. "Okay," she conceded, clearly not believing me for a second. "What can I do for you?"

I stepped forward. "It's actually what I could do for you."

Her breath faltered. "Oh?"

God, I loved messing with her.

"You promised me a maybe."

Her face went through a series of emotions. First, confusion, followed by what appeared to be understanding, and then a sly smile tugged at her lips.

"I don't recall actually promising it, but, yes, I do recall agreeing to…what was it again?"

Now, who was messing with whom?

"Ponies," I said. "I want to take you to see the famous Ocracoke Ponies."

I actually just want to take you right here on this floor, but ponies sounds all right too.

"Right." Her pointer finger rose to her lips as she dramatized her decision-making process. "Well, I guess I could take a bit of time off. I mean, if you think it would help inspire me." Her eyebrow rose in a way that made me think this was a deciding factor.

"Oh, yes, definitely. Absolutely inspiring," I said, going along with her insanity. "No hotel should be erected in Ocracoke without seeing the famed ponies first."

"Great." She grinned. "I'll grab my purse."

"Grab a swimsuit, too," I added.

She immediately turned back around and gave me a dubious face. "You know, you already told me that part of the hustle, right? I know the ponies don't actually roam the beaches anymore."

I laughed. "I know. But it's a nice day. I thought we'd end with dinner on the beach."

"So, why do I need my swimsuit?"

She seemed pretty nervous over a silly swimsuit.

"Because it's the beach," I answered.

She bit down on her bottom lip.

"What?" I finally said.

"I didn't bring one."

I let out a laugh. "You didn't bring one?"

She shook her head.

I motioned toward her. "You're like Miss Hawaiian Tropic, and you didn't bring a swimsuit to a beach town?"

She held up a single finger in my direction. "Okay, first, don't call me that."

I tried not to chuckle.

"And, second, I guess I didn't plan on doing anything but working."

"That's really sad."

"I don't suppose you have a mall I could run to real quick?"

My eyes ventured to the window. "No, but I have the next best thing. Come on." I held out my hand.

"What? Where are we going?"

"Shopping."

"Together?" The idea seemed to mortify her.

We headed toward the double doors of the hotel, and I waited for her to lock up, impressed that she'd finally figured out the tricky key.

"Does that freak you out? Me coming with you?" I asked, leaning against the door as she dropped the keys into her purse.

Her eyes found mine and slowly made their way down and back up again.

Oh, yeah, it does.

"No," she lied.

I couldn't help the wide smile I now carried. "Good. Then, let's go."

We walked side by side down the road, a custom I was growing rather fond of.

"So, where are we headed?" she asked.

"Just over there." I pointed.

Her eyes followed. "Oh, yeah, I meant to check that place out the day I arrived but ended up at your place first, and… well, I was a bit flustered afterward."

That statement made me smile. "Flustered?"

"I'm not used to being hit on like that," she admitted.

"What?" I found myself taken aback. "I mean, not that I relish in the idea of men throwing themselves at you on a regular basis, but I hardly think that's true. Maybe you just don't notice it. Like the architect."

She shrugged. "I work a lot."

I grinned. "That's your answer? You work a lot? I work a lot, too, but I still manage to—"

Her hand went up. "Please don't finish that sentence."

A chuckle escaped my lips. "Fair enough. Hey, we're here."

Her eyes turned upward. The bold new sign Millie had designed, which proudly displayed the store named Beachcombers, caught her eye.

But only for a fraction of a second.

I pulled the door open and ushered her in.

"That was definitely a rule-breaker," I said softly in her ear as she went.

"What was? Allowing you to open the door for me?"

"No. Getting jealous over my after-work activities." I grinned.

Her gaze turned to mine. "Then, so is asking about men flirting with me."

Shrugging, I followed her in. "You brought it up."

"Oh my God!" Millie's voice brought my attention forward. "Is that…no."

My eyes rolled.

"It couldn't possibly be!"

"Millie," I warned, but she carried on with the theatrics as Leilani watched the exchange between us, probably wondering if this was just another blonde I'd slept with.

"It is! It's my good friend Taylor. But what's this? What's he doing here, in my store? He never comes here."

"You're being ridiculous."

She smiled. "I know. But it has been a while since you've passed through those doors."

"No, it hasn't," I argued. "I was here…" I tried to think back as both women waited.

"See?" Millie's smile widened.

"Okay, fine. But can you blame me? Look at this place. What in the world would I buy?"

Leilani did just that, her wide eyes roaming as she took it all in. It really was an impressive shop filled with beautiful clothes, handcrafted items, and gifts, but there was definitely a female vibe, and I wasn't feeling it.

"Well, I'm glad you're here. What can I do for you? Or are

you just here to introduce me to your new friend?" she asked, turning her attention to Leilani.

I was grateful for the hospitality from Millie. I knew everyone had been nervous since the arrival of Leilani and her ideas for this hotel project, but so far, aside from me, she'd been met with nothing but kindness.

I swallowed hard.

That was a sobering revelation.

It was true. From my brother to the committee to everyone she'd met in the town, not a single person had acted out in anger toward her.

Not one person but me.

"Uh…" I stumbled for a moment, still lost in my thought. "Leilani seems to have forgotten her bathing suit back home. Do you think you could help her pick one out?"

Millie's eyes lit up in excitement. "Of course!" She motioned to the back of the store, and Leilani quickly followed. "I've just started carrying this line—super on trend but not too hard on the pocketbook." Millie suddenly looked like she'd said something wrong. "Not that you have to worry—"

Leilani smiled warmly. "I love a good bargain."

A look of relief spread across Millie's face as I leaned back against the checkout counter.

"Oh, good, because, when I spotted those designer shoes, I got a little worried I wouldn't have anything suitable for your high standards."

Leilani batted her hand as they both dived into the racks. "Please," she said. "I've had these for ages, and it took three paychecks to afford them."

The statement surprised both Millie and me.

Leilani was an heiress after all. The title alone assumed a certain sort of lifestyle. I mean, we'd all grown up watching Paris Hilton.

"I used to have a pair just like them," Millie boasted.

"Bought them right off the runway in Paris, but I sold them and all their little brothers and sisters to afford this place."

Leilani took a moment to look around. "I think you made the right choice. And I love the color scheme you went with."

"Really?" Millie said, the pride she felt over this shop showing all over her face. "Because I had an interior designer from Nags Head come down, and she suggested something completely different than this, but it just didn't feel right."

Leilani shook her head, her eyes briefly landing on mine. "Sometimes, you just have to go with your gut."

I wasn't sure if she was referring to her hotel or me, but either way, my stomach flip-flopped like a freaking teenager hoping to get to second base. I continued to wait around as the two women made small talk until Leilani had several swimsuits picked out and headed into the changing room.

The effort it took not to picture her stripping down naked was monumental.

"So, what's the deal between you two?" Millie asked, her voice barely a whisper as she joined me at the wooden counter. She pretended to be interested in organizing several displays of jewelry, but really, she was just being nosy.

"What do you mean, what's the deal?"

She shook her head, smiling. "I mean, are you playing nice, still hoping to sabotage her plans—"

My eyes nearly bugged out of my head as they jerked to the changing room across the store. "Dude!"

Her smile only deepened. "Or are you really into this woman?"

Before I had a chance to answer that question, Leilani peeked her head out of the dressing room, and I felt my mouth fall to the floor.

"Do you think you could grab a larger top for me in this one? I'm always a size larger up here," she asked Millie, showing her the mini red bikini top that barely covered her breasts.

Fuck. Me.

I didn't even try not to stare. I mean, what man could?

If anything, I was just training myself for the torture I'd endure later on in the day.

The beach?

What the hell had I been thinking?

"Sure," Millie said, giving me an amused grin before she ran to the racks. She handed Leilani the top she needed.

By the time she returned, I was pretty sure there was drool forming around the corners of my mouth.

"Oh, man. You've got it bad, don't you?"

"We're just friends," I answered immediately.

She laughed. "Okay."

"What? I can be friends with a female," I demanded. "We're friends. And we were platonic friends way before you met Aiden."

"Yeah, but you never looked at me like that," she said quietly, giving a head nod in the direction of the changing room where Leilani was currently trying on a plethora of teeny, tiny bikinis.

So much for not picturing her naked.

"That's because you're my friend," I said the words before I even realized they were coming out of my mouth.

A satisfied grin spread across Millie's face. "Exactly."

"See? I told you," I boasted as we pulled back onto Highway 12, having just spent an ample amount of time watching the once-wild ponies of Ocracoke.

I caught a warm smile from the passenger seat.

"Yes, you were the perfect gentleman. And I even got another history lesson."

"Well, I couldn't take you to see the infamous Banker ponies and not tell you the legends of how they got their name."

She laughed. "I swear, you must know everything about this island," she said.

I shrugged. "It's my home. Tell me you don't know a ton of random facts about Hawaii."

Her eyes narrowed as she thought it over. I'd already begun to pull over to the small turnout that led to the beach I wanted to take her to. It was a local spot I'd been visiting since I was a kid.

"I guess so," she answered. "Although I think I would know more if my grandparents were still around. And my mom."

I nodded. "There are definitely parts of my family history that are spotty because my father is gone."

Her eyes lifted to mine. I guessed it was the first time I'd mentioned him.

"How old were you?"

"Young," I replied. "Too young to remember..."

Much.

I paused for a moment, gathering my thoughts. "But my mom has always been more than enough, and I had Dean."

"He seems like a good guy, your brother?"

I smiled. "Yeah. Perhaps a bit nosy, but he's all right. No brothers or sisters for you?"

She shook her head as both of us headed out of the car. "I remember asking for a little sister once when I was young, but my mom said—jokingly, of course—that they had their hands full with me. I don't know if they just didn't want any more or if there was some other reason, but I grew up as an only child."

"Sounds lonely," I said as I grabbed the cooler from the back of the truck.

We continued our tradition of walking side by side, but this time, our heels dug into the sand as we climbed the dunes toward the beach.

"It wasn't," she replied. "Or, at least, it wasn't until..." Her voice faded.

"How old were you?" I asked, echoing her words from earlier.

"Fifteen," she said.

I winced. What a terrible age to lose a mother.

Not that there was ever a good time, but at fifteen, with all those awkward hormones and emotions to navigate, it was a delicate time, to say the least.

Even I'd needed my mom's shoulder to lean on more than once.

"My father was making the globe-trotting, mega-millionaire thing sort of work back then, coming home when he could, but after my mom died, he just gave up on anything family-related."

"Hence the reason you mentioned the hotel staff before?"

She nodded. "Yeah, they were basically my family for those last few years of high school. Sad, huh?"

I stood straight and looked her in the eye. "No, not sad at all. You found a family when your own let you down. I'd call that pretty damn brave."

A small smirk tugged at the corners of her lips before her attention turned to the cooler I'd dropped on the sand next to me. "So, what does Taylor Sutherland bring to the beach? Beer and chips?"

"You seriously think I'd bring you all the way out here with just a cooler full of beer and a measly bag of chips? What kind of friend do you take me for?"

Her hands found her hips, reminding me that, before we'd left Beachcombers, she'd slipped a bathing suit on under her sundress. Just remembering her breasts peeking out of that bikini top had me giddy with anticipation, wondering what was waiting for me underneath it.

Not for me, I reminded myself. *Definitely not for me.*

"Well, I was hoping you'd pack a little more, but I wasn't sure. You are a bachelor. For all I know, it could be leftovers from your fridge."

I gave her an exasperated look. "And, if it were, you'd be delightfully surprised because I am an excellent cook."

"Really?" Her brow rose. "Well then, show me what you've got."

Now, it was my brow that rose...and waggled. She laughed out loud.

"That's definitely breaking the rules," she warned.

"You're no fun."

"You're the one who made them up," she replied with a shrug.

I know, I thought, remembering just how tight that bikini top had been while stretched over those perky breasts of hers. *Don't remind me.*

To prove to her just how good my cooking skills were, I popped open the cooler and began pulling things out.

When her eyes widened, I realized I might have gone a little overboard.

Okay, I probably should have realized that late last night when I had lost sleep, cooking for a girl I was convinced was no more than a friend.

Yeah, I definitely had it bad.

"You made all of this?" she exclaimed as I pulled out homemade chicken salad, rolls, several side dishes, and of course, dessert.

"I like to cook," I simply said.

"Well, you'll be happy to know, I am a girl who likes to eat."

"Thank God." I laughed.

We both dug in, and I felt a distinct sense of pride as I watched her sink her teeth into the food I'd made especially for her. I rarely cooked for other people, aside from my brother's early morning visits, and it was nice to feel appreciated and see the joy in someone else's eyes.

Or maybe just hers.

We ate in comfortable silence for a time, enjoying the warm afternoon sun and each other's company.

Nothing was hurried or rushed, just like a day at the beach was supposed to be.

"I would have never guessed you were such an amazing cook," Leilani finally said, nibbling on a brownie. "What are some other random facts about you that I might not know?"

"Well, let me think," I said, leaning back on my elbows. "I was a scrawny kid. Bet you didn't know that."

She laughed. "No way."

"Yep." I grinned. "Smallest kid in my kindergarten class. But there were only three of us, so it wasn't great odds, but I was still pretty small. I didn't fill out until middle school."

"Only three? That's crazy." She briefly paused, probably trying to visualize a class size that small. Finally, she spoke up again, "Give me another."

"Okay," I agreed, turning toward her. "I guess this one might be hard to believe, given my love for my town, but up until a few years ago, my plan was to eventually leave Ocracoke."

"Really? Why?"

"You heard the part about three kids being in my kindergarten class?"

She giggled.

"Seriously though, I just wanted to be somewhere different—or so I thought. I thought there was something missing, like I was—"

"Waiting for your life to start?"

Our eyes met.

"Yeah."

"I feel that way, too," she admitted. "Like I'm just holding my breath, waiting for my real life to begin."

"And has it?" I asked.

"I'm starting to wonder."

The air seemed to crackle around us, making my skin prickle and my heart race.

God, I wanted to kiss her again. What I wouldn't give to feel those lips against mine, to slip my hand under that short, little skirt, and to finally give in to all those fantasies I'd been having of us together.

But, instead, I opened my mouth and asked her a question, "What about you?" I felt like the ultimate loser. I'd never been one to beat around the bush when it came to making the moves on a woman. But, Leilani was different.

Leilani was more. "What are some random facts about you?" I asked.

Her eyes blinked several times before she answered, obviously still stuck in the moment I'd just yanked us out of, "Um…oh!" She grinned, moving her leg so that her ankle was in plain view. "I have a tattoo!"

I leaned forward, running my finger on the tiny lightning bolt that adorned the inside of her ankle. Her breath caught the second I touched her, which only made me want to linger there longer.

Her gaze met mine. "That's a rule-breaker," she managed to say but only just. She was so caught up in my touch she could barely get a word out.

Grinning, I pulled back. "Which house?" I asked, nodding to her tattoo.

Seemingly impressed, she replied, "Ravenclaw. You?"

"Take a guess," I said.

She looked at me, her lips scrunched to the side as she took an appraisal of me.

"Gryffindor?" she said.

"That's correct! Or at least, that's what my niece told me when she made me take the test one day in the office. I actually bought the first book, but I haven't had the time to start it yet. Lizzie—that's my niece—and her mom are obsessed with all things Harry Potter. Well, that, and a whole plethora of things I don't understand."

"Well, the fact that you're willing to take the time to learn about something for your niece is pretty cool."

"Lizzie's pretty cool," I said adamantly. "You'll have to meet her sometime."

Her smile held warmth. "I'd like that."

"What's another one?" I asked, liking this little game we'd started. It was fun to get to know her a bit better, and as an added bonus, it was an easy distraction from wanting to tear her clothes off.

Well, almost.

"Oh, um…" I could see the wheels spinning as she thought of another random fact. Suddenly, her eyes went to the waves nearby. "I haven't been swimming since I was a teenager."

"What?" I exclaimed.

Her hands found her face. She melted into them, covering her head in shame. "I know; it's horrible."

"That's…" I couldn't even find the words. "Like, a decade!"

"I know!"

"Why? And are we talking all kinds of swimming? Pool, ocean? Not even a quick dunk in a Jacuzzi?"

She just shrugged her shoulders.

Her eyes finally met mine, and I couldn't help the grin that tugged at my lips. It only grew when her adorable face appeared, so bewildered over her silly confession.

"I was kind of a nerd in college," she explained. "And I guess I just forgot?"

"You forgot?" I echoed her words like they were just too ridiculous to be heard. "Who forgets to swim?"

"I don't know," she laughed. "I mean, you saw the tattoo. I'm an indoor girl. Books and Netflix—"

"Now, I understand why you forgot your bathing suit," I said with a chuckle.

"I didn't forget it," she fessed up. "Up until today, I didn't actually own one."

"You're the worst Hawaiian I know."

Her arms wrapped across her chest. "Oh? And how many of us do you know?"

"Well, just you. But you're really ruining the stereotype I had."

She laughed. "And you're ruining the stereotype I had of Southerners."

My brow lifted. "Oh, yeah? And what exactly did you envision a Southerner to be when you flew all the way over here?"

Her eyes roamed down my body, like they often did, giving me a giant dose of confidence. "Well, I expected more of a Southern drawl," she said.

I shrugged. "You're going to have to go inland for that. I've got what's called an Ocracoke brogue—or what's left of it. It's a dying dialect, but if you want to hear it all out, come over to Sunday dinner with my mama."

"Is that an invitation?"

"I believe it is."

"Good."

"Now, about that swimming hiatus," I said, rising to my feet.

"What? No!"

I held out my hand. She warily eyed it.

"Why do you think I made you buy a bathing suit?" I asked.

"So, you could gawk at me while I tried it on?" she fired back.

I let out a chuckle. "That was, by far, the best part of my day."

"You're breaking the rules again, Taylor." She grinned.

"You're changing the subject, Leilani."

"Do I have to?"

"Of course you don't," I said. "I'd never force you. But don't you want to?"

Her eyes fell to the waves breaking just feet from our picnic, and finally, she reached up and took my hand.

Success.

When she rose to her feet, I heard her exhale a large breath from her lungs, like she was expelling nervousness from her body. I kind of liked that I set her on edge.

"We need to get undressed first," she said, her voice barely above a whisper.

Staring down at her, I managed to blink several times before answering, "Sorry, what?"

A slow grin stretched across her face. "Water," she said before adding, "Swimsuits?"

None of these words seemed to be working on me. I was still stuck back on the part of the conversation where she'd mentioned getting undressed.

A laugh escaped Leilani's lips before she rolled her eyes, and she playfully slapped my arm. "You're horrible. And you're breaking the rules again."

I shrugged as she began pulling off her dress. "You're the one talking about getting naked."

Her dress halfway over her head, I heard her laugh. "I didn't say anything about getting naked!"

"Sorry," I said, taking her all in. The naturally tan skin… the legs that seemed to go on forever…the bikini. "Can't talk right now. Having a heart attack."

And back down went the dress.

She tried to appear flustered, mad even, but she couldn't hide the smirk that pulled at the corners of her mouth. Even when she placed her hand on her hip and said, "Nope, we're not doing this."

"What? Why?"

Her forehead wrinkled as her brow rose. "Why? Because you clearly can't follow the rules."

And you clearly love it when I don't, I wanted to say.

But I didn't.

She was right.

We were supposed to be just friends, and I was breaking the rules I'd made.

But, damn, it was fun.

"Come on." I offered my hand once again. "I'll be good."

She cocked her head to the side, contemplating my request, before finally sliding her fingers into mine.

"Okay," she said. "But, only because I want to be able to say I swam in the Atlantic Ocean."

I nodded. "Deal."

"And you won't make any inappropriate comments when I take off my dress?"

"Nope," I said.

I'll be thinking them though, I thought.

All of them.

At once.

"Total saint," I promised.

I wasn't sure she believed the last part, which I gave her credit for, but she began disrobing all the same. To keep myself occupied, I did as well, stripping off my shirt and kicking off my shoes.

When I turned back around, I found Leilani gawking at me.

With a smug grin, I chose not to point out the fact that the rule-breaking was now completely on her.

"Ready?" I asked, trying not to look at her for too long, for fear that things down below would become too hard far too quickly.

Brilliant idea, I scolded myself. *Take the hot new friend that you're desperately trying not to bang out to the beach where you'll both be half-naked and wet.*

Fucking genius.

"Yep," she said just before a mischievous grin appeared on those rosy red lips of hers. "Race you to the shore!"

And then she took off.

Just when I'd thought I had this nerdy, indoor girl pegged.

I took off after her, laughter welling up from my insides as my legs dug into the sand to try to catch up.

Damn, she was actually a lot faster than I had given her credit for.

But I was a seasoned runner.

We darted around the shore, and finally, as my feet splashed into the water, I grabbed her around the waist, her voice squealing out in delight, and I declared myself the winner.

Her legs kicked, sending salt water into my face.

"No, no, no!" She laughed. "I beat you fair and square!"

"Did not!"

"Did so," she announced. "I said, first one to the shore, and clearly, that was me!"

I'd waded us out past several waves. The water reached mid-thigh for me but probably waist deep if I were to let her go.

"Hmm," I said playfully. "You see, that's kind of a problem for me."

"Oh, really?" She joined in the fun, not caring in the least that I hadn't let her go as I ventured out a little deeper.

"Yeah, you see, I'm kind of a sore loser."

"Really?" Her lips formed a sort of knowing smirk. "I would never have guessed."

"I know. Such a surprise."

She rolled her eyes.

"Anyway, I tend to act out."

"Act out?"

I nodded. "When I lose. Not violently, mind you. But I might be known to just—" My hands around her waist were her only warning before I lifted her up and tossed her.

When her face broke the surface of the water, her dark hair now wrapped around her like liquid silk and those chocolate brown eyes searching, I knew I was going to get some serious payback.

"That was not nice," she grinned, shaking out her wet hair.

"Like I said, I'm not a great loser."

I watched as she bobbed over to me. We were deep enough now that she couldn't touch the bottom, but I could.

A small advantage that she didn't seem to need.

As soon as she got close enough to me, she pounced. Her legs went around my waist, and all her weight went to pushing me under.

Instantly, I was fish food.

When I came sputtering up for air, I was ready for war.

Instead of tossing her this time, I tried her tactic. Dunking. But she was prepared for that. Wrapping her legs around my waist, she'd made herself dunk-proof.

This girl was smart.

But she'd lost the element of surprise, and this time, I wasn't going to go down without a fight.

We wrestled around, laughing and yelling at each other, neither gaining much ground until one thing started to become painfully aware.

Just how close we were.

Her body, covered by that bikini—which would probably keep me up all night—was pressed so tightly against me that I could feel her heart beating inside her chest.

And the fact that we were in water? It just made it ten times worse.

Because, every time she moved against me, she slid.

Up and down.

Now that I was aware of the proximity, that only made me imagine what it would feel like to have her sliding around on top of me in a bed.

Leilani's breath caught, and I realized why.

All that rubbing and dirty thoughts had caused the semi-wood I sported whenever she was near to go full out.

And she'd noticed.

In a big way.

But, instead of pushing away from me like she normally would, citing our dumb rules or making a silly joke, she just sat there in my arms, lost in the moment with me.

Could she feel it, too?

The sizzle in the air. The crackle in the atmosphere when we touched.

How could I be just friends with someone who made me feel so much?

That was the ultimate question.

The one I was too scared to answer.

And so, this time, it was me to put on the brakes, and I stepped back.

Because, like I'd told her earlier in our little game in the water…

I was a sore loser.

And, if Sierra was right and love and life really were a game, I wasn't sure I could play and afford to lose this one.

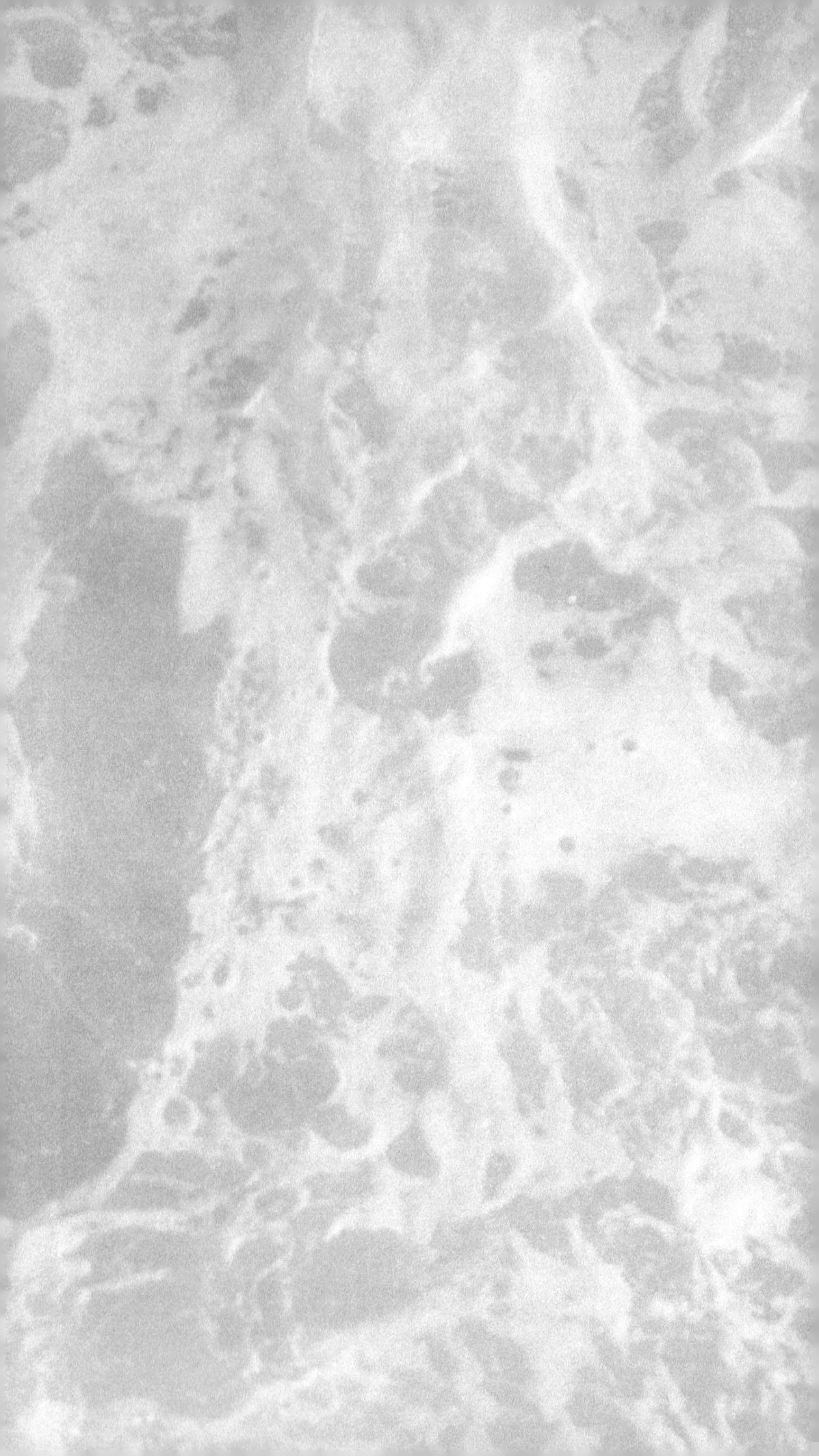

CHAPTER TEN

Leilani

After that moment in the water between Taylor and me, the one I couldn't stop thinking about, I was in desperate need of advice.

And there was only one place I would go searching for it.

"Oh my God, do you know what time it is?"

I checked my phone. "Um, yeah. It's midnight here, so it should be, like, barely dinnertime there."

Piper laughed. "Yeah, I know. I'm just messing with you. What's up? I haven't heard from you in a while. Are you burning the midnight oil, trying to get that place ready for your dad?"

"Yes," I said at first, but then I let out a big sigh and finally said, "No."

"No? Are you all finished then?"

"Are you kidding?"

She made a sort of noncommittal noise. "I just figured I'd ask. Maybe you were out, celebrating your success?"

"I wish."

"Okay." She was obviously sensing my distress. Her best-friend vibes were strong. "Well, let's start with the basics, shall we? How is the project going?"

I slumped down on the bed in my suite, and I stared up at

the ceiling. I'd managed to change out of my wet clothes from the beach and shower after I got home, rinsing all the sand and ocean water from my body.

But the memory of that moment in the water…

"It's behind," I answered, clearing my throat. "I'm seriously behind."

"Why?" she asked. "Are you having problems with the locals like you anticipated?"

I snorted. "You could say that."

A silence passed between us before she spoke again, "You know, this kind of skeptic nonsense might work with others but not with me. So, why don't you cut the bullshit and tell me what's really going on?"

"God, I miss you." I laughed.

"My feelings for you right now are a little muddled, so spill."

"I think I'm falling for someone."

Well, that one shut her right up.

So much so, that, after a while, I actually had to respond with, "Hello?"

"I'm sorry. Did you just say you were falling for someone?"

"Yes,"

"And by someone, you do mean, an actual person? Like flesh and blood? Not a TV character on *Game of Thrones*?"

I rolled my eyes. "No, this time, it's not *John Snow*. Promise."

She waited, still expecting further clarification.

"Or anyone else of a fictional nature."

"Sorry," she said. "I just had to make sure. You haven't had an actual crush on someone in…well, eons."

My mouth gaped open. "I have, too!"

"Have not," she countered. "Name one."

Sitting up on the bed, I fired back, "The IT guy from work."

She made another sound that made it clear that she was

not impressed. "Gary? Oh, please. You were not at all interested in Gary from IT!"

"I dated him! I'd call that interested."

If someone were to give out an award for the biggest eye roll, it would be awarded to Piper because, even with her being in Hawaii, I felt the effects of her peepers twirling around in her head from that statement.

"There is a difference between going out with someone because you're too polite to say no and being so over the moon for someone that you can hardly breathe. Now, tell me," she said, "which one describes your relationship with Gary?"

I thought back to our less than stellar date to the aquarium where he'd tried to impress me with the name of every fish in the place.

And yes, I do mean, every single one. He really liked fish.

"Um…"

"Exactly. So, you want to tell me about your mystery man now?"

"Well, now, I'm kind of scared to," I confessed, finally settling back into my pillows at the top of the bed.

She laughed. "I know I'm doing a good job when I've scared you. What's it this time?"

"Well, what if he's not worthy enough? What if you deem him as just another Gary?"

"Oh, please, Lani," she said. "The fact that you're even bringing him up makes him so far from Gary, it's not even funny. If he were anything like Gary, you would have sent him packing the day your dad gave you that ultimatum. Come on, it's midnight, and you're up, thinking about a guy and not the project you have to present to your father in five weeks. Definitely not a Gary."

"Yeah, okay," I agreed, giggling. "I feel kind of bad for Gary now."

"Don't," she said. "He's marrying a gorgeous girl from marketing in a few weeks."

"Oh," I replied, feeling kind of relieved. "Well, good for Gary then."

"Her name is Dory."

"Shut your mouth!"

"I kid you not," she said. "They're having an entire under-water-themed wedding. A bunch of the IT guys were telling me about it the other day in the break room. I've been flirting hard with several of them, trying to see if I can score one of their plus ones…"

I couldn't help but chuckle. "Well, you'll have to give me a full report if you do go."

"Oh, believe me, I will. So, are you going to tell me about this guy, or am I going to have to pry it out of you as usual?"

Direct and to the point. That was Piper.

"Well, actually, you already know a little about him," I said.

"I do?"

"Yeah, remember the guy I met the first day I was here?"

Her voice changed, and even I could hear the sudden note of surprise in it. "You mean, the guy you gave a stern talking-to? The one who was so angry with you? That guy?"

"Yep."

"Wow. He talked to you after that? What does he look like?"

My stomach instantly fluttered. "You kind of know that as well."

I waited for her to put two and two together.

"He's the sexy guy in the photo you sent me? Damn. Does he have a brother? Because, if so, do you need an assistant? Maybe these North Carolina men really do need some checking out."

I laughed. "He does have a brother, but he's married."

"Boo."

"I thought you had an IT guy to woo," I said jokingly.

"Believe the words that are coming out of my mouth"—she said—"none of our IT guys look like that."

I smiled to myself. "I'm pretty sure Taylor is one of a kind, Piper. Sorry."

"Man, you really do have it bad for this guy."

"I know," I said. "That's why you have to help me."

"Babe, I know it's maybe been a while, but I'm sure you'll figure it all out." She laughed. "It really is like riding a bicycle."

"Not that!" I exclaimed. "I'm pretty sure I still know how to do that." I thought back to how it'd felt to be wrapped around Taylor, his body so hard and ready for me. "Yes, I definitely know how all that still works."

"Great."

"Good." I let out a huff of air from my lungs.

"Then, why do you sound so frustrated?" she finally asked.

"Because I don't think any of this is a good idea," I finally blurted out.

"What?"

"Me, him—us. It's not a good idea. Did I tell you we work together?"

"Uh, no. You didn't mention—"

I didn't let her finish. The dam had been broken. The floodgates were open. I was letting it all out now. "The town appointed him as my go-between. Him! Can you believe that? Of all the people in this town, they sent him! The one man I couldn't stand!"

"But, clearly, you can. Stand him, that is."

"Of course I can!" My hands went up in the air. "Did I mention we kissed?"

"No!".

"Yep. We kissed. It was amazing. Like life-altering. Until I stepped back and told him I didn't need any distractions."

"Ouch."

"I know. I'm an idiot. So, now, we have rules."

"What rules?" she asked, obviously trying to keep up with my convoluted life.

"We're not allowed to date each other."

"I see."

"And," I added, "We're not allowed to date anyone else either."

"Huh? Who made up that one?"

"He did."

"Oh, really?"

"He said it was only going to distract us further. I agreed because…well, that was the day that I saw him with the blonde at lunch."

"Lani, you are making my head spin."

"Sorry," I said, realizing I had been talking way too fast. "He just makes me crazy."

"Love can do that."

"Love?" I echoed. "Who said anything about love?"

"You didn't have to. It's written all over your face."

I scrunched my lips to the side. "You can't see my face, genius."

"No," she agreed. "But I don't need to. I can hear it in your voice, Lani. You're in love with this guy. Or you're well on your way."

The very idea scared me.

"But I barely know him, and I'm only here for five more weeks," I said.

And, again, when she smiled, I could hear it in her voice just as loudly as the love she supposedly heard in mine.

"Then, make the most of it," she encouraged. "Isn't that what your mom would have done?"

"Enjoy every moment," I whispered, remembering the words she'd said to me over and over throughout my childhood. It's something I'd shared with Piper many times in our long reminiscent talks. "But what if he doesn't—"

She didn't even let me finish the sentence. "Then, at least you'll know you tried."

I'd come here to experience something new.

Something different from the ordinary.

Maybe what I had been looking for all along was him.

"Get out of the car, Lani," I said to myself for the fifth time.

I'd been sitting in this borrowed car, just outside of Taylor's house, for what seemed like a century, trying to get up the nerve to walk up to his front door.

After practically no sleep following my lengthy conversation with Piper the night before and basically not a bit of work done during the day because I couldn't keep myself away from the hotel windows in hopes that I'd catch a glimpse of him working at his desk, or heaven forbid, even chatting it up with a gorgeous tourist, I had known I had to do something.

Yes, I had it bad.

So bad in fact, that by the time I'd made it back to the inn, I'd driven myself so mad with indecision that I basically spilled my secrets to the first bystander who walked by.

Poor Molly didn't know what had hit her.

Luckily, the young mother had been more than eager to help me in my hour of need.

She, like Piper, had believed I should seize the moment.

So, here I was, seizing the moment.

Yep, definitely seizing it.

I stared out at his front door again.

If I stayed in this parked car much longer, someone might report me for suspicious activity, and wouldn't that be lovely?

Oh, no, Taylor, I wasn't stalking you. I was actually just gathering up the courage to knock on your door—you know, to see if you wanted to break some of those rules and get naked with me?

My head fell to the top of the steering wheel. "Come on, Lani. This is ridiculous. Get up."

I blew out a breath and reached for the handle.

This was why I'd wanted this job in the first place.

I thought of Taylor on that first morning, bare-chested on the boat dock.

Okay, maybe not this exact reason.

But I'd wanted this promotion, this freedom, so I could finally do all the things I'd only dreamed of.

I'd been living inside for far too long.

Hell, I'd barely been living at all up until now.

It was time for all that to change.

It was time for this life of mine to begin.

Finally finding the confidence I needed, I pushed open the car door and went for it. I walked toward that front door, thankful for Molly and her meddling. She'd not only supplied me with an ample pep talk, complete with homemade baked goods that I'd totally devoured and the car that had gotten me here, but she'd also supplied me with Taylor's address, something I hadn't known until tonight.

Standing at his doorway now, I could see him everywhere —from the well-kept entryway that boasted several potted plants to the weathered plaque on the door that proudly displayed his last name.

Smiling, I wondered if it, too, came with its own history lesson.

There was only one way to find out.

So, I knocked on the door.

And I waited and waited.

And, finally, when that front door creaked open, I found myself face-to-face with someone I hadn't expected.

"Sierra," I said, trying to sound pleasant even though my spirit was being crushed by her very presence.

The smile on her face, the carefree one she'd answered the door with, faltered. "Lani," she replied.

How did she know that nickname?

"Who's at the door?" Taylor's voice made my body freeze in place when all I wanted to do was run.

"This isn't what it looks like," Sierra said.

And, for a moment, I believed her. For a moment, I

thought I felt a connection, a brief flash of something that felt like friendship—or at least, the beginning of it—but then my gaze flickered past hers, and I saw Taylor standing at the foot of the stairs, his eyes telling me everything I needed to know.

"It was stupid of me to assume you weren't busy," I said, my words fumbling over one another like dominoes. Kind of ironic because that was exactly how my life felt right that second.

My foot took a step back, and I saw Taylor's take one step forward.

"Leilani."

I waited for him to finish, to beg me not to go, but his wide eyes and silence seemed to drag on endlessly.

I guessed there was nothing else to say.

I'd misinterpreted the signs.

I'd turned harmless flirting into something it wasn't, and now, here I was, ready to open my heart to someone who was clearly interested in someone else.

I was a fool.

A fool who was about to cry.

So before that happened, I willed my body into motion and turned back down that walkway, back to the car that had seemed so difficult to get out of just moments earlier, and then I drove away.

I drove away from Taylor and the girl he'd called nothing more than a friend, and I drove to the only safe place on the island.

My crappy hotel.

But it wasn't mine, now, was it? It was my father's. Just like everything in my life.

Stepping out of the borrowed car that I'd been gifted until morning, I decided this was as good of a place as any to stay for the night. I really didn't want to return to the inn less than an hour after I'd left. Molly would find out soon enough about my fallout with Taylor, I was sure.

Until then, I really could use these precious hours to wallow.

A crack of thunder above my head made me jump, and I hurried toward the entrance.

"Leilani!"

It didn't take a genius to guess who that was. I turned around and saw Taylor jogging up to me from the parking lot.

"Whose car is that?" he asked, his breath heavy as he reached me.

"Did you come all this way to ask me that?"

"No, of course not."

My less than chipper greeting must have thrown him, but I wasn't budging. I just stood and waited for him to explain his presence.

The blank stare should have been familiar. He'd perfected it not fifteen minutes earlier.

I could tell he was about to say something. He reached out for me, and his lips parted, but just as the words were forming, the sky opened, and it began to rain.

Hard.

So, I made a run for it.

Grabbing my keys, thankful I'd finally mastered the tricky lock, I got the front door unlocked as the rain fell around me and pushed my way inside. Dropping my soaking wet purse on the ground, I pulled off my coat and let it fall into a heap on the floor as well.

I might have huffed a bit in the process.

"You're cute when you're mad."

I might have also forgotten to shut the door.

Turning, I saw an equally soaked Taylor standing just inside the entryway. Thanks to the wet shirt currently sticking to his body, I could see each defined muscle of his stomach like there was nothing there.

It was like my own personal wet T-shirt contest, and Taylor was my obvious winner.

Focus, Lani.

Remember knocking at his door? Remember Sierra?

"I'm not mad," I said, my chin held firm as my arms folded across my own soggy T-shirt.

The movement didn't go unnoticed by him, and I saw a definite grin pass across his face.

"Okay. Then, you're cute when you're jealous," he said, amending his previous statement, which only made my mouth gape open.

"I am not jealous!" I exclaimed.

"No?" He took a couple of steps forward.

"No," I answered. "I don't care what you do with your free time. Or whom you do it with."

His grin widened. "Now, that sounds a bit like jealousy to me."

A couple more steps were taken in my direction. I took several back.

"Why were you at my house tonight, Lani?"

It was the first time he'd ever called me by that name. I liked the way it sounded on his tongue.

But it didn't change the fact that he'd been with someone else tonight.

"I wanted to run some things by you. You know, for the hotel."

His eyes followed the curve of the ceiling before finding mine once again. A knowing smile spread across his face as he took another step or two. It was like being stalked by a lion.

"You wanted to run some things by me? At nearly eight o'clock in the evening?"

I shrugged, trying to play it off. "Sure. Why not?"

"How did you get my address?"

I swallowed down the lump in my throat. "Molly."

"And the car?" he asked. "You never answered who it belongs to."

I took a few more steps back until my butt hit the corner of the desk I'd set up. "Also Molly's," I said. "Shouldn't you know that? You seem to know everything about everyone."

He grinned, ignoring my question entirely. Of course he knew who's car it was.

Jerk.

"And you just came over to…how did you put it? Run some things by me?"

"Yes," I answered. "Exactly."

He took one last step forward, his body pressing against mine. I should push him away, but I didn't.

I should hate him, but I couldn't.

He leaned in close, so close that I could feel his breath against my skin. "I've said it before, but I'll say it again. Sierra is just a friend; a friend who is getting over a hard breakup and needed a night away from her grandparents'."

I didn't believe him. "Then why did you look so guilty when you saw me?"

His face blanched. "It wasn't guilt you saw, Leilani. It was fear."

"Fear?"

"I thought I could follow the rules with you because you pushed me away. You didn't want this. You didn't want me. I was a distraction, and you were only asking for friendship. But when I saw you standing at my doorstep, I knew this thing between us, it was real and—"

"And?"

"It scared me."

"It scared me, too," I confessed.

"But you know what scared me more?" he whispered, his voice so smooth that my heart did a somersault in my chest.

"What?" I breathed out.

"Watching you walk away."

His words made my breath catch in my throat, and looking up at him, I felt the air suddenly change between us. Just like the storm raging on outside, something was building between us.

Something big.

"Lani, we have less than five weeks. I can't offer you anything past—"

"I like it when you call me Lani." I smiled lazily.

"Concentrate!" He laughed, his arms wrapping around my waist.

"Look," I said, "I know we have only a finite amount of time, but I'm okay with that."

"You're okay with the fact that you live over four thousand miles away from here?"

"No," I answered. "But can't we choose to just not think about it?"

He looked conflicted, but his grip on my waist tightened. "It's either that or we go back to being friends."

"You were a horrible friend anyway," I said.

He smirked but didn't seem convinced.

"We both said the other day, that we felt like we were waiting for our lives to start. Maybe we just need to learn how to take leaps when the universe offers them," I offered.

He cupped my face, sincerity written all over his. "I just don't want to hurt you."

"Then don't," I simply said.

He stared down at me, the resolve in his dark green eyes becoming clearer with each passing second as he pulled me closer. "I'm going to kiss you now, Lani," he said, sending a thrill of anticipation down to my very core. "And when I do, you can just consider that friendship of ours null and void, because after I'm done thoroughly kissing you, we're going to spend the rest of the night breaking every other stupid rule we made."

His lips found mine before I even got the chance for a rebuttal.

Not that I'd had one.

Because, holy hell, this man could kiss.

His fingers wove into my hair, pushing me back onto the

desk. It wasn't the sturdiest piece of furniture, but it held as I sat back and let him devour me.

It was as if he was in a frenzy one minute and taking his time the next. As if he couldn't wait to see what was next. He lifted my still-wet T-shirt for the bare skin that lay beneath but then stopped short to pull me closer, so he could kiss me a while longer.

It drove me mad.

It made me wild with need, and by the time he finally reached up and tugged at the top of my shirt, pulling the deep v-neck down so that he could drag his lips past my collarbone and toward the valley between my breasts, I thought I might combust from the raging inferno he'd ignited between us.

"I've wanted to do this," he said, his hot breath against my skin as his fingers danced along the edge of lace bra, peeling back the delicate fabric inch by inch "this and so much more, since the moment you entered my office that first day."

His mouth closed around my nipple and I jumped, the feeling of his tongue circling around my sensitive flesh so intense that I couldn't keep still.

And I didn't want to.

I wanted to move with him.

Against him.

Underneath him.

And with all those thoughts swirling in my head, suddenly, my hands had a mind of their own. Finding the hem of his very wet shirt, I began to pull it upward, wanting to feel all those delicious muscles I'd been dreaming of.

"If you start undressing me now, this show is going to be over a lot quicker than I anticipated."

His eyes met mine, his sexy grin making my belly swarm with butterflies. He swiped his thumb across his jawline as my hands were frozen across his bare waist.

"There are just things—" I said, trying to explain.

"Things?"

"Yeah. Fantasies?"

His brow rose.

"Do you remember that day you stomped over here, all jackass-like?"

He laughed, tiny creases forming around his eyes, making his smile that much more adorable. "Not quite how I remember it, but go on."

"You'd just finished doing something with the boats. Giving them a bath maybe? I don't know."

"Right," he said with a chuckle. "We'll go with bath."

"Anyway, you were wet." I bit down on my bottom lip as my gaze fell to his T-shirt. "Kind of like you are now. Only then, you didn't have a shirt on, and I could see tiny droplets of water cascading down your chest. It took every ounce of willpower I had not to leap forward and lick each one right off your—"

His shirt went up and over his head in one fell swoop, and he dropped it to the floor without a second thought. "Show me," he demanded.

A shudder went through me at the deep command in his voice as I took him all in. He truly was magnificent.

And he was about to make all my fantasies come to life.

But, first, I needed to level the playing field a little.

Reaching for the bottom of my own shirt, I pulled it up and over my head, my bra quickly following.

Taylor growled in appreciation, his eyes taking in every inch of the new view as I bent down and got to work. His shirt had done a good job of soaking up a decent amount of water from his skin, but I made do, running my tongue along the waistband of his jeans where that sexy V near his hip bone started. His breath hitched as I worked my way up, kissing the well-defined planes of his abdomen. Soon, his hands were in my hair, and his body shook from obvious restraint.

"Lani," he groaned, grabbing my chin and tilting it upward. He looked desperate.

Desperate for me.

"I know I said a lot of things earlier, but if you don't want to, if you're not ready"—he swallowed hard and cupped my cheek—"we can stop."

If I hadn't started falling for him before, this right here, this would have done it.

"Can I trust you?" I asked, already knowing the answer.

"Yes." He smiled, looking deep into my eyes.

"Then, let's break some more rules, Taylor Sutherland."

"Thank God," he breathed out before kissing me once more. "We need a bed."

"What?" I asked, looking around, so consumed with lust that I thought this was as good a place as any. "Why?"

An amused smile spread across his face as his hand slid underneath me and grabbed ahold of both butt cheeks. "Because"—he gave the table a hard lean, and it creaked in response—"what I have planned for tonight is going to require something a lot sturdier than this."

My heart fluttered. "Well, the rooms aren't exactly in great condition."

He gave me a look, one that basically said he'd fuck me anywhere, just point him in the right direction.

It wasn't my heart that fluttered that time.

"But," I replied, making his eyebrow rise, "I was playing around in one of the rooms with fabrics and such, and—"

"Where?"

"Top of the—"

I was airborne before I even got the chance to finish my sentence.

"Taylor!" I squealed. My legs wrapped around his waist as we hastily made our way toward the room.

"You've been busy," he said, a hint of wonderment in his tone the moment we crossed the threshold.

"Oh," I said, suddenly feeling embarrassed as he took in all the work I'd done.

There were fabrics and tile samples in the corner, but the middle of the room, that was where I'd really outdone myself.

"I wanted to see what it could be," I explained as I watched his eyes move about the room—from the four-poster bed I'd refinished in matte black to the soft white linens and the fresh plants nearby. It was by no means finished, but I could see it.

"And what do you see?" he asked, letting me slip down his legs, my feet touching the floor.

A small smile crept across my face. "I see two lovers sneaking away for a weekend. Two busy lives finally taking a few moments for themselves in this hotel. They'll walk into this room and feel like they can breathe for maybe the first time in years."

His eyes darkened as his fingers traced the skin down my bare shoulder. "And what will they do once they've taken that deep breath, Lani?"

"Maybe the man will strip off all of their clothes," I said, feeling emboldened by this wicked game he was playing.

Obviously, he was, too, because he didn't waste any time, taking my words at face value. He reached for the waistband of my skirt first, and I mentally high-fived myself for wearing it as his hands easily peeled it off my body.

I was left standing before him in a barely there satin thong I'd worn specifically to his house in hopes that he might see it.

We might not be at his house anymore, but, oh boy…

He saw it, and that lusty twinkle in his eyes, it made me feel like the most beautiful woman alive.

"Damn," he swore, brushing his thumb across his bottom lip as his eyes took in every inch of me. "I kind of want to just stand here and look at you." A mischievous smile spread across his face. "But," he said, his hands going to his belt buckle, "I really want to find out what happens after the couple takes off their clothes."

Oh, holy crap.

I'd never been so in love with the sound of a belt buckle hitting the ground before.

Now, it was my time to stare.

If Taylor half-naked had made my fantasies go wild, seeing him in all his glorious splendor was enough to send my brain into overdrive.

"I have so many new places I want to lick," I found myself whispering.

He chuckled, stepping in close. "And I'm going to let you, believe me. But, first—"

He slowly lowered himself down my body as his fingers curled around the thin edge of my panties. Tender kisses scattered over my hip bone as he eased them down to the floor, revealing the sensitive flesh beneath.

On his knees now, he looked up at me, this gorgeous god of a man, and said, "What happens next? After the man strips his woman bare?"

I could barely think, my mind a lust-filled haze, so consumed with the feel of his hands sliding up my ass, his mouth so close to my core.

"He breathes life back into her," I answered. "With his mouth, his hands, and his strong, hard body. Over and over until neither of them can ever forget what it feels like to be here, in each other's arms."

His eyes darkened once more, and a tiny squeak escaped my lips when he popped up with me in his arms. He turned, placing me on the delicate white bed next to us.

I looked up to find he'd disappeared. Concerned, I rose up, only to find him wrestling with something in his pants pocket.

He turned to find me giving him an amused expression. "Condom," he explained, holding the little foil packet up between two fingers.

My cheeks reddened. "Oh."

It had been so long, I was ashamed to admit that I hadn't even thought of that particular part of the puzzle.

Obviously, he had.

Because, for him, it probably hadn't been nearly as long.

What if I was just a notch on a very crowded bedpost for him? Was I okay with that?

He could sense my shift, crawling beside me, and he pushed back a piece of my hair. "Did this just become too real?" he asked.

"No," I lied. "I just—"

His brows rose, his eyes giving a look that said he could see through all the bullshit I had tried to push his way.

I let out a sigh. "It's been a while since I—"

"You don't have to explain yourself," he said.

"No, I want to," I said, trying to find the right words. "I don't do one-night stands, and I don't do the casual, multiple-partner thing."

His smile broadened. "Are you trying to say, you don't want me to date anyone else?"

I swallowed hard. "We did say we were going to break all the rules," I reminded him.

He kissed my forehead. "Well, that is one we can leave firmly in place."

"Really?" I perked up.

"Really," he confirmed, cupping my cheek. "It's not just a vision you're seeing in this room, Lani. When I'm with you, I feel like I can breathe…maybe for the first time in my life. I don't want to share that with anyone."

This time, when our lips met, it was me who reached for him and pulled him close. It was me who took the condom from his hand and tore it open, so another moment wouldn't pass without him inside me.

Seize the moment, I'd been told.

I'd seize every damn moment I had with this man.

Starting now.

Taylor made quick work of the condom, rolling it down his impressive length. I reached up and splayed my hands over his chest as he positioned himself, rubbing his fingers over the tender, slick folds between my thighs.

Pressed possessively above me, he whispered in my ear,

"I've never wanted anything more than I want you in this moment."

My fingers curled around his shoulders, and I cried out as our bodies became one. He filled me so completely, so absolutely, that I didn't think I'd ever recover.

"Jesus," Taylor breathed out. "So fucking tight."

I knew it had been a while, but I seemed to remember that was a good thing. Especially since Taylor's eyes seemed to be rolling back in his head a little, and his pace quickened.

That only made my eyes want to roll back in my own head.

We became an entangled mess of limbs, panting and moaning to the frantic beat of our lovemaking.

I'd thought being with Taylor would make all my fantasies come to life.

But the reality was so much more.

With him, I could envision endless fantasies, never-ending possibilities… A lifetime of pleasure.

"You feel so good," he said, pushing my knees tight against my chest, so he could thrust deeper.

The angle sent shock waves down my spine.

"Oh, yes!" I cried out, feeling almost feverish from the frenzied pace he'd set.

Sweat dripped down our bodies as he drove me closer to climax. I could feel it coming, like a freight train, ready to consume us both.

My skin prickled, my belly tightened, and my breath caught.

And then bliss.

Pure, unequivocal bliss.

There was no other word to describe the way I felt when that orgasm exploded through my entire body. My core tightened as endless waves of pleasures passed over me. I felt Taylor buck, his body going rigid as his fingers weaved into my hair, and he gave in to his own earth-shattering finale.

"That was..." he breathed out, his forehead resting against mine, our bodies still joined.

"I know," I said before adding, "I hope you have a couple more condoms in that wallet of yours."

He pulled back, a smug grin written all over his face. "Just a couple?"

A smile pulled at the corners of my mouth. "You might need to go back to your place for reinforcements."

A passionate kiss fell upon my lips.

"Now, that's what I'm talking about."

I was in for a late night, and I'd never been happier to pass up sleep.

Exciting new things?

Check, check and *check*.

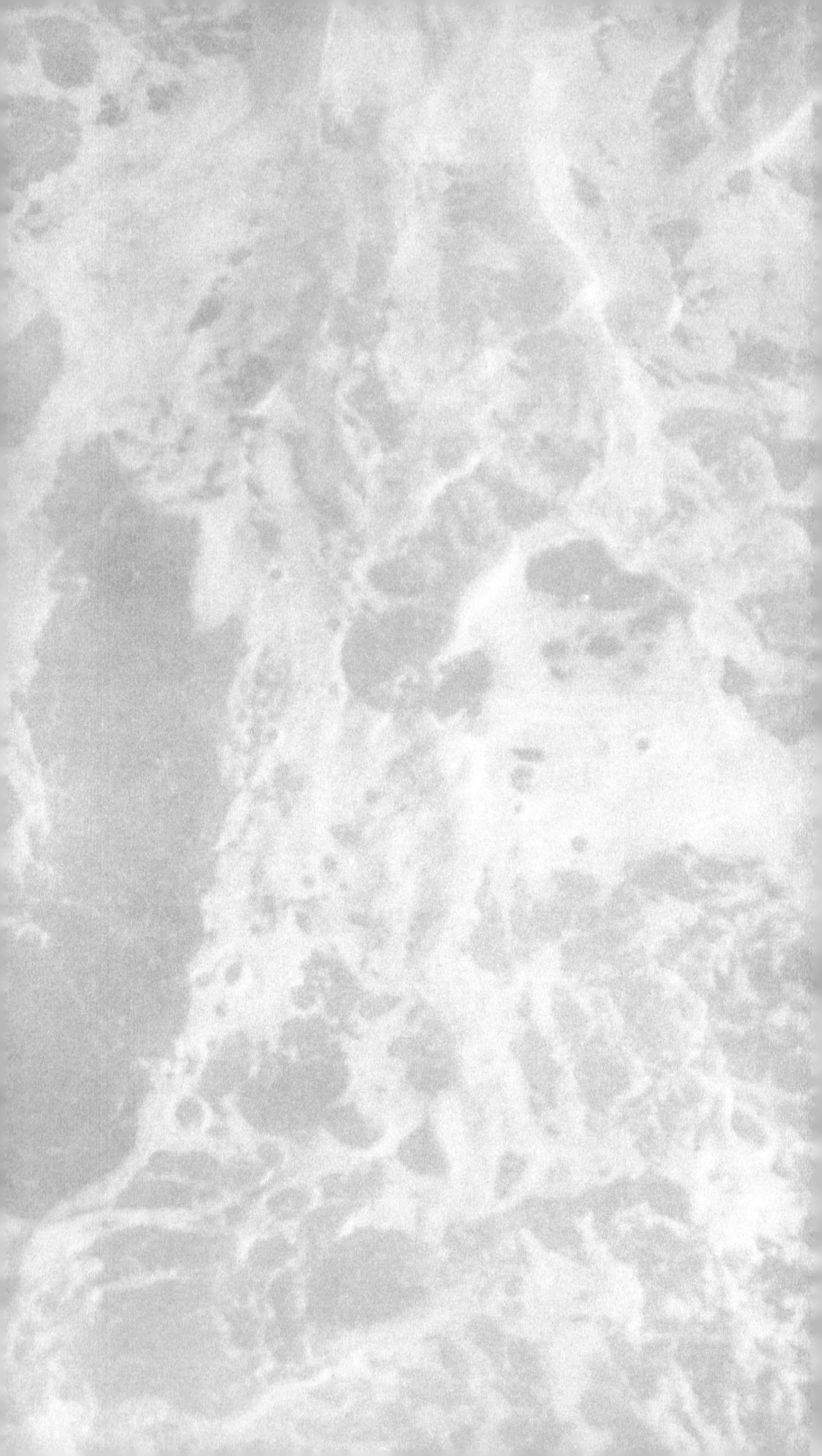

CHAPTER ELEVEN

Taylor

I awoke the next morning, the familiar salty sea air gently waking me from the best night's sleep I'd had in years. Opening my eyes, I reached for her, a gesture that felt almost second nature even though I'd never done so before this moment.

But Lani wasn't there.

Sitting up, I found myself alone in the messy bed we'd made our own last night, making love into the wee hours of the morning until we fell into each other's arms, exhausted, achy, and sated.

But, now, I felt the pull again, the desire.

The hunger.

Searching the room, it didn't take me long to locate her. Standing just outside on the balcony, dressed in my T-shirt that nearly came down to her knees, she scanned the water as if she were in desperate need of answers this morning.

Rising, I immediately went to her.

She must have felt my presence because, the second my arms wrapped around her waist, she seemed to melt into me. Her head turned, and I kissed her temple, such an intimate gesture but one I felt she needed.

"You okay?" I asked, sensing turmoil buried deep inside her, like her mind and emotions were mirroring the choppy waves below.

She turned in my arms, and I saw a glint of something in her eyes.

Sadness perhaps?

But it was gone and replaced before I had the chance to decipher it.

"Yep," she answered, a wicked grin spreading across her face. "Just tired."

I couldn't resist that smile. "Tired, huh?" I said, pushing her back against the railing of the balcony. "Why is that, Lani?"

Her cheeks reddened. "You know why."

My hand slipped under the T-shirt she wore, finding the curve of her ass and grabbing it with a satisfied grin on my face. "I do," I acknowledged. "But it doesn't mean I don't like hearing you tell me all about it. In detail, if you'd like."

She laughed, but it wasn't the laugh I was used to. This one didn't reach her eyes, and I found myself willing to do anything to bring it back.

"Hey," I said, taking a step back. "What if I took the day off today and we spent the whole day together?"

Her gaze widened. "What? You can't do that."

"Sure I can. I am the boss," I assured her.

"But what would your brother think?" She bit down on her bottom lip, obviously uncertain with the idea.

"He'll think it's about time. I haven't taken an entire day off in well over a year."

That seemed to surprise her. That was, until she realized she was running out of excuses. "But I'm already so far behind."

She got me there. Too bad for her, I was always a quick thinker.

"Think of it as a research trip. You need to get more acquainted with the area."

She responded with silence.

My smile widened.

"Oh, come on," I said. "I'll let you pick. We can do anything, and the history lessons can be optional."

"I love your history lessons," she said with enthusiasm.

Now, it was me who was lost for words.

"I could take you out on one of the boats," I said, my voice hoarse with emotion. I didn't know why, but hearing her say she loved my stupid history lectures had really gotten to me.

And I was having a hard time processing the emotions coursing through me.

"Can it be a long boat ride?" she asked, an idea obviously forming in that mind of hers.

"Uh, sure. Why?"

"Well, there is this resort up the coast that we built—"

"The Lighthouse Inn and Resort," I said.

"You've heard of it?"

I grinned. "The Outer Banks isn't that big. When a hotel is built, especially by a company as big as Hart, we all know about it, even all the way down here."

"Oh, right. Well anyway, my dad personally oversaw that one, and he never does that. So I kind of want to go see it."

"Check out the competition?"

She shrugged. "Yeah."

An idea of my own sprang to mind. "What if I took more than a day off?"

"What?"

"Why don't we make a weekend of it? That way, you can get the ultimate feel for the place. We can stay in a room and make sure the bed works." I gave her a good waggle of my eyebrows for that one, making her giggle.

"I mean, I guess I would technically be working."

"Exactly," I agreed.

"And it would be nice to see a room."

"Mmhmm." I leaned in closer to her, giving her a tender kiss on her neck before working my way down. Thankfully, my T-shirt on her was gigantic, making it easy to pull off her shoulder so that I could continue the path I'd started.

"Okay," she agreed, the word coming out more like a moan. "But can we leave in a couple of hours?"

I grinned against her naked skin, pulling the T-shirt even lower. "Absolutely."

"For an heiress, there sure are a lot of things you haven't done," I told her as we made our way to the hotel in Corolla.

"I told you," she said as we walked the short distance between the dock and The Lighthouse Inn, "I've been on a boat before."

"Yes, but you barely remember because you were five."

She stopped short, her eyes reaching out toward the water. "Things sort of stopped when my dad became the big CEO. He tried to be a dad," she said. "For a long time he tried, but it wasn't the same. And all the stuff we used to do—the family outings and the adventures—they were few and far between because his visits were few and far between."

I took her hand, squeezing it in mine. "I'm sure you have some wonderful memories with your mom though. Things you did together when he was away?"

It was like she'd just been struck across the face. All the color fell from it, and she instantly turned away.

"Yeah," she answered. "We did. The beach. Um, she liked to go to the beach."

She might have done a good job of hiding it from me before, but right now, her emotions were bleeding through, and I couldn't ignore it any longer.

"Lani," I said softly, pulling her toward a bench off to the side of the walkway, "please tell me what's going on."

"Nothing," she persisted, but the concerned stare I gave back told her I wasn't budging. Letting out a sigh, she caved. "My mom…she died fourteen years ago. Today."

My heart broke for her, so much so that I didn't know what to say.

Did I feel grief when this day rolled around each year for my own father?

Sure.

But, for me, it was different.

I grieved over a man who had died when I was a toddler. To me, he was basically a ghost. And yes, that was tragic in its own right, but for Lani, I imagined the pain went so much deeper because she felt her mom everywhere.

"Tell me about her," I finally said, knowing nothing I said could ever make it right.

She settled against me as we sat on that bench, halfway between the docks and our final destination, not in any hurry at all.

"I remember her being wild when I was younger, but I think she lost a bit of her spirit when my dad traveled so much," she said. "And she loved the beach; that part is true. She used to say it gave her life—the sound of the waves and the way the sand felt between her toes."

"I'd have to agree with her there. I couldn't see myself living away from the water," I said.

She smiled. "After seeing you wield magic today over the sea, I couldn't picture you anywhere else either."

"Captaining a boat is not wielding magic," I argued with a shrug. "It's just a learned skill."

"Not the way you do it."

I found myself grinning and placed a chaste kiss on the top of her head. "What else? Tell me more."

"She was an amazing hula dancer."

"No shit?"

A laugh escaped her lips, and I felt a sliver of the worry I had over her fall away.

"Yes," she said. "She was actually quite good. It was how my parents met."

"Your dad did Polynesian dancing?"

She laughed again. "No. She was hired to dance at one of the original Hart hotels. My dad couldn't take his eyes off her. She gave him lessons for their first date."

"I can't imagine your father trying to hula."

"That makes two of us."

"Did she ever teach you?" I asked, already picturing my dark-haired beauty in a grass skirt, her hips moving to the beat of drums.

"Yes," she answered. "But I haven't practiced in a long time. It's like going to the beach. After she died, I just stopped. It was easier to ignore the things she'd loved rather than face the fact that she wasn't there to do them with me anymore."

"So, you haven't been too busy to go to the beach?" I said.

She shook her head. "No," she answered, her eyes trained on the coastline.

"I'm sorry if I forced you to face something you weren't ready for."

Turning toward me, she met my gaze. "You didn't," she answered. "If anything, you gave me the push I needed. I've finally realized I've been doing the exact same thing my dad has been doing for years."

"And what's that?"

"Avoiding," she replied. "Only I've been avoiding small things, like beaches and hula dancing."

"What is he avoiding?" I asked, cupping her cheek.

"Me," she answered. "I think that every time he looks at me, it's just another awful reminder of what he lost."

I let out a heavy sigh, unsure if I could ever meet her father without pummeling him to the ground first. "When my brother lost his arm, he went through a long period of grief. He said it was like mourning the life he'd once had. For three years he went on like this, never letting us in, just sort of adrift. He said the grief nearly consumed him because he became obsessed with the past—how things used to be and how they were nothing like that now."

"But things weren't great back then either," she said. "When she was alive, I mean. It wasn't magic and rainbows. He was still gone all the time. It still sucked."

"The mind has a way of forgetting the bad times and overemphasizing the good ones, I imagine."

"I just wish he'd see me," she confessed.

"I know," I answered, hating that she was hurting, knowing that I cared far too much, and realizing I had no idea how I'd be able to let go of her in five weeks.

"Holy shit," Lani whispered under her breath as we entered the swank hotel. "This place is amazing."

"Is this what they consider an inn at Hart International?" I asked, taking a quick glance around the lobby, which was so massive that it could probably encompass the entire first floor of Molly's inn, no problem.

"Yeah, the use of the word *inn* threw me, too. I've never seen the word used in any of our other properties. I'm guessing it's a regional thing. But, then again, we have hotels all up and down the East Coast, and none of them are called inns."

"Maybe it's an effort to stand out against the other hotels," I suggested as we made our way to the check-in counter.

It was a slow process. Leilani meticulously inspected every aspect of the lobby—from the groupings of chairs to the flooring to the wood beams that stretched high above us.

"I would think it'd do that on its own," she said.

"True," I agreed. "But hotels in the Outer Banks aren't exactly the best. It's why there are so many rental houses."

She looked at me, a slightly amused expression painted across her features. "I know, why do you think I'm trying to revamp the one I have?"

I chuckled. "Well, come on then. Don't let me distract you any further. Go forth and work, woman!"

She joined in my laughter but grabbed my hand before finally stepping up to the check in counter. I caught her eyeing the gorgeous wood desk, probably making a mental note to research it online later.

"Can I help you?" a friendly young woman asked, her smile so wide that I could see every last one of her teeth.

I opened my mouth to respond, the gentlemanly manners my mother had instilled in me kicking in, but Lani beat me to it. "Hi. Yes, we're checking in."

She gave me a sideways glance that said she had this, and I could stand down.

So, stand down I did.

It was her father's hotel after all.

"Great!" megawatt-smile girl replied. "And what is the name on the reservation?"

I smiled wide, preparing for the stunned look on the woman's face when Leilani dropped her name.

"Taylor and Leilani Sutherland," she answered.

I coughed, nearly swallowing my own tongue.

"Oh, honey," Lani said. "Are you okay?" She patted my shoulder, as she gave me a wide eyed glare.

"Yep," I answered. "Totally fine, *Pookie Bear*."

A slight smirk tugged at her lips. "Sorry," she apologized to the woman across the desk. "We're newlyweds. We just can't help ourselves with the adorable pet names."

"Newlyweds! Really?" The woman was so excited; you would think she'd just had her own damn wedding instead of us.

Except we hadn't had one either.

Damn, I was confused.

"Just yesterday!" Lani said, perfectly playing the blushing bride. "We eloped! Can you believe it?"

She looked at me, and I found myself smiling, hopefully not awkwardly.

"We didn't even have rings, but none of that matters, does it?"

"It sure doesn't," the woman replied, completely enamored by our totally bogus story.

I had absolutely no idea why we were doing this or what the point was, but I had a feeling, that where Lani was concerned, I'd go anywhere and do just about anything.

"Well, I don't normally do this, but I'd love to offer you an upgrade as congratulations on behalf of the resort."

Lani reached across the counter. "Oh, wow. Thank you!"

"Of course." The woman smiled. "It's my pleasure!"

We finished up, and I handed over my credit card, not wanting to blow our cover by Lani giving hers and revealing her real last name. Soon, we had room keys for a swanky suite with sweeping ocean views.

"Nice job, Mrs. Sutherland," I said, taking her hand as we made our way to the elevator.

"Why, thank you, Mr. Sutherland."

"Was that just for fun or—"

"Oh, it was definitely fun," she said, a tiny snicker escaping her lips. "But I grew up in a hotel, remember? A Hart hotel to be exact."

"So, you knew that would get us an upgrade?"

She shrugged as we entered the elevator, thankfully alone. "Not exactly, but I had a pretty good idea."

"You're pure evil, Leilani Hart." I grinned.

Her brow rose as the elevator dinged, announcing our floor. "Oh, you have no idea. Wait until you see what I'm wearing for dinner," she teased, stepping out into the hallway, leaving me to follow behind.

I was about to ask her for a few details when she pointed down to the floor and uttered, "Oh, man! Look at that carpet!"

I chuckled under my breath. I'd lost her to the hotel again. But it was okay. I kind of enjoyed seeing her in her element. It was a healthy dose of excitement, scrutiny, and professional fascination. I could see what she approved of by a simple twitch of her brow, her face lighting up at the subtle color choices. But when we came to something she disagreed with? She'd scrunch her nose in disapproval and simply move on.

"Not a fan of those sconces?" I asked as we finally arrived at the door to our room.

She shook her head. "A surprising choice for my dad. He's usually a less-is-more kind of guy when it comes to decorating. Let the property speak for itself and all that."

I let out a laugh, taking one last look at the gold monstrosities. "They are a bit much."

"That's an understatement."

"Maybe he let someone else pick them," I suggested as I reached for the key card in my back pocket.

"I doubt it," she said. "He's not really the compromising type."

I couldn't help but smile. "Hmm."

"What does that mean?" Her eyes were bright and playful.

I pushed the door open. "It's just, you're not exactly the most compromising type either."

Her mouth opened wide. "I am very compromising."

"Really?" Still standing in the entryway, I didn't budge. I knew she was dying to get inside and check out every inch of that suite, but I couldn't help but mess with her.

"Yes," she said, sticking to her guns, her arms defiantly wrapped around her chest.

Of course, I couldn't help but notice the way it pressed her breasts high and tight against her low-cut top.

"Name one instance in which you compromised. Because I think my fleabag hotel is still being turned into…what did you describe it as? A hidden spa oasis?"

Her head tilted to the side, her face lit up with amusement. "I don't think I ever said that. And I'm sorry, but whose hotel is it?"

That mischievous grin I so loved sparkled deep in her eyes. It was a look I was starting to crave. It meant that all those perfectly placed feathers of hers were starting to ruffle, and she was looking for trouble.

And I was just the guy to give it to her.

"My town," I said. "My hotel."

A wicked grin crept up her face as she pushed me forward into our suite. "Who owns The Cozy Hotel, Taylor Sutherland?"

I'd thought I'd never want to hear those words again.

The first time they'd fallen from her lips, I'd felt such anger.

Anger that I hadn't accomplished anything in our brief meeting together.

Disappointment that I had been schooled by a woman I'd just met.

And frustration that I couldn't take her right there, on that very floor.

But, now, I could.

"Why don't you show me?" I said, taking a step back.

She eagerly followed, fully willing to do just as I'd asked until her eyes caught sight of the room.

And then I lost her.

"Wow! Look at this place!"

I couldn't help but laugh as I took a backseat to her first passion. But I knew, when she was done geeking out over bed linens and furniture choices, I'd make her forget all about it with a single, scorching touch.

"You know, my eyes are up here."

My brow lifted as I met Lani's amused gaze across the table. "Yes, and they're beautiful, but if you expect me to look anywhere else tonight when you're wearing a dress like that, you're crazy."

She smirked, seemingly very pleased with herself. "I guess I did promise something very wicked, didn't I?"

"Yes," I affirmed, giving her another once-over.

From the moment she'd stepped out of the bedroom of our suite, wearing that tight little black number, I'd been imagining all the different ways I'd take it off her later.

I was up to twenty-eight.

I was extremely creative.

"And, if you keep doing that," I said, watching her lean forward, her breasts nearly spilling out of the top.

"Doing what?" she asked innocently.

"Driving me crazy from across the table like that," I explained. "Keep poking the bear Lani, and I'll be forced to do something about it."

Her smile widened, and she did exactly what I'd hoped she'd do. She leaned forward, pressing those luscious breasts together, the ones I'd kissed and sucked not hours before, and gave me the challenge I'd been wanting.

"Good evening," a voice said, startling both of us.

We looked up to find a chipper waiter at our table.

"May I take your drink orders?"

Lani seemed to be trying to hold back laughter while I rolled with it.

"Yes," I answered, "but first, do you think you could do us a favor?"

"Of course," he answered.

"My wife and I are newlyweds," I said, taking a tip from Lani's book. "And we'd really love to sit next to each other and face that beautiful ocean view together. Would you mind switching her table setting?"

Lani seemed a little confused by my request, but the moment she sat down next to me and my hand slid up her leg, things started to shift into place.

"Thank you," I said to the waiter, giving a wide smile while he took our drink orders. Once he left to retrieve them, I turned my attention back to my adoring fake wife.

"You wouldn't," she whispered as my fingers slipped under the skirt of her dress.

"Oh, I would."

"But there are so many people."

"Mmhmm," I agreed, taking a quick glance around. We were fairly close to the table next to us. Not too close, thankfully, but a moan or two would definitely be heard. "Then, I guess you'd better be quiet."

She opened her mouth, but not a single protest came out as her legs spread wider under the table.

That's my little daredevil.

Her breath caught as my fingers found the tiny scrap of fabric between her thighs and moved it aside.

"You're so wet, Pookie Bear." I grinned.

"You're going to get us kicked out of this restaurant, honey," she said, her voice barely a whisper.

"No," I answered as my index finger began slowly circling her clit. "This is easy."

"Easy?" The single word came out more like a puff of air as her whole body reacted to my touch.

"Sure," I said. "We just need to keep talking. People won't notice if we keep talking. It's when we stop that we stick out."

"So, you expect me to carry on a conversation, too?"

I slipped two digits deep inside her.

"Oh, holy shit," she hissed under her breath.

"I think I can carry most of the conversation," I said, slightly leaning forward on my elbow to provide a little cover. "Besides, I don't plan on this taking long. I do know how to get you off."

To prove my point, I pumped my fingers in and out, rubbing my thumb over her clit. I could feel her thighs closing in, clamping around my arm, her core tightening.

"Did someone order a pinot grigio?"

"Yes!" Lani cried out, her hand slamming against the table as her body exploded around me. She swiftly recovered, noticing the man standing next to us. "Yes, I did order a pinot grigio. Thank you so much!"

I pressed my lips together to keep from laughing as the

bartender delivered the wine and scotch to our table, my fingers still rubbing her as the shock waves rolled through her body.

"Oh my God, that guy probably thinks I'm nuts." She laughed, her face flushed from her climax.

"Or just the most enthusiastic wine drinker on the planet."

Our eyes met, and I couldn't help the desire I had for her in that moment. It was overwhelming.

It always was.

"Room service?" we both said in unison.

"I'll flag down the waiter," I said.

"I'll run to the restroom and freshen up."

Shaking my head, I placed a smoldering kiss on her lips. "Don't you dare. I want you exactly like this when we get upstairs. Wet, dirty, and —"

Her hand shot up in the air, grabbing the attention of the waiter herself.

Within three minutes, we were walking toward the elevator, practically devouring each other in the process.

"You know," she said, whispering in my ear, "I bet there are a few things we could do in an elevator, too."

Fuck. Me.

I'd never been so eager for the sound of an elevator to arrive.

Until it did.

The moment the doors opened, I knew something was wrong. Lani's body tensed, like she was frozen in place with fear. Looking up, I saw a man staring at us from inside the elevator.

A man even I recognized.

"Daddy," she breathed out, her voice shaky and weak as I met the eyes of Stephen Hart.

But it wasn't him she was staring at. It was the woman on his arm. Her gaze seemed to ping-pong between them, as if trying to make sense of the two of them together.

Did she know the woman?

Or was it just the fact that he was with a woman at all?

"Are you here to see me? How did you know I'd be here?" he asked, patting the woman's arm as they stepped out. He took a step forward without her and approached his daughter.

"What? No," she said. "I'm here, doing research for my own design project. I didn't even know you were here."

His eyes briefly darted to mine. "Research? I see."

"Well, you told me to make nice with the locals," she answered snidely before throwing her attention back toward the woman next to her father. "Why is Becky here?"

So, she did know her.

Her father let out a sigh. "She's here with me."

A mixture of betrayal and disbelief was written all over her face. "For business?"

"No, Leilani. Rebecca is my fiancée. We're getting married. I've been meaning to tell you, but—"

"But what? You didn't have the time? You forgot? What excuse is it going to be today, Daddy?"

"I didn't know how," he said.

His fiancée stepped forward to reach for his hand. Lani noticed, of course, and turned her head away.

"Well, now, I know. I'm sure you'll have your assistant update me on the details of the rest of your life as they happen. Now, if you'll excuse us," she said, reaching for me. She didn't have to go far; I was right there. "We were about to retire for the evening."

"Leilani," he said, his voice firm and fatherly, "aren't you going to introduce me to your friend?"

She swallowed hard, blinking several times as she forced a smile. "You know, Daddy, I want to, but I just don't know how."

If Lani was going for brutal, I'd think she'd won because the devastated look on her father's face as we walked away almost made me feel bad for him.

Almost.

That was, until I saw Lani.

And then I wanted turn right around, run after the bastard and kill him.

"Babe," I said softly as she crumbled in my arms, sobs echoing through the small space as I shielded her body and tried to alleviate her pain.

By the time we reached our floor, tears had drenched her face, her breath so rushed and hurried that she was nearly hyperventilating. Bending down, I did the only thing I could think of. I picked her up and carried her to our room, letting her rest her head against my shoulder but wishing I could do so much more.

For her, I'd take it all.

All the pain, all the suffering.

Everything.

I made quick work of getting into our suite and headed straight for the bedroom. As gently as possible, I set her down on the bed, the covers already tossed back from our love-making earlier. Knowing I couldn't leave her, I kicked off my shoes and slid next to her, wiping her tears as they fell from her eyes.

"Shh," I whispered.

She looked up at me, so unguarded and fragile. "Why doesn't he want me?" she finally asked.

And I felt my heart break a thousand times over.

"I don't know," I answered honestly, knowing I couldn't sugarcoat this for her. The man I'd met just minutes earlier didn't deserve it.

But the woman lying before me did.

She deserved everything and more.

"That woman," she said, her voice filled with venom, "Becky, she's my age. We went to school together. He promoted her just last month, made her the project leader for the major renovation property in Chicago. Guess she's taking a little time off. I bet she's the one who picked out those horrible sconces," she said with a huff. "Figures. Can't expect much for a girl who got a B-minus in Introductory Design."

"Lani," I whispered.

Another huff. "I know," she said. "I'm being petty. But, I mean, do you blame me?"

"No, I just don't think it's Becky you're truly mad at."

Her lips quivered. "Mad? No," she answered. "Creeped out a little, yes. But mostly, I'm just angry."

"Why?" I asked, knowing we were getting somewhere.

"Because, all this time, I thought he was avoiding me because of my mom. Because it was just too hard, you know?"

I nodded.

"But now, I know he's had Becky. He's moved on. So, why?" she said, her eyes filling with tears. "Why am I still not good enough to be a part of his life, Taylor?"

"I don't know," I answered.

But I intended to find out.

<hr>

It didn't take long for her to fall asleep. Crying took a lot out of a person, and she'd wept a river over her father tonight.

Leaving her wasn't easy, but this was something I needed to do.

Grabbing her phone out of her purse, I searched her Contacts, pulled up the asshole's phone number, and sent the text.

Surprisingly, it didn't take long to receive a reply; one that I quickly erased, but not before I saved his number in my own phone. It might come in handy the next time he decided to hurt his daughter like this.

Grabbing the key card off the table where I'd left it, I headed out, hoping I'd be back before she woke.

I didn't want her to be alone.

I wasn't the first to arrive at the bar, and seeing his reaction as I entered instead of his daughter, as my text had suggested, he didn't seem nearly as surprised as I would have thought he'd be.

As I joined him at the bar, he didn't bother introducing himself. "I figured it was you," he said. "My daughter is stubborn, like her mother. She likes to ignore me for a month or two before extending another olive branch."

"You act as if you know her so well."

He flagged down the bartender, a casual gesture that made it appear like we were talking about sports or pop culture, not the fact that he'd all but abandoned his daughter for the last fourteen years.

"I know her well enough."

My hands tightened into fists at my sides. "The woman who just cried herself to sleep in my arms would suggest otherwise."

His eyes narrowed on me. "What are you to my daughter, Mr. Sutherland?"

I was taken aback. "You know my name?"

Who was this guy?

"Of course I do," he said, dismissing my shock with a wave of his hand. "I bought property on your island. You think I didn't do research before doing so? I investigate every business, every property. I'm meticulous, unlike my daughter who appears to just be sleeping with the locals rather than doing her job."

I rose to my feet. "You don't know a damn thing about Lani!" I roared.

"And you do?" He seemed amused.

"A hell of a lot more than you do," I said, slumping back in my chair. "Lani is working her ass off to meet your deadline. God knows why. You don't seem to give a rat's ass either way. I mean, don't you realize what an amazing woman she is?"

"You seem to."

"I do," I said, which brought me to my point—the very reason I'd brought him down here, to this bar. "I need you to decide," I said.

"Decide?" The old man seemed confused.

I was about to make it crystal clear for him. "You need to decide if you're in or out when it comes to Lani because I will not allow you to continue to hurt her like this."

"You won't?"

"No, I won't."

"And who are you?" he asked, his gaze dead set on mine.

"What? What do you mean, who am I?"

"I mean exactly what I said, Mr. Sutherland. I asked you what you were to my daughter. A friend? A lover? What do you mean to her? Since you never gave me an answer, I'm asking again. Who are you to demand this of me, her father?"

"I…" I had no words.

A satisfied grin spread across his face. "I think the question you're asking is actually one meant for you, Mr. Sutherland. Because as her father, I am always in. Even if our relationship is difficult or strained, I will always be in; even if she doesn't want me to be. But you? You have a choice, so what will it be? Are you in or out?"

My mouth hung open as I stared at him and then back toward the elevator that would take me to Lani.

Every molecule in my body wanted me to tell that man that I was in it for the long haul.

That I'd pack up my life, leave my family, and move across the entire damn world for his daughter.

But, as I stared at the elevator, I couldn't do it.

I couldn't say the word.

Why?

Because, deep down, there was still a part of me that believed that this would never work. Love wasn't as simple as my brother believed it to be.

Like all good love stories, ours would just eventually end.

And where would that leave me? Just like Sierra and my mother…

Alone. Absolutely alone.

CHAPTER TWELVE

Leilani

I awoke to darkness, the sound of the suite door being opened and shut.

"Taylor?" I called out, rising up in bed to look for him.

"I'm here," he said, the silhouette of his broad body moving toward me.

I felt the bed dip as he came to sit beside me.

"Where did you go?" I asked, wondering just how long I'd been out.

Oh God, I thought, remembering all the tears as my fingers traced my puffy cheeks and swollen eyes. *I must look like a hot damn mess.*

Like he was reading my mind, he reached up and took my hand in his. "You look just as beautiful as ever." He smiled warmly, flipping on the bedside light. "And I was out, grabbing provisions."

"Provisions?"

He nodded, reaching into a small paper bag with his other hand. He drew out a pint of Ben & Jerry's, instantly making me laugh.

"You're a man of many talents," I said.

"My mom is a widow," he said plainly. "There were often

tears when I was growing up. I'd do just about anything to make them go away."

I pictured a smaller, sweeter version of Taylor sitting on his mother's lap, sharing ice cream on a warm summer afternoon.

"And ice cream worked?" I asked, fairly certain my heart was melting faster than the ice cream in his hand.

He shrugged. "Ice cream and humor."

"No history lessons for Mrs. Sutherland?" I asked, reaching for the pint of Karamel Sutra. I didn't want it to go to waste after all.

"Who do you think taught me all of them in the first place?" he said, handing me a spoon. "You won't meet a person more passionate about Ocracoke than my mom. Our family was one of the first, you know?"

"I didn't."

"Yep, generations of Sutherlands have lived on that island. If you want to hear a history lesson, just give her a hand with Sunday dinner. That's how I got hooked."

A smile spread across my face. "So, that's where you learned all those cooking skills."

"It was purely selfish on my part. I figured out early on that if I helped out, we would eat sooner."

I shook my head, laughing. "I highly doubt that."

"It's true." He chuckled. "I'm a pretty selfish guy."

I swallowed hard. "No, you're not," I said, knowing exactly what selfish looked like. I'd seen it firsthand tonight, in the eyes of my own father. "You're the exact opposite, Taylor."

He seemed to sense the change in emotions, the carefree banter gone, replaced by something heavy and deep. He reached out for me, his hand gently stroking my cheek. "I'd take it away if I could."

I blankly looked up at him.

"The pain," he said, taking the ice cream from my hands and setting it aside. "I'd take it all, Lani."

Pressing my cheek into the heat of his palm, I assured him, "You do, just by being here."

He slowly shook his head from side to side. "I wish I could do more."

"Make me forget," I said without thinking. Reaching for him, I said it again, "Make me forget, Taylor. Just for a couple of hours, for a night. Make me forget everything that happened and—"

He kissed me. "You don't have to beg," he said breathlessly, his eyes intense and dead set on mine. "You don't ever have to beg me to—"

He didn't finish his sentence, and I could feel the mystery of his words hanging in the air as our lips met.

What was he going to say?

"You don't ever have to beg me to…"

Have sex with you?

Fuck you?

Love you?

My heart beat wildly as he pushed me back against the mattress.

Surely, he hadn't meant that.

We had less than five weeks.

He didn't give me much time to consider it as his hands found the thin straps of my dress and made quick work of sliding them off my shoulders, allowing him to pull my dress the rest of the way off. His gaze grew heavy as he looked down at the lace bra I wore beneath.

"Jesus," he swore. "I don't think I'll ever grow tired of this view."

Reaching up, I removed his collared shirt, working the buttons, one by one, until I could run my hands all over that chiseled chest of his. Smiling to myself, I replied, "I totally agree."

Trying hard to keep his word, to make me forget, he took his time, kissing every inch of skin as he made his way down, removing my bra and panties.

It worked.

By the time he was slipping my lace thong down my calves, I was delirious; so drunk on him that I couldn't think about anything but how good it would feel to have him again.

And again.

Over and over until I couldn't move from the sheer pleasure of our lovemaking.

I watched as he got naked, licking my lips as his pants fell to the floor, knowing every inch of that manly body would be all over me in seconds.

"When you look at me like that, naked and ready for me," he said, shaking his head, a cocky grin stretched across his face, "it just might be the sexiest damn thing I've ever seen."

Knowing I was taunting him but not caring in the least, I spread my legs, giving him a view I knew he couldn't refuse.

It was like watching a lion on the hunt. I was his prey, and I'd just been captured.

Willingly.

Our mouths fused together as his hands pulled us close.

Before I knew it, he was in me. Filling me. Claiming me. Making me his.

"Taylor, yes!" I cried out.

This was magic. This was paradise.

This was exactly what I'd been missing in my life.

Him, me.

Us.

Grabbing my waist, he suddenly flipped us, so I was on top. I loved this position. It gave me power, and as I moved, riding his cock, I felt beautiful, sexy, and daring.

And I could see in his eyes as he watched me that he agreed.

Our hands joined then as he leaned up to kiss me. Chest-to-chest, body-to-body, soul-to-soul, we made love.

And I forgot.

I forgot about my shitty childhood and all the loss I'd felt.

I forgot about the hours before and my father's new life.

And I even forgot about the minutes leading up to our lovemaking and the one tiny detail we'd both definitely forgotten.

Sleep had a way of refreshing you in more ways than one.

It was like, while your brain was idle, soaking up those precious hours of rest, it was playing an ongoing game of Tetris, tediously putting those random nuances of life into place that maybe hadn't made sense during the day.

Or that perhaps you'd forgotten.

When my eyes popped open that morning, the first thought that flew into my brain was of that stupid condom.

Or lack thereof.

Sitting up in bed, I realized I wasn't the only one with this realization.

Taylor, who usually seemed like a fairly laid-back guy, was currently shirtless, pacing the room like a caged bear.

Back and forth, back and forth, he went.

"We forgot—" he began.

"The condom," I finished, meeting his worried gaze.

He slumped down in the corner chair, the sunlight from the window casting a beautiful glow across his broad chest. "I don't know how I forgot. I've never…"

I didn't know what I'd expected, definitely not happy jubilation or glee, but after last night, after the connection I'd felt, I guessed I'd just thought he'd be calmer.

But it didn't matter anyway.

"I have an IUD," I said, making his eyes jolt back to mine.

"You do?" A glimmer of hope appeared in his eyes.

I nodded. "I know I said it'd been a while, but I'm still responsible."

"More responsible than me," he said, the guilt written all over his face.

"Hey," I said, rising from the bed and grabbing his button-down from the floor.

He watched me, like he always did, but I could see he didn't think he deserved to. Not bothering with the buttons, I just pulled it on and walked over to him, his hungry gaze taking in every inch of me.

"We both forgot."

I slid onto his lap, and his hands glided up my legs, wrapping around my waist.

"There was a lot of that going on last night," I told him.

A satisfied smile crept across his face. "Well, at least I can do something right."

I leaned forward, close to his ear. "Oh, believe me, Taylor Sutherland, there are many things you can do extremely well."

He chuckled. "I feel like that particular gift has left me lacking in other areas as of late."

"Like what?"

His head tilted to the side. "Like the fact that I haven't fed you in nearly twenty-four hours."

I opened my mouth to protest, remembering the ice cream, but his eyes motioned toward the bed, and I followed. There, sitting on the nightstand, was the sad, melted pint of Ben & Jerry's we'd forgotten about minutes after he brought it to me.

"I'm going to order us breakfast," he said with determination.

"But..." I pressed against him, feeling him harden in response.

He groaned. "You're evil."

"You did call me the daughter of the devil when I first arrived, didn't you?" I grinned.

"I don't think I'm the one who came up with that particular name, but considering the way you move those hips, I'm not surprised."

"Can't we just stay in bed all day?" I begged.

He glanced at the clock next to the melted ice cream container. "Checkout is in a couple of hours."

"What if we just stayed another day?" I suggested, my arms stretching around his neck. "Maybe two?"

"Not that I wouldn't enjoy that, but what happened to you being behind? Don't you need to get back?"

I rose to my feet, the loss of his body heat feeling strangely hollow. "I'm not sure I'm going to continue."

It was like a vacuum had sucked all the air out of the room as I watched his reaction. Confusion, disappointment, disbelief.

"No," he finally said.

"No?" I echoed. "What kind of answer is that? You can't tell me no!"

He stood up, determination in his eyes. "Someone has to. Jesus, Lani. You can't give up. Not now, not so easily."

Anger took hold of me, and I retaliated. "Why? Why can't I? It's my dream, Taylor! I get to say when and how it ends, and believe me," I yelled, the tears already welling up in my eyes, "that's all it's ever going to be. Just a dream. Because my father is never going to take me seriously, and now that he has Becky, why would he ever leave the company to me? I've been replaced. He has a new family, a new successor. I'm nothing!"

So much for forgetting.

But I guessed we never could really forget, could we?

We just hid the pain, squirreled away in the recesses of our mind, until one day, it came racing back to the surface, ready to play.

Too bad mine hadn't dug a bit deeper. Hid a bit longer.

It would have been nice to live in a state of naive bliss for a while.

"Hey," Taylor said softly, pulling me into his big, strong arms, trying to take away the pain, just as he had the night before. "We'll figure this out."

I shook my head in disbelief. "I don't know how. My dad

expects complete project plans on his desk in four and a half weeks. That's barely enough time to do one design, let alone two."

He tilted my chin up, giving me a questioning look. "Two?"

My cheeks went pink, as I realized I'd just given away my secret. But, now that I had, I wasn't sure why I had been keeping it from him in the first place.

"I'm having Halladay work up two plans for the hotel," I explained. "One that is a cohesive vision of the spa retreat I had planned."

"And the other?" His brow lifted.

"And the other is a nod to the original hotel; art deco with a modern twist."

"Are you serious?" His green eyes were alight with excitement. "Why didn't you tell me?"

"Well, for one, I didn't want you to disappear. I was afraid that if I told you, you'd consider your job done and stop hanging around so much."

He grinned. "You couldn't get rid of me if you tried. And two?"

"Because I'm still not sure it's going to work," I said.

"What? Why? If you're designing it, it will be brilliant!"

His enthusiasm was contagious, and I couldn't help but smile.

"I don't get the final say, and as you can see," I said, holding my hands out to use the room as an example, "we kind of have a certain style we adhere to."

"So, change it," he pressed. "Do something different. Be the change, Lani. Show your dad just how amazing you are!"

"I want to. I really do. But, if he hates it, if he rejects the first design, I have to have a backup; otherwise—"

"Otherwise, you're afraid someone else will come along and take it out of your hands."

I nodded. "Someone like Becky and her ugly gold sconces."

I could see the wheels in his head turning.

"Okay, so we go back to Ocracoke and we work our asses off."

My brow arched. "*Our* asses?"

"Do you think I'm just going to leave you high and dry?"

My heart swelled. "No, I guess I don't."

"Good," he said, his smile so genuine and pure that I felt it in my soul. "Then, let's order some food."

I pushed him backwards, catching him off guard; otherwise, he wouldn't have budged an inch. "Not yet."

"Lani," he warned, but it was obviously in vain because his body moved along with mine, stepping back toward the chair we'd just vacated. "We don't have much time."

"Good." I grinned, shoving him down. He tumbled into the high wingback chair as I knelt before him, nestling my body between his thighs. "I'll be quick."

I hadn't realized how much I loved the open water until I stepped on a boat with Taylor Sutherland.

Watching him man a boat without a shirt on didn't hurt either. He was truly in his element out here though, and I could see why so many young tourists had fallen for him over the years.

It was a total turn-on.

Of course, those blonde bitches will have to go through me now, I thought slyly.

And then my gut churned.

Or at least they would for the next month or so.

And then…

I didn't really want to think about that.

"You look like you're deep in thought over there," Taylor said, giving me a wide grin as he walked over to sit by me. "You're not having second thoughts, are you? About going back?"

I smiled. "You mean, am I wishing I were still shacked up in that hotel room, naked, with you? No. Definitely not."

He chuckled.

"I am wondering why you're sitting next to me and not over there," I said, pointing toward the helm or the wheel or whatever the hell it was called, "driving us."

His brow rose. "That's cute."

I playfully punched him. "Seriously, aren't we going to drift off or something? I've seen movies. I know how people get lost at sea."

"Okay, first, ow."

I rolled my eyes.

"Second, I'm kind of hurt on how little you trust me. I do actually know what I'm doing."

"Which is?" I asked.

"Waiting," he explained. "Did you even notice that I'd shut off the engine?"

I listened for a moment, and indeed, the world was quiet, free of the loud roar I'd grown accustomed to. "Oh, huh. How about that? What are we waiting for?"

He ignored me. "And, third, we've got a pretty sophisticated navigation system back in the office. Even if I didn't know what I was doing," he said, holding up a finger to silence me before I even had a chance for a rebuttal, "which I do, my brother could find us. So, are you happy?"

My lips pressed together. "I would be if you told me what we were waiting for because, right now, I'm envisioning sharks."

He chuckled again.

"Not helping, Taylor!"

I watched as his eyes scanned the water, the boat gently rocking back and forth. Grabbing my waist, he turned my body, angling my head to where he was looking, and said, "There. Do you see them?"

I squinted, but the glare was almost blinding. "See what?" I asked.

Reaching up, he pulled off his sunglasses and placed them on me, shielding my vision from the brightness.

"You'll have to wait a second for them to surface again, but—"

"Oh my gosh!" I nearly screamed as two dolphins popped up out of the water.

"Shh!" He laughed. "You'll scare them away!"

"Really?"

He shrugged. "I don't know. Do I look like a marine biologist?"

I laughed, my eyes still trained on the spot he'd pointed out. "How did you know they'd be here?"

His arms wrapped around mine. "There are several spots I bring some of my fishing tours to if it's the right time of the year. I actually wasn't sure we'd see them; it's pretty late in the year. They migrate to Florida for the winter."

"Smart animals." I smiled, rising to my feet to take a closer look on the other side of the boat.

There were only a few of them, but they were magnificent, and I couldn't help but watch how they moved and played in the water as a single unit.

A family.

"Thank you for this," I said, turning back toward him.

He pulled me close, tucking me beneath his chin, like we were two puzzle pieces that fit together perfectly.

"Anything for you," he answered, making my belly flutter.

"Anything?" I found myself saying.

"Teach me to fish?"

Laughter broke from his lips. "What?"

I could barely be heard over the roar he was making. "I just thought, if I was going to be seen hanging around the town fisherman for the next month, I might want to learn."

His laughter died down as the reality of our time together set in. I watched as he swallowed hard, his eyes meeting mine.

"Yeah, I'll teach you," he said, his fingers trailing down my face.

I felt like both of us were waiting, the words right there on the tip of our tongues.

What if I didn't go?

What if I went with you?

But neither of us said it, neither of us capturing the moment while it dangled there in front of us, waiting to be caught.

Instead, we stood frozen in fear, worrying over what would be when our time together ended and life returned to normal.

But then again, what could ever be considered normal after meeting a man like Taylor Sutherland?

CHAPTER THIRTEEN

Taylor

"So, what is this thing we're doing today?" Leilani asked. "And why am I dressing up like a pirate?"

I chuckled, giving her a once-over as we both dressed, having commandeered the suite she'd made over in the hotel for our very own. We had also spent a few nights over at By the Bay over the last week, enjoying Molly's scones and the killer dual-head shower.

We had yet to spend a single night at my place, however—a fact that neither of us had decided to bring up.

It was kind of like her impending deadline—when she would go back and present the plans to her father. We knew it was coming. We worked on it daily, yet we didn't actually talk about it.

Ever.

"It's a fall festival. By the Bay used to host it at the inn, but it got too big over the last few years, so they moved it to the streets."

"That sounds dangerous."

"You really are a city girl, aren't you?" I laughed.

"Okay," she said, slipping into the long, old-fashioned dress, "but that still doesn't explain why we're dressing as pirates."

I smiled. "Only one of us is dressing as a pirate, Pookie Bear," I corrected her, knowing I'd always get a rise out of her when using that particular pet name. "You are just a woman."

Her eyebrows rose. "Just a woman?"

"Sorry! What I meant to say is, you aren't a pirate; you're a woman. A specific woman."

She didn't look impressed.

"History lesson?" I said like it was a plea for mercy.

A smirk tugged at her lips. "Okay."

"Every year at the fall festival, there is a theme when it comes to costumes. Molly, who still runs the whole thing, tends to go a little off the rails sometimes. Last year, being pregnant, she picked the color pink."

"Pink was the theme? Like, just the color pink?"

"Yep. The whole town looked like an ad for Pepto-Bismol. It was crazy. Anyway, this year, she's a little saner, and she went with historical characters. Anyone in history is fair game."

"And you chose a pirate?" Again, her tone was less than pleased.

"Not just any pirate. I'm Blackbeard!"

She looked confused. "Like Jack Sparrow?"

"What?" I laughed. "No! Well, kind of. Jack Sparrow was actually created after the original and very real Blackbeard."

"Really?"

"Really."

"Was he super sexy like Jack Sparrow? Oh, can you wear guy liner like he did?" she asked, a mischievous grin spreading across her face.

"I think we're getting off topic," I said.

She looked down at her plain dress. "You know, I think we are. How about we talk about the fact that you're some super-cool pirate—"

"He was actually a pretty horrible dude. He murdered—"

She gave me the death stare.

"I'm sorry. Continue."

"And I'm a woman. Just a woman."

"I thought that wasn't okay to say."

"Taylor!" she hollered.

I tried not to laugh, but it was hard. She was just so damn cute when she was flustered.

"You're not just a woman," I finally told her. "You're Blackbeard's wife."

"I'm what now?"

A satisfied grin tugged at the corners of my lips. "There are all sorts of legends and stories about the many wives of Blackbeard. It is rumored that he had up to fourteen wives, but most believe this was just a stunt he did to lure women onto his boat."

"That's…weird."

"Like I said, not a great guy."

"And yet, here we are, paying tribute to this horrible dude. You couldn't have picked the Roosevelts?"

My head twisted to the side. "You know, I could have, but I was kind of hoping to get laid after this, and I wasn't sure that look would do it. Plus, Dean had this costume, so really, it was a win-win."

"Okay, smart-ass," she said with a chuckle, "tell me about Blackbeard's wife."

"There's not much to tell," I said. "Her name was Mary Ormond. She was the daughter of a plantation owner, and I'm guessing he wasn't a great guy since he offered up his sixteen-year-old daughter to a thug."

"Maybe they loved each other," she said.

"I don't think a guy like that believed in love."

She walked toward me, slipping her hands around my waist. "Maybe she changed his mind."

Her words made my breath falter.

"Maybe she did," I found myself saying.

"Whatever happened to her?"

"No one really knows. Some accounts say he offered her as a gift to his crew."

She shook her head, disagreeing. "No," she said. "I think they ruled those seas together until the very end."

I remembered her out on the boat just a week earlier, her happy laughter as I'd tried to teach her how to wield a fishing line.

Would she stay with me to the very end?

If I asked her to?

"So, this is what small-town Americana looks like, huh?" Lani said as we strolled down the now-closed Silver Lake Drive, which had been completely transformed for the annual fall festival.

"I'm not sure we're the perfect example, considering we have more boats than kids and our population is mostly retired people, but sure, welcome to small-town life." As I finished my sentence, a kid whizzed by on a bike, making her smile.

"Sure seems like there are a lot of kids here."

I gave her a wink. "We bussed those in especially for you."

She laughed, rolling her eyes.

"The fall festival has become a popular event. Lots of people ferry in for the day, and some even rent houses and stay for the weekend."

"Really?" That piqued her interest. "That's useful information."

"Oh, yeah? Why?" I asked. "Planning something special for the hotel next year?"

Her mouth opened but shut immediately. "No," she finally answered, her head downcast. "Just thought I could include it in my notes for the future staff."

Right, because she wasn't going to run the hotel. Just design it.

Soon, she'd hand it off to someone else, and just as swiftly as she'd arrived, she'd be gone, off to another place and another part of the world.

I swallowed hard and did what I always did in these moments when things got too real.

I ignored it and changed the subject.

"Oh, hey," I said, motioning toward the other side of the street, "there's Molly!"

Coward, a voice in my head shouted.

I ignored that, too.

Despite being the lead for today's festivities, Molly seemed to be as cool and collected as ever, dressed as Cleopatra in a gold-and-black gown that made the bubbly blonde look mysterious and super glamorous.

"Oh my gosh, I love your costume!" Lani said, greeting Molly like the friend I knew they'd become to each other. I watched as the two women hugged, feeling extreme pride over the woman at my side. "You make a gorgeous Cleopatra!"

"Thank you!" Molly said, running her hands over the silky black wig. "I'm glad someone thinks so."

I got the feeling that *someone* had a name.

"Jake in the dog house?" I guessed.

Her arms folded across her chest as her eyes picked him out of the crowd. I followed her gaze, seeing him walking toward us, and I immediately broke out in a grin.

I could see why she was so put out.

"Did you come here straight from work, Jake?" I asked the moment he stepped up to our small group.

He gave me a friendly pat on the back and said a quick hello to Lani, whom he'd apparently already met several times at the inn.

"No," he said. "I'm in costume."

We all gave him a blank stare.

"What?" he asked. "There are tons of famous doctors in history."

"Name one," his wife demanded.

"Uh…" His brow rose, the effort showing as he tried to come up with one. "Oh! Norman Shumway!"

"Who the heck is that?" Molly asked, not looking pleased at all.

"He's the father of heart transplants, and considering that is what I used to do, that kind of makes him my hero."

I looked at him and back at Molly.

"Fine!" Jake threw his hands up. "I didn't want to wear that costume, Molly! Happy?"

A satisfied smirk spread across her face.

"She wanted me to wear a skirt, Taylor. A fucking skirt. In public!"

I couldn't help but grin as I watched Molly's eyes roll. Lani seemed to be enjoying the show as well.

"It was not a skirt, Jake. I'm Cleopatra. You were supposed to be Mark Antony! Couples go as couples; that's how it goes. See, Leilani and Taylor are dressed as…" Molly took a look at our outfits, and her brows furrowed. "Who the heck are you? A pirate and his very prudish wench?"

Lani laughed out loud. "We're Blackbeard and his wife, Mary Ormond, who was most definitely the love of his life."

I gave her a devilish grin. "That part is still up for debate."

"Definitely up for debate," she agreed, licking her lips in a way that made me want to groan.

"Ah," Jake said, his gaze dodging between Lani and me. "Well, that's great. Molly, you want to go check on your mom? See how she's handling Ruby?"

"Yep."

They made a beeline across the street, and I couldn't help but chuckle as Lani wrapped her arms around me.

"I think we made them uncomfortable."

"Yeah? Well, they've been making me uncomfortable my entire life, so it was nice to be the gross one for a change."

"Could you imagine being with someone that long? Like they have? Molly and I have chatted a few times, so I've gotten the readers digest version of their love story. It just seems so romantic, you know?"

I swallowed hard.

Until her, I couldn't imagine being with someone for longer than a single night.

"I—"

"You know this is a family event, right?"

I turned, breathing out a sigh of relief as my brother and his wife walked over, and I nearly fell into his arms in thanks.

Lani and I were great at a lot of things. Together, even more so. But talking about us as a couple?

That was one skill we seriously sucked at.

"Hey," I said before giving him a once-over. "Whoa."

"I know; I know," he said, doing a cocky little spin. "Take it all in."

"Isn't he hot?" Cora blurted out, nearly jumping up and down.

Lani giggled, having never met my sister in law, but I had a feeling, if they had a few minutes together, they'd become instant friends.

"*Hot* isn't really the word I'd use, but, yeah, he looks all right. John Smith, I'm guessing?"

"Yeah. How'd you know?" Dean asked, looking fairly impressed.

"Well, it wasn't based on you, idiot," I said, motioning toward his dime-a-dozen white peasant blouse and black jeans. "You look like a Disney reject. But your beautiful wife, that's a different story."

"Hey now," Dean warned.

"You really do look stunning," Lani said of Cora's intricate Native American costume.

"Thank you," Cora said. "My dad actually has a few things from my great-grandmother who was Cherokee, but there was no way he was going to let me borrow those, so I made do. Hey, have you guys entered the King and Queen Competition?"

Lani cocked her head to the side. "The what?"

"Yeah…no, we won't be doing that," I said nearly at the same time.

She seemed to be slightly more interested at my almost-instantaneous dismissal.

"It's not as bad as it sounds," Cora promised. "I honestly think Molly couldn't come up with a better title."

"So, what is it?" Lani asked.

"It's a competition," Dean explained. "One we happen to be the reigning champions at." His eyes rose in my direction. "Huh, is that maybe why you don't want to enter, brother? Intimidated?"

I blew out a loud breath through my teeth. "Hardly."

"Then, what's the reason?"

All three sets of eyes were on me, and I felt sweat dripping down my back.

"I, uh…"

"Isn't it a couples thing?" Lani asked, saving me.

I sent her a silent, *Thank you,* from across the circle.

The question seemed to throw Cora a bit, but she answered it all the same, "No. I mean, usually. But there are several friends who enter."

"Molly and I were partners for years," Dean said before adding, "You know, before we were actually—"

"We got it," I answered.

"So, what say you, Taylor? In or out?"

I tried not to think about the last time I'd been asked that question.

Lani's father had asked me that question weeks ago and I was still too afraid to answer.

Turning my attention to Lani, I lifted a single challenging eyebrow and watched as her shoulders shrugged, giving me all the answer I needed.

"We're in."

"We have to perform?" she almost shouted as we sat down on the grass near the mouth of the bay.

"Now, you know why I never enter."

She let out a heavy sigh. "I feel like I really should have asked more questions before giving you the go-ahead for this, but honestly, I heard *Queen,* and my brain kind of went to mush."

Chuckling, I handed her the hot sandwich she'd ordered from the street vendor as I dug into mine. "So, that's why we're in this mess?"

"I can't help it. The little girl still buried inside me always wanted to be royal! And, besides, I didn't see you protesting much!"

"My brother has a way of antagonizing me."

"I noticed." She grinned. "Okay, so how exactly are we going to pull this off? Can we do anything? Like, could we get up onstage and recite Shakespeare if we wanted to?"

I shrugged. "We could. I wouldn't suggest it if you want to actually win, but sure, the rules just say there must be two of you, and you must preform...something."

"Okay, that's simple enough. But I need to change. Do you think your friend Millie could let me into her store?"

"Uh, yes—right after you tell me what you have planned."

A smile curved around her face. "Maybe later. I'm starving."

"We look ridiculous," I said as we waited on the side of the makeshift stage that had been erected on the street for the fall festival's King and Queen Competition.

The sun had begun to set, and a large crowd had gathered around for this evening's show.

It was something I sometimes stayed around for, lingering in the back for the last several years when my brother had hopped onstage and competed with Cora, but not this year.

Nope, this year, I'd had to open my big mouth.

This year, I was front and center.

"We don't look ridiculous," Lani encouraged me, giving me a once-over. "Well, maybe you do since you refused to change, so I guess that means we kind of look ridiculous, standing next to each other…"

"See?" I said, my eyes sweeping over her.

She'd gotten rid of the drab gown from the 1800s for something a lot cooler.

Or hotter rather.

We'd managed to track down Millie, who'd been more than glad to sneak us into Beachcombers to help Lani find a more suitable dress for what she had planned.

And, if it wasn't for that plan, I might have bailed on this whole thing.

"So, what is your job?" she asked, going through her directions one last time as the couple before us, who happened to be my brother and Cora, finished.

"Stand there and try to look sexy?"

She smiled. "I don't think I said sexy, but sure. Just dance. You can dance, right?"

"Uh," I managed to say.

"Oh! They're announcing us!"

I was so screwed.

As Cora and Dean exited the stage, having just finished singing "I Got You Babe" by Sonny and Cher to a roaring crowd, my brother gave me a pat on the back and wished us luck.

God, I hated him in this moment.

Just dance—that was all I had to do.

All I had to—

The second Leilani stepped on that stage, I lost the ability to breathe.

It was like watching a butterfly take flight for the first time.

Her smile was dazzling as she walked with the confidence

of a tiger onto center stage, just waiting for the music to begin, waving to little girls in the front row, while I stood there like a deer in headlights, just staring at her.

We'd both joked at how ridiculous we'd look onstage—me still in my Blackbeard costume and her now looking like a fucking goddess, dressed in a white bikini and a flowery print sarong tied around her waist—but the truth was, I could have been wearing anything next to her, and it wouldn't have mattered.

She'd steal the stage regardless.

And that point was proven the moment the music began, and I discovered just how much her mother had taught her all those years ago.

I knew I was supposed to dance or do something. This, after all, was a couple's competition. But all I could do was watch her. The mesmerizing way her hips moved to the drumbeat and the sensual sway of her hands. I'd never really understood the idea of hula dancing—how a person could tell a story with movement. But watching her made me a believer.

I loved every moment, and the crowd did, too, breaking into a fury of noise when the routine was over.

Jumping into my arms, she exclaimed, "Oh my gosh, that was fun! I think they liked us!"

"I think they loved you!" I corrected her as she gave one final wave as we headed offstage. I pressed her against the nearest wall, her breath still heavy from dancing. "What would you say if I dragged you back to my place and we skipped the rest of the performances?"

A devilish grin appeared across her face. "But what about my crown?" she asked.

"There is no crown, babe. Just a gift card to Billy's, and honestly, I don't think I can make it much longer after seeing you up there like that."

She looked incredulous. "You mean, I did all that, and I don't even get a damn crown?!"

Laughing, I pulled her toward the door. "Hey Dean, we forfeit. Enjoy your shrimp salad!"

I heard a chuckle from my brother as we made a run for it. I was thankful my house was only a block away because we were tearing at each other's clothes before we even reached the front door.

"Are you sure there aren't any blondes in there?" she joked the second I fished out my key.

"Funny," I said, unlocking the door with one hand. The other was shoved under her bikini top, about to make a serious wardrobe malfunction if I didn't get us inside.

"I want you to dance for me like that every day," I said, pushing us both past the threshold.

"Okay," she wholeheartedly agreed.

"But, right now, I just want to fuck you against this door."

"God, yes."

Slamming the door shut, I did just that, shoving her skirt up high on her waist as her finger worked the button on my pants. Our breaths were heavy, our hearts wild and our touches frantic, as we reached for each other, knowing what we craved most was just moments away.

Thankful she was wearing a bikini and not that ridiculously long dress anymore, I pushed aside the small strip of white fabric, and with one powerful thrust, I was exactly where I wanted to be.

I took her hard and fast, both of us needing that release more than we needed air in our lungs. When we were sated and spent, I carried her to my bedroom, and I fell asleep with her cradled in my arms, feeling like the luckiest man in the world.

But then morning came, and reality set in when I awoke to the smell of bacon.

In or out, Taylor?

The unanswered question loomed once again in my mind.

"You look like shit, little brother," Dean said as I marched into work later that morning.

I gave him a look as I grabbed my morning coffee. "You know, you say that a lot."

He shrugged. "Can't help it if you look like shit all the time. Late night?"

Dumping half the container of creamer into my cup, I snapped back at him, "I don't want to talk about it."

Clearly not getting the hint, he kept going, kept prodding and poking. "You seemed pretty chipper when you and Leilani left the festival, practically pawing at each other. You got second place by the way, although I don't see how, considering you basically just stood there like a damn idiot the whole time, but—"

"We had breakfast together," I finally said, unable to meet his eyes.

A palpable silence filled the room before the sound of my brother's laughter broke it. I blinked several times before turning in his direction, only to see where I needed to aim my assault.

"That's what's got you in a wreck this morning? You had breakfast with a woman? Come on, Taylor. When are you going to grow up?"

I blew out a frustrated breath as I tried to remember all the reasons I shouldn't kill my brother.

My mom would hate me.

My niece would be sad.

"You don't get it," I finally said.

"No," he replied, leaning back in his desk chair, "I don't because you never talk to me about anything other than the business and family stuff. I'm your brother, Taylor, and yet I barely know you."

I scoffed, taking a sip of coffee and turning my head as I set a pace around the room. "That's not true. You know plenty."

"I know the cursory stuff. I know you put way too much

creamer in your coffee and that, up until recently, you hit on every blonde tourist who crossed your path. I know that you make a mean omelet, and you still go to Mom's early on Sunday to help her cook the family supper. That is, when you're not busting your ass, working overtime here."

"You know that?"

"Of course I do," he answered. "But what I don't know is why you've completely shut yourself off to the possibility of love. What rocked your world so massively that you think something as simple as sharing the first meal of the day with a woman is a death curse?"

"Dad was making breakfast," I said faintly.

I caught his movement as he swiveled his chair toward me. "What?"

"The morning it happened, he was making us all breakfast. And then he…he was just gone."

Dean shook his head. "How could you possibly remember that? You were too young."

"I remember," I said, the memory replaying like an old home video. It was hazy, no words or conversations.

Just tiny bursts.

My father's face as he'd turned back from the stove and smiled at me.

My mother running across the kitchen toward his collapsed body.

And then the screams.

The terrible screams.

"I thought you said you didn't have any memories of Dad," Dean said, looking somber and sullen, his hand reaching for the back of his neck as he leaned forward in his chair, no longer the picture of casual ease.

"What was the point of telling you that the only memory I have of him is right before he died?"

Dean shook his head, clearly distressed. "We could have talked about it," he said.

"Talked about what? What is there to talk about, Dean? He died; it's over."

"It's clearly not over. It's been decades man, and you can't stand to have breakfast with the woman you love. You think that's normal?"

I slammed my empty coffee cup down on the counter. "Coming from a guy who gave up on life, that's rich. If it wasn't for Cora, you'd still be moping about this goddamn island while I worked my ass off, running the business to take care of you."

"You're right," he agreed, rising to his feet. "I had issues. Still do. I nearly fucking died, Taylor. And when I needed to sort that shit out, you stepped up and did more than your fair share to allow me to do that. So, is that what you need? Time? To work out whatever the hell is going on with you?"

"What?" I looked back at him like he was going insane. "I don't need time! I don't have issues to work through. I'm not you!"

My words hurt, and I could see the physical pain in his eyes as they stung their way into his heart.

"Oh, really? Then, how did breakfast go this morning? Planning on doing it again tomorrow? What about the next day?"

Now, it was him doing the hurting, and I couldn't help but fight back.

Only this time, I didn't retaliate with words.

I went for his throat instead.

"What the hell—oomph!" he yelled out the moment I tackled him.

Was it a dick move, trying to kick the ass of my brother who happened to be an amputee?

Probably.

But he was the one who would go on and on about wanting to be treated just like everyone else.

Right now, he was being an asshole, and this was how I dealt with assholes.

Dean, the vigilant peacemaker, seemed determined to end this fight before it began, stepping back, fighting me off and holding out his hand as he tried to reason with me. "Taylor, you're being ridiculous. We're not kids anymore. This isn't the living room where we just simply push back the furniture and wrestle out our problems."

"The fuck it isn't," I answered, taking a swing.

His eyes went wide as he realized I wasn't standing down.

"Seriously, Taylor!" he yelled, dodging me. "Would you take a look at yourself? Do you really think this is normal? If you'd just take a few days and—"

"I don't have issues!" I roared, my chest heaving as I tried to tackle him, but I forgot who I was fighting.

Even missing an arm, my brother was a beast.

And he didn't back down in a fight.

Shoving me back, he warily eyed me. "Everyone has issues," he said, his breathing heavy. "And I think it's time you come to terms with yours."

"I told you, I—"

"You have a week off," he said, his voice firm.

"You can't just tell me when to take time off. You're not my boss!"

"I'm not your boss, but I am your partner. And, right now, you're worthless to just about everyone. So, go—"

"Dean, this isn't cool. You can't—."

"Get out of here, Taylor. Don't make me call Macon and press assault charges on my own brother."

My mouth fell open. "You wouldn't."

His eyes met mine. "You want to try me?" he asked. "Maybe a night in the slammer would give you an issue or two since you seem to be so free and clear of them."

A dark scowl took hold of my expression. "You're an asshole, Dean."

He shook his head, his breathing still heavy. "That might be true, but I'm an asshole who cares about you."

"Crappy way of showing it."

"Maybe by the end of the week, you'll change your mind."

"Don't count on it," I said, making my way toward the door, my chest still heaving from our altercation.

"And, Taylor?" he said just before I pushed my way out. "Don't do anything stupid."

I let out a sadistic laugh.

Now, why would I do that?

CHAPTER FOURTEEN

Leilani

"Hey, Lani? You okay?"

Molly's concerned words pierced through the trance I'd been in for what seemed like forever. How long had I been staring at these flames slowly crackling away in the fireplace of the inn?

"What?" I managed to say, finally able to tear my eyes away.

My innkeeper and new friend gave me a sideways glance, walking the rest of the way into the parlor. She took a seat on the couch next to me, although I was on the floor, wrapped in a fuzzy blanket, looking extremely pathetic.

She picked up the empty coffee cup, giving it a quick sniff. "I came by to do my last check on everything before bed. Did this have whiskey in it?" she asked.

I shook my head. "No," I answered. "Although it wasn't for a lack of trying. Do you know how hard it is to find liquor in this town after six o'clock?"

She laughed. "Try being a teenager here." Giving a quick nod toward the kitchen, she winked. "Next time, there's whiskey up above the refrigerator. I use it in some of my recipes sometimes, but I've learned to hide it from the guests."

"Now, you tell me. That was the one place I didn't look."

Her eyebrow lifted. "So, what did he do?"

Closing my eyes, I could still feel his lips against my skin, hear his voice as he'd called out my name.

Had it all been a lie? A ruse? A fucking game?

"He bought my hotel," I finally said.

"What?" The word came out far louder than either of us had expected. "Man, you go away for a few days and all hell breaks loose."

I nodded, the news still shocking to even me, and I'd had twenty-four hours to let it marinate in my brain. Yet still, I couldn't process it. Obviously realizing this was going to be a longer conversation than she'd planned, she settled in next to me.

I was grateful for the company. I'd missed her while she was gone. I hadn't realized how much I'd come to value our little talks in the hallways and just before breakfast. Although they were brief, they always managed to cheer me up and brighten my day.

Just like the woman sitting next to me.

The last few days without her had been basically hell.

"So let me get this straight," she began. "Taylor, the guy who is head over heels in love with you, that guy bought your hotel?"

I let out a stilted laugh. "You mean, Taylor, the guy who basically ghosted me a week ago and then didn't even have the common decency to tell me to my face how he'd screwed me over. Instead, he waited for my dad's assistant to send over the official letter of purchase." My voice was barely a whisper now as I tried as hard as I could to fight back the tears I'd been holding back.

I would not cry over this man.

I would not cry anymore over this man, I thought.

"What?" Molly seemed shocked, finally noticing the letter in question sitting on the coffee table. Picking it up, she read through it, seeing the proof of his betrayal for herself. "The last time I saw you, you two seemed pretty happy."

I thought back to that day at the fall festival.

We had been happy.

Deliriously so.

We'd raced back to his house, barely able to contain our pulsating need for each other. My heart had raced as he pushed me through the open door, only to make love to me against it moments later.

He'd never taken me there before.

I had known it meant something.

It had to have.

So the next day, as I had sung to myself over a pan of sizzling bacon, wearing one of his old T-shirts, I'd let myself dream.

But instead of boardrooms and exotic hotels, this dream was different.

Different and amazing.

And all mine.

I'd pictured myself here, in this town, somewhere down the road.

Not just for a few days or a week but a year. Two years. Ten.

I'd pictured our life on this island, and for once, I hadn't been scared.

For once, I hadn't felt alone.

Until I had seen his face when he came down the stairs, and I'd realized something was seriously wrong.

Maybe fantasies weren't supposed to come true after all.

All my fears had been confirmed the next day when I'd sat at the inn for hours, waiting for him to pick me up for Sunday dinner at his mother's house.

He never showed.

After several unanswered calls and texts, and a full twenty-four hours of radio silence, I began to get worried. Had something happened?

Racing into the office of Sutherland Fishing Co. the next morning, I found only Dean.

"Have you seen Taylor," I'd asked. "Is he okay?"

A sad expression had passed across his face. "He's fine, Lani."

I had my answer.

I hadn't tried to contact him since.

"Have you asked him why?"

"No," I answered. "I don't have to. From the beginning, he made his intentions clear. The town comes first. I was never part of his permanent plans."

Her voice was warm and comforting. "Lani, I know you're hurting, but think this through with me. If Taylor had this money—which is a lot by the way—sitting around from the beginning, why didn't he just buy the hotel from your father weeks ago?"

I shrugged, unwilling to justify his betrayal. "Maybe he needed a distraction."

"Maybe he's pushing you away," she said. "And, in effect, running from the one thing he wants more than anything."

It was a romantic notion, but one I couldn't comprehend. Not when my heart was breaking and my chest ached.

And—

"You know, Jake ran once," she went on, her eyes wistful, deeply emotional. "We'd barely graduated from high school, but even then, I had known. We had known. He was mine, and I was his. We would have our whole lives together."

"What happened?" I asked.

"His mom died," she answered. "His mom died and everything changed. He changed. And then he ran."

"Taylor isn't running," I said firmly. "He's getting exactly what he wanted. Now, everything will go back to how it was before I came. His precious hotel will stand, unchanged, and so will the town."

"Do you think that's what he really wants?"

"I have a very official-looking letter that tells me he does."

"Maybe you should go ask him yourself. Men are…" She scrunched her nose, as if she was trying to find a particular word but then just gave up. "Frustrating," she finally said. "Sometimes they need a little extra push to get them to fess up their feelings." Laughing lightly, she added, "I guess women aren't innocent of that either."

"Is that what you did with Jake?"

She laughed. "Oh, yes. I pushed him all right—right out of town."

My brows lifted. "You kicked him out?"

Her head tilted. "It broke my heart to do it. But, as much as I loved him, we needed time. And I figured if we found each other again, it would be right next time. And it was. So, yeah, I pushed him. But I also pushed myself in the process. We both grew."

I shook my head, feeling like I was swimming in doubt. It was a nice notion, the idea of time.

But time was never a luxury Taylor and I had.

Especially now…

"No. He's made his decision, and he chose wrong. I don't need any further explanation than that, and I don't want to wait around for a man who doesn't want me, especially since…" My words got caught in my throat. It was barely an idea but one I'd been grappling with all day. It was the real reason I'd given up my fruitless search for whiskey.

"Especially since what?"

I swallowed hard, knowing that once I said it, action must be taken. "Especially since I think I might be pregnant."

I honestly didn't know what I would have done if it wasn't for Molly. She hadn't asked many questions or passed any judgment.

She'd simply asked what I needed, and when I'd said, "A friend," she was there.

Having never done this before, she was a guiding light as well as the shoulder I needed to lean on. While I suspected I might be pregnant, I wasn't sure if I could actually confirm it.

Molly, having already been down the surprise pregnancy road assured me enough time had passed.

"I got my first positive test when I was a day late," she'd said. "I took about ten more after that, and Jake took a blood test when he didn't believe the pile I threw on his desk. But, yes, the home tests are pretty accurate these days."

I sort of nodded my head in a daze.

Great, that's great.

Luckily, my good friend Molly also took care of procuring the much needed pregnancy test as well, having some stored away in her own bathroom at home. When she returned and handed one over, I couldn't help but give her a questioning look.

"We're trying for baby number two," she said, giving a casual shrug. "I order them online so that the entire town doesn't know."

"Small towns are weird," I commented.

She let out a small laugh. "Indeed they are. Do you know how to use one of these?"

Looking down at it, I felt a small lump form in my throat. This wasn't exactly how I pictured this moment in my life.

"I think I can figure it out, but can I make a call first?"

She shrugged. "I'm not going anywhere. You do whatever you need to."

"Thanks."

Fortunately, the inn was all but empty, the only midweek visitor being me, so we had the whole place to ourselves. Leaving the door to my suite open, she wandered out, making herself busy in other rooms to allow me some privacy.

I didn't need it, but I appreciated the gesture.

This all felt a little overwhelming, and right now, I just needed to hear one voice before I did this.

Pulling up her number, I sat down on the bed, draping the yellow quilt over my legs, and waited for Piper to answer.

"Please tell me you're going to give me several details about your juicy new love life," she said, not bothering with a greeting. "'Cause it is a Sahara over here, if you know what I'm saying!"

I smiled, although it was a halfhearted one as I pushed back tears.

"Piper," I managed to say.

Her voice sobered instantly. "What's wrong? Who died? Oh my God, what's wrong?"

"No one died," I said, hoping to calm her. "But I do have something to tell you."

"Okay," she said cautiously. "Why do I get the feeling it's not something good?"

I shook my head, feeling my heart beat in response. "I think I might be pregnant."

"You think, or you are? Have you taken a test yet?" she asked. "And how did this happen? Did he talk you out of a condom? That rat bastard! I will come to that island myself and—"

"Piper!" I nearly yelled.

"Sorry!" she said softly. "You know how I handle stress."

"You panic?"

"Exactly! So, why are you calling me?" she joked. "You know I can't handle this crap."

"Because you're my family, and I'm scared."

"Let's talk you through this, okay?"

I breathed out for maybe the first time in a minute. "Okay."

"You used condoms?"

I nodded my head at first, and then I realized she couldn't see me. "Yes, but—"

"Yes, but what? There should be no *yes, buts* when it comes to sex."

"I have an IUD. So, we stopped."

"What IUD?"

"Um, the IUD I got in college. You should remember; you went with me."

The moment of silence made me seriously question my remembering skills.

"That IUD?" she exclaimed. "Have you gotten it replaced?"

My heart started to beat wildly. "No. Why would I have? It's good for, like, twelve years."

"Five! It's good for five!" she screamed.

"What? No! I got the one that lasted forever, remember?"

She groaned, and I wasn't sure if it was a groan over how incredibly stupid I was or that she was starting to seriously feel bad for me.

Either way, it wasn't good.

"No," she explained. "You went in there, dead set on the copper IUD, because you didn't want any hormones in your body."

"I remember that."

"And then the doctor told you about the possibility of losing your period all together if you went with the five-year option."

Suddenly, everything started to come back.

"Shit," I said, my stomach becoming queasy. "But I did have my period every single month. Like clockwork." It was one of the reasons I panicked so quickly. My period was like a very punctual out of town guest. It came like clockwork.

Except for this month.

This month, it was a no-show.

"I remember calling my doctor to complain when my period came, despite her bragging that it wouldn't, and she just played it off as no big deal and said it would just work itself out eventually. I hung up, called her a quack and never thought about it again."

I stared at the pale yellow walls, realizing my monumental mistake. "I'm such an idiot. This is all my fault."

"Hey," she said, her voice soft and filled with warmth. "It's going to be okay. It's not like you had a one-night stand. This guy is one of the good ones, right?"

My lips trembled. "Right," I said, trying not to think of the letter still resting on the table downstairs.

He's one of the good ones.

"So, see? Maybe it's not so bad. And, besides, we're getting ahead of ourselves. You haven't even taken the test yet."

"Right," I said again, unable to think of anything else.

I didn't need to take the test.

Some things you just knew.

And I knew beyond a shadow of a doubt that I was carrying Taylor's child.

"Are you going to be okay?" she asked after an unusual amount of silence passed between us.

Looking down at my belly, I protectively nestled a hand over it. "Yeah," I said, feeling more determined than ever. "I'll be just fine."

When we hung up moments later and I called Molly back in the room, I no longer felt like the trembling, lost little girl sitting in front of the fireplace.

Now, I was a woman, ready to take on the world.

"Let's do this," I said, surprising even Molly.

"Well, okay then."

I was still scared, still fearful of the future, but when that positive test appeared, I knew one thing for certain.

I would never be alone again.

"Taylor, I'm having your baby."

I took a deep breath and let it out.

"See?" I said to absolutely no one. "Totally easy."

Saying it out loud didn't sound so bad. Of course, I'd been

saying it to the very sympathetic air in the hotel lobby for what seemed like days.

Actually, it had been days.

Days of slowly wearing down a circled path around this large space as I tried to figure out what to do.

Should I tell him or just walk away, leaving him completely in the clear?

No ties, no commitment.

No responsibility to either of us.

It didn't seem fair—to keep it from him—but then again, neither was stealing my hotel. The hotel I was currently trying to vacate. I hadn't heard from the new owner, but I assumed that was what he wanted—for me to leave.

But the process was moving slower than I'd anticipated. As it turned out, I'd grown quite attached to this dingy old place and the island that surrounded it.

That singular moment in Taylor's kitchen when everything in my life had suddenly seemed to click into place, continued to haunt me. I felt connected to this island, to Ocracoke, and the people I'd met. As silly as it seemed, when I had stood there that morning, making bacon and frying eggs, I'd felt relief.

I'd been working so hard, chasing a dream I thought I'd wanted for so long.

Prove my worth and show my father I was good enough.

Those were the only goals I had seen.

But what would happen after that? Did I really want to follow in my father's footsteps? Nonstop travel, endless meetings, no time for anyone?

Was that the life I was hoping for?

Somewhere along the way, as I'd fought for the goals I thought I wanted, I'd actually found the life I was supposed to have.

Right here. With Taylor.

And then it had been ripped right out of my grasp with a single soul-crushing letter.

Now, I had to find a new dream. A new life. Because it wouldn't be found by taking over my father's company.

I wouldn't be that parent.

What kind of parent would Taylor be?

That had yet to be determined.

But, first, I had to tell him.

Just as I was contemplating how I was going to accomplish this, my phone rang. Heart racing, I looked down at the screen, only to discover it was Piper.

"Hey," I said. "What's up?"

"You were hoping I was someone else, weren't you?" she said.

"No," I said, a definite pout to my voice.

But we both knew I was lying. After my confirmed test the other night, I'd called her back to deliver the news, and we'd had a heart-to-heart, in which I'd confessed the current and very real status of my relationship with Taylor.

It had taken all I had to talk her out of catching the first flight out of Hawaii so she could hunt him down and kill him.

After I'd reminded her that my child would actually need a father, she'd managed to calm down. At least for a while.

"Well, unfortunately, I'm not calling to give you good news."

"Oh?"

"I'm stuck in Georgia," she said, as if that was supposed to mean something to me.

"What the hell are you doing in Georgia?"

"Coming to see you, obviously."

A faint smile tugged at the corners of my lips. "You're coming to see me?"

"Of course I am! Do you think I'd let you get knocked up without me?"

I laughed. "Well, that part has kind of already happened."

"You know what I mean, dork. I'm not letting you go through this without me."

"You know, if my father catches you out here—"

"He'll what? Fire me for taking vacation time? Besides, that hotel isn't even his anymore, so I don't give a shit what he thinks."

"I couldn't agree more," I said before following up with, "So, why are you grounded?"

"Haven't you seen the news?"

I looked around, like that was some sort of explanation. "I've been shacked up at the hotel for days, trying to pack up and force myself to leave." I let out a small huff. "No, I haven't seen the news."

"The tropical storm—"

"The one that is supposed to brush by the tip of Florida? They grounded you for that?"

"No," she said. "It turned. And it's headed right for the Carolinas."

After talking Piper into going back home and convincing her I'd be okay without her, I pulled up a local news channel on my phone, hoping to get some more details on what we were facing.

As a native of Hawaii, I'd had some experience with hurricanes and tropical storms, but it was extremely limited. The last major storm to pass through had happened when I was very little, but I remembered the stories.

And they were terrifying.

Homes ripped right from the foundations, people stranded for days, the loss of life.

As the website loaded, I clicked on a video and held my breath.

"Officials are calling this storm a late-season killer. Not only because of the timing—coming at the very end of hurricane season—but also due to its deadly force. What once was a tame tropical storm has now grown to a Category Two, and meteorologists warn it could get even bigger."

"Damn," I whispered.

The video cut from the anchorman to a satellite photo, and I got my first shot of the monster coming for the Carolina coast.

"No word from state and local government on mandatory evacuations, but they appear to be imminent."

Evacuations?

I looked around at the hotel, the one place I felt safe, and a sudden wave of panic took hold of me.

Where would I go?

I couldn't stay here, not with…

My hand dropped to my belly.

With my phone in my hand, I pulled up the only number I could think of. The name attached to it had once felt like a beacon of hope, a source of calm, and a shield from everything that could harm.

But I couldn't rely on false hopes and flimsy shields any longer.

And I was over the disappointing men in my life.

So, instead, I dialed another number and made plans to get the hell out of Ocracoke. For good.

***

Turned out, the people of Ocracoke were like a well-oiled platoon, ready for battle when it came to hurricanes.

"Just another day in the 'Coke," Molly said with a shrug after I met her and Jake at their home just a few hours later.

She'd kindly agreed to be my ride out of town, admitting that she'd already planned on dragging me out herself if I didn't come willingly. Honestly, Jake and Molly had been my source of sanity over the last few days. They'd even driven me up the coast for my first ever OB appointment.

Apparently, doctors took things a bit more seriously when you had both an IUD and a positive pregnancy test. The whole appointment had been borderline terrifying as the doctor said words like *miscarriage* and *high risk*, but then she'd given me a pat on my shoulder and tried to soothe my fears as she'd gone over all my options.

I'd decided to have the IUD removed, hoping to reduce the risk of miscarriage later on.

I'd left, wanting Taylor more than ever, despite the fact that he'd hurt me more than anyone.

"Aren't you scared?" I asked Molly, feeling kind of ill prepared with my small duffel bag and purse.

The rest of my luggage would be shipped by Molly when they returned.

Assuming they had something to return to.

"Of course we are, but if we let it get to us, we'd never be able to live here. Hurricanes and storms are just a part of life around here. Sometimes, they pass us by, and we can breathe a sigh of relief, and other times…well, they don't, and we have to do this."

And by this, they meant pack up all their valuables—including family pictures, jewelry, and anything else they didn't want to be swept away or lost—and simply walk away, hoping for the best.

And that was just their home.

That didn't even include the two businesses they were leaving behind.

"It just all seems so—"

"Hard?" Jake intervened, giving the tailgate one last shove to make sure the minivan was properly shut.

I nodded.

Leaning against the back, he looked back at his beautiful blue house and gave a warm smile. "I've lived all over the country," he said. "California, Chicago, and I traveled a bit, too. But nothing compares to here. And it's not the stunning views you get while enjoying a pint at Billy's or even the salty sea air I love when I take my morning runs. It's the people. My people. And, yeah, it sucks, having to pack all our shit up and leave the house we've built together, wondering if we'll ever see it again, but I know that when we come back, whatever we find, we'll all be in it together."

I swallowed hard, knowing, after this, I'd most likely never return to this island again. Because that was what us Harts did.

If it hurt, we avoided it.

And this island and all its memories hurt more than I could bear.

"You ready?" Jake asked, reaching out with his arms to grab my bag, but he stopped short, his eyes moving past me to the road beyond.

Tires crunched the gravel drive behind me, making the hairs on the back of my neck stand on edge.

My heart felt him before I even turned around.

Taylor's door pushed open and he stepped out, determination in his eyes as he stalked over. "You're coming with me," he demanded.

My eyes widened as my breath quickened. I tried to slow it, but I couldn't. "The hell I am."

Every step he took closer to me, I felt my resolve weakening.

And it pissed me off.

"Yes, you are. Get in the car, Lani."

"Only my friends can call me that," I spit out.

A menacing grin took hold of his lips as he grabbed my bag from my hands. "We were never friends," he reminded me.

"No, we definitely weren't. We were much better off as enemies."

He didn't wait for permission. He simply turned back toward his truck and tossed my bag behind the passenger seat. Then, he turned back and waited. "I'm not leaving this fucking island without you."

Letting out a frustrated huff, I gave Molly a parting look.

"Are you okay?" she asked. "Jake can force his hand, if you'd like. It might be kind of fun to see them wrestle."

She meant it mostly as a joke, but I knew if push came to shove, these two would go to blows for me.

The corner of my mouth turned upward, but I declined. "Thank you, but I've been avoiding this for too long as it is. He deserves to know, especially since I'm leaving."

She patted my shoulder and then pulled me into a hug, knowing I needed it. "Good luck."

"Thanks," I said before heading toward the truck and an impatient-looking Taylor.

After I hopped into the passenger seat, he joined me, putting the car in gear and pulling back onto the road.

"You going to wear that scowl on your face the entire car trip?" I asked, my arms firmly folded across my chest.

"You gonna bitch the entire time?" he countered.

"Well, seeing as how I didn't really get much of a choice in the matter, maybe." And then, for shits and giggles, I added, "But, then again, I haven't been getting much choice in a lot of things lately."

He didn't have a witty comeback for that one and remained silent the rest of the way out of town.

"How'd you know where to find me?" I asked as we coasted down Highway 12.

He kept his focus dead ahead. "It didn't take a genius to figure out who you'd turn to for a ride out of here." His fingers gripped the wheel hard and his jaw ticked with annoyance.

"Well, Molly is a reliable friend."

"Yeah, she is."

The traffic was heavy, everyone making a run for it at once. It made getting on the ferry a cumbersome task, but eventually, the line ambled forward, and we were parked in a sea of vehicles, waiting to move across the sound toward the mainland of North Carolina.

"I'm assuming you're meeting up with everyone else at the regular place?" I asked once he'd shut off the engine, and the silence had become too much to bear.

"You know about our meeting place?"

I smiled, glad to have the upper hand at least once. "Molly and Jake told me," I explained. "I was going with them, and then once the storm let up, they were planning on dropping me off at the airport."

His eyes finally met mine. "You're leaving?" he asked, his voice suddenly hoarse.

I looked away, tears prickling my vision. "There's no reason for me to stay," I simply said.

"No," he agreed quietly. "I guess there isn't."

CHAPTER FIFTEEN

Taylor

Coward.

That was what I was.

A fucking spineless coward.

I was pushing the woman I loved away, basically hand-delivering her to the airport with a giant sign on my forehead that said, *Don't come back*, thanks to the things I'd done over the last week.

Coward.

It was the only word to describe my actions.

My brother had been right.

I had issues.

Major ones. But they didn't center around my inability to love because of some hang-up with my dead father.

No, I'd gotten over that. With Lani, love was easy. So easy that I'd barely even registered the fall.

Until the morning in the kitchen.

I'd climbed down the steps and seen a future.

My future, if I wanted to take it.

She could be mine; I could be hers. Here on the island, just the two of us.

"Are you in or out?"

That was the question her father had asked me.

God, I wanted to be in.

In on breakfast and never-ending history lessons. In on stupid fall festivals and lazy nights on the couch.

I wanted to be so in that it hurt.

But a life on this island wasn't the life Lani was supposed to live. She was meant for more than these four square miles of nothing, and I knew that, if I let her stay, she'd regret it.

Just like I regretted never going to college and making something of my life.

Sure, it'd abated with time. Regret had turned into something sort of like acceptance, which had then morphed into a reasonable life.

But was it the life I would choose again, if given the chance to do it over?

I wanted Lani to have every chance.

So, I'd done the unthinkable. I'd done something stupid and rash, but it was the only way to guarantee she'd never give up on all those lofty dreams of hers.

I'd bought her damn hotel.

It'd turned out, saving her father's cell phone number had come in handy after all. It'd cost me almost every dime I had, including most of what I'd squired away to keep the family business afloat. When Dean saw our next financial statement he'd be furious, but at least, now, she would have a real future.

"So, we have a deal?" I said, every word coming from my mouth feeling like another betrayal. Another knife jabbed into my heart.

"Yes," Mr. Hart answered. "I'll sell you the hotel—for a hefty profit."

My teeth gritted. "And you'll give her the promotion?"

He let out a sigh. "I don't really see how this part of the deal benefits me."

"If she stays here, you'll lose her. For good. She'll give up everything, including her legacy. Her dreams."

"So, by buying my property, you're being the bigger man?"

"I'm simply giving her a chance."

"No," he argued. "It seems I am the one doing that, Mr. Sutherland. You're just breaking her heart."

"Will you give her the project or not?"

"The Chicago project will be hers," he confirmed. "It would be nice to not have Rebecca traveling back and forth so much."

I shook my head. "Happy doing business with you."

Jackass.

It was painful, more painful than I could comprehend, to know she'd be leaving this island, hating me. But, at least now, I knew, when I watched her go, she'd go with her dreams intact and her whole life ahead of her.

So, was I in?

Yeah, I'd always be in when it came to her.

But it sure as hell didn't feel good.

Especially since she hadn't spoken a word to me in nearly six hours.

We rolled up to the hotel that was the meeting place for many of the people in town during an evacuation. It brought a sense of peace to those who didn't have family to visit, and we could huddle together as a group while we prayed over our town and waited for the all clear to return.

"You going to buy this one, too?" Lani asked the second I parked, giving the well-known hotel name a once-over.

"Funny," I said through gritted teeth.

Guess I deserved that one.

Reaching back behind the seat, she grabbed her duffel and pushed open the door handle.

"Where do you think you're going?" I asked.

"To get a room," she said. "Did you think I'd be staying with you?"

Honestly, yeah, I'd kind of hoped.

"Make sure you give them the right name, *Pookie Bear*," I said with a bite.

"Oh, don't worry," she answered. "I wouldn't want to be confused with a snake. Oops, I mean a Sutherland."

I watched her leave, headed for the hotel lobby as I pounded the steering wheel with the palms of my hands.

Repeatedly.

It didn't help one bit to dampen my frustration.

But it passed the time, and by the time I was done beating the shit out of my car and headed into the lobby, Lani was on her way up to her room, doing her best to ignore me in the process.

Check-in was quick, and soon, I had a room of my own.

I took the elevator up to my room, trying to forget the last time I had been in one. I remembered thinking, as I'd held Lani in my arms, her tears soaking my shirt, there was no possible way I could ever hurt someone like her father had hurt her.

And yet, four weeks later, here we were.

With the small backpack of clothes I'd packed on my shoulder, I rode the elevator to my designated floor and walked the short distance to my room, only to stop short when I saw a familiar face standing next to it.

"Need a hand?" I asked, seeing her fiddling with her key card.

Frustrated, she looked over at me, her shoulders slumping at the mere sight of me. "Really? You couldn't be on a different floor? They had to put you right next door?"

I shrugged. "Sorry. I didn't pick the room."

"Of course you didn't."

I looked at her still standing by the door. "So, do you need help?"

The question seemed to stir something inside her. "No," she answered. "I don't need anything from you."

I let out a huff, stepping up beside her to my own door,

and simply shook my head. "Well, you know where to find me."

My key worked fine, the green light flashing, and I turned the handle, stepping into the nondescript room. I'd no sooner thrown my backpack on the bed before a loud knock sounded at my door.

Pulling it open, I had to step aside as Lani pushed her way in, her face filled with anger and frustration.

"Why'd you do it, Taylor? Why?! I've been racking my brain for days, trying to figure out why you'd go through such lengths to woo me, seduce me, make me feel—" She caught herself. "Anyway, why'd you do it?"

My arms folded across my chest as she paced in front of me. "I wasn't sure you'd pick the right design. I had to put the town first."

"Bullshit!" she shouted. "That's complete bullshit, and you know it! You could have bought that hotel at any given point, long before I came into town. So, why now, Taylor? Was it fun to string me along? Or maybe you were just tired of blondes? Figured you'd try something different for a change? Did you and my dad have a nice laugh over that one?"

"You were going to stay if I didn't!" I roared, my chest heaving from the effort. "You were going to stay." The words echoed from my lips, quieter this time. "And I couldn't let you abandon your dreams for a worthless nobody like me. So, I made a deal with your father."

"You talked to my father?"

"I knew you'd go if I bought that stupid hotel, but I had to make sure you had something waiting for you."

"What?"

"He'll give you what you want now, Lani. A promotion, the company—everything. You don't have to prove yourself anymore."

Her eyes met mine, a heady mixture of disbelief and pain. "So, you ran." It wasn't a question. She turned her head, shaking it in disbelief. "Molly was right. Men are so frustrating. You really did run."

Silence fell as she continued to stalk back and forth, gathering her thoughts. Finally, she turned to me, her gaze a powerful blend of emotions. "Dreams change, Taylor," she said. "You would have known that if you'd given me the common courtesy to ask what mine were, but instead, you decided for me, refusing to give me the right to think for myself."

"I..."

She was right. All the regret I still carried from the life I'd been denied so long ago, I'd put that on her. It wasn't her regret I had been worried about.

It was mine.

And it was time to let go.

"Do you want to know my dreams?" I asked.

Her gaze was so full of mistrust that it made my heart ache.

"Yes," she said, her body stilling for the first time since she'd walked through the door.

"I want a life filled with happiness," I said. "One where I look back and I feel nothing but fulfillment and wonder. I want someone by my side that is strong-willed and puts me in my place when I need a good ass-kicking. I want that woman to be you, Lani."

Her breath caught. "What else?"

"I want you to turn that hotel into everything you imagined it could be, and I want us to run it side by side."

"But it's yours now."

"No," I corrected. "It's always been yours."

"I can't pay you for it," she said. "The money I have, it's not my own."

"It doesn't matter. I'll gift it to you right now if that's what you want."

"You what?" Her voice ricocheted across the small space. "Are you crazy?"

"Probably, especially considering I used the business as collateral."

"Oh my God," she moaned. She grabbed her abdomen and looked like she was going to be physically ill.

"Are you okay?"

"No! You bought my hotel and now there's a storm coming that could obliterate it! Do you see the problem here? We could be destitute."

I smiled. *She had said we, hadn't she?*

Stepping closer, I tested the waters to see how hot they still were, sliding a tentative hand around her waist. When it didn't get slapped away, I pulled her close, feeling her melt against me.

Jesus, I'd missed this.

"You're an idiot," she whimpered against my shoulder.

"Yeah, but I'm your idiot," I said, lifting her chin upward. "We'll figure it out. Promise. Think of it as an adventure, for just the two of us. You, me, and our hotel."

Her eyes widened, her cheeks ballooned, and then she bolted to the bathroom and spilled her guts into the toilet.

I tried to push my way in, but she continually kept shoving me back out, saying, "Get out! You do not want to see this!"

I finally managed to get in and calm her down. She didn't let me near her though until I went and retrieved her toothbrush from her things so she could do some damage control, as she'd called it. I got her upright, sitting down on the edge of the bathtub. I wiped her forehead with a damp cloth.

"Was it something I said?"

Her face blanched, making me wonder if I needed to clear the room again.

"No," she said. "Well, kind of."

My brow lifted.

"All those dreams of yours? They're my dreams, too. I don't want to work for my father anymore. But the hotel? It won't exactly just be you and me."

"Oh?"

"I'm pregnant."

This time, I was the one who felt queasy as the room sort of started wobbling, my world shifting from the news I'd been given.

"You're pregnant?" I had to say it out loud for it to be true.

My eyes went to her stomach, like I was looking for some sort of physical sign, but it was just as flat as it had been a moment earlier.

I was going to be a father.

Tears stung my eyes before I realized she was rambling, trying to apologize for the gift she'd just given me.

"It's my fault," she said. "I thought my IUD was still good, but—"

I placed a single finger against her lips, and she quieted instantly.

"It's the best news I've ever heard."

"Really?" she said, a sob escaping her lungs.

"Really," I confirmed as I wiped the tear that had trickled down her cheek.

She did the same to me, running her fingers across the stubble that had grown along my chin.

"I like the beard." She smiled, cupping my face in her hand as she gave me an appreciative look.

"Yeah?" I grinned. "It's called *I just gave up the woman I love and can't stop drinking* look."

Laughing, she briefly kissed me. "I think we should rename it to *I stupidly gave up the woman I love but she wouldn't go, and now she's forcing me to keep this beard* look."

"Kind of a mouthful, but—"

Her eyes glimmered, and it was that moment that both of us realized just how long it had been since we'd been in each other's arms because half a second later, our lips were locked, and I was hoisting her up in the air to carry her toward the bed.

"Can you—I mean, will it hurt the baby?"

She laughed. "Do you think I'd be ripping open your jeans like this if it could?"

"Good point."

Clothes fell to the floor as I found my home, my center, my world, all wrapped up in her arms.

"I love you, Lani," I said as our bodies joined together once again.

"I love you, too, Taylor," she echoed back.

And we spent the rest of the night making up for lost time.

***

Waiting out a storm was brutal.

Waiting out a storm while you were far away from home was even worse.

I was used to the abuse, having evacuated more than my fair share of times over my lifetime on the island.

But, for Lani, this was definitely a first.

"Do you think it's okay?" she asked, watching the news from her perch on the edge of the bed, a place she'd made her home over the last week. "I mean, can't they just give me one shot of Ocracoke? Just one? They keep mentioning damage in the Outer Banks, but they don't say where! I need to know where, stupid weatherman!"

I slid up behind her, straddling her from behind. Running my hands over her shoulders, I proceeded to massage her tense muscles, hoping to force her into relaxing.

It seemed to be working, as her body began to melt into mine, and I inhaled the citrusy smell of her shampoo clinging to her hair.

"We'll find out soon enough," I said. "The storm has already passed. We're just waiting for the all clear."

"All clear? What does that even mean?"

I smiled, pulling her already-tense body back to mine. Pregnant Lani was a high-strung Lani.

Jake had already informed me that these were all good

signs—the mood swings, the extreme nausea. It showed the pregnancy and the baby were strong.. Although the IUD had been removed, there was still risk of miscarriage and a whole host of other things I didn't want to think about. She could have all the damn mood swings she wanted if it meant her and our baby stayed healthy.

I was tough; I could take it.

"They just need to make sure the roads are passable. It takes a while for the water to recede. And, if there are places that washed away—"

She let out a frustrated sigh. "I hate waiting."

"I do, too."

We all did. We'd done our best to keep busy, gathering together for group activities when we could, but even then, all anyone could talk about was home. No one truly knows what a hurricane is like until they've been down this road, and felt the agony of an evacuation.

"Does anyone have any updates?"

"Are the phone lines up yet?"

"Did anyone see any photos online? On the news?"

The waiting was getting to everyone.

What we did know was that the hurricane hit at a Category Two. Thankfully, it hadn't gained any speed or hit us any harder than that, but still.

But a hurricane was a hurricane.

And the specific damage to Ocracoke was still unknown.

We'd seen footage that made me nervous…washed out roads, broken power lines, damaged homes. I tried to keep my fears at bay because scaring Lani was the last thing I wanted.

I was keeping a good game face on, but inside, I was terrified of what we were going home to.

Jumping up off the bed, I said, "Hey, why don't we go for a walk?"

She was staring at the floor rather than the TV—my first

clue that something was wrong. Finally, her big brown eyes met mine. "Taylor, I'm scared."

Kneeling down beside her, I looked up and grabbed her hand. "About what? The hurricane? Us? The baby?"

She let out a gentle laugh, a single tear falling down her cheek. "Way to make a pregnant woman's heart rate jump."

I grinned. "Sorry."

She squeezed my hand and took a deep breath. "What if we fail? What if I fail and the hotel is a giant flop? Worse yet, what if it doesn't and it's a huge success and I become just like—"

"You will never be like your father."

"But how do you know?"

"I know," I said firmly, remembering the nonchalant way he'd handed over his daughter's hotel, his biggest concern being his fiancée's travel schedule. "You are nothing like your father."

"It's not just about us anymore," she said, placing a hand on her belly.

Smiling, I settled my fingers over hers. "That is why we won't fail," I promised.

A gentle knock sounded at our door, and I gave her a pat on the knee before rising to my feet to answer it.

Dean was on the other side, looking uncomfortable.

We hadn't exactly made up since our major blowout in the office. For the last two weeks, we'd done an amazing job of avoiding each other—sitting on opposite ends of the table at group dinners, making sure we were in different groups for outings. Our mom was thoroughly disgusted with us and our petty childish behavior.

"Hey," I said.

"Hey," he answered back.

Silence settled between us before I heard a very intentional throat being cleared. Dean rolled his eyes as I leaned my head out the door, finding Cora in the hallway.

She waved. "Hi, Taylor," she said, looking highly embarrassed.

"Hi."

She gave her husband a death stare, her eyes going wide and her head tilting at an odd angle. Dean seemed to grumble a little deep in his throat before finally turning back toward me.

"I wanted to tell you that the all clear has been given," he said.

"Oh," I said, nodding. "Uh, thanks."

Cora cleared her throat again.

"And," he said, his throat working overtime, "I wanted to apologize for being an"—he looked over to Cora once again—"overbearing asshole."

A rumble of a laugh escaped my lips.

I waited for him to go on, but then I felt my own woman slide up behind me, and I knew my upper hand was gone.

Especially since I hadn't told him about the hotel yet.

"It's cool," I said. "Really. And honestly, you were right. I needed to work through some things."

"Yeah?" he said, sounding pleased with himself.

"Yeah," I answered, hoping to postpone the hotel discussion until later. Like maybe next year. "But we'll talk more later."

"So, you're not going to tell me how you bought a hotel without consulting me?"

Busted.

My eyes widened as I heard Cora laugh outside in the hallway.

"How'd you—"

"Public record, dipshit," he growled.

"Oh, right."

His eyes narrowed as I waited for the shit-storm I knew I deserved.

"Just don't screw it up," he said before walking away.

"That's it?" I hollered down the hall.

"I want a discount," he hollered back. "A big one. And free babysitting forever."

Laughing, I turned toward Lani, feeling like a giant weight had been lifted off my shoulders. "Are you ready to go home?" I asked.

"As ready as I'll ever be," she said, her nervousness bleeding through.

"Whatever we find, we'll deal with it together," I said.

"Together," she confirmed.

We drove back to town in a tight group, a caravan of strength.

I held on to Lani's hand as we passed the Welcome sign before cars began to disperse, each in different directions toward home.

Who knows what they would find?

Lani and I headed for the marina first.

My house was the least of our concerns.

It was eerie how quiet it was.

The birds had even picked up and left town before the approaching storm.

"Oh God," Lani whispered under her breath as we drew closer.

Cleanup crews had done what they could, clearing downed trees in the roads to make them passable, but the rest? The rest was up to us.

The storm had pushed the sand up high onto the banks of the bay, making a mockery of the sandbags we'd placed around the office and the hotel.

"Did you do that?" she asked, pointing to the sandbags and the crisscrossed tape I'd managed to throw up on the windows.

I nodded.

Her face softened.

"I don't think it helped much though," I said as we pulled

up to the parking lot, not bothering to find a space. It was so littered with debris that I wasn't sure I could make out the white lines anyway.

"We'll check out the hotel first and then go to the office later."

"Okay."

Walking up to the front door, I held out my hand for the key. She gave it willingly.

"If I tell you to get out, you get out. Understand? If there's anything dangerous or—"

"I understand," she said, not arguing at all, her eyes already spotting several broken windows.

Sliding the key into the lock, I twisted.

And then I pulled.

"Need a hand?" she asked, making me smile. "Sometimes, you just need a professional."

"Very funny," I said, handing over the key.

"It's actually really tricky. It took me days to—"

Her words stopped instantly the moment the door swung open… and tears began to flow instead.

Inside, we could see the full extent of the damage brought by the storm.

Water and structural damage, windows gone.

You name it, and the storm had taken it.

"Taylor," she cried as I pulled her into my arms, "what are we going to do?"

"I don't know," I answered truthfully, looking around at our giant mess. "But we'll figure it out," I told her, needing to hear the words as much as she did.

Somehow, we'd figure it out.

Thankfully, my house being a few blocks inland, seemed to have escaped the brunt of the attack from the storm, and for the night, we had a place to stay. We settled into bed, and I held her close to my chest, vowing to do anything I could to make it right.

This woman and the child growing inside her were my life now.

And I'd protect them, no matter what.

Waking up early the next morning, I did something I'd thought I'd never do.

I made breakfast. For a woman.

Sadly, it wasn't quite the breakfast I was known for, and when Lani came downstairs to find the table adorned with candles and dry Cheerios, luckily, she found the gesture charming and endearing.

"I promise, when I have time to pick up groceries—assuming I can get to a grocery store sometime soon—I'll make you something amazing."

"This is amazing," she argued. "Besides, with this morning sickness, I'm not sure I can stomach much more than this."

"Well then, consider this done all on purpose."

She laughed, taking a few nibbles of her cereal before her face fell.

"What is it?" I asked, rushing to her side. "Do you need to throw up again?" I'd gotten used to her sudden bathroom jaunts.

"No, but the thought of our crumbling hotel isn't helping. I think back to how it was a few days ago before the storm, and in comparison, it was actually kind of luxurious."

My head fell. "I know," I said. "But we'll get it back to where we want it. It's our dream, remember?"

"Yeah"—a hint of a smile peeked through her sullen expression—"it is."

Rising up onto my feet, I grabbed my keys, the jingle catching her attention. "I'm going to head over there now. You just stay here and rest."

"I'm not staying here while you go work yourself to the bone!"

"Babe—"

"Don't *babe* me!"

"You're pregnant. I can't let you."

She folded her arms across her chest and rose to her feet, giving me a single raised eyebrow. "I am not the first pregnant woman on the planet, Taylor."

"No," I answered, crossing my own arms over my chest. "But you're the first woman pregnant by me, and like hell am I going to let you near a building that could be infested with mold and God knows what else!"

She scrunched her nose, looking thoughtful. "Okay, that's fair. But I can't sit here all day and I won't let you do all the work by yourself."

I tapped my foot against the hardwood floor.

"Remember, compromise?"

I let out a frustrated sigh. "Fine, but outside work only. And if you come in the building, you wear a mask. Got it?"

She smiled, clearly happy with her win. "Got it."

"I'm never going to win a single argument for the rest of my life, am I?"

She draped her arms around my shoulders. "Did you really ever win before?" she asked.

When I squeezed her ass, she let out a little squeak before running upstairs to get dressed, leaving me with a shit-eating grin on my face. I felt like the luckiest man on earth.

Within fifteen minutes, we were on our way to the marina, ready to conquer what was sure to be days and days of cleanup.

Unfortunately, the Sutherland office hadn't weathered the storm all that well either. Although it seemed to be structurally sound, thanks to years of meticulous upkeep on our part, there was some serious water damage and several broken windows.

Just more to add to the long list of things to get done. If I tried to think about it too much, the list started to become overwhelming.

So, I was taking it one step at a time.

With a baby coming, all my finances tied up in these two buildings, and no income for the foreseeable future due to widespread damage all over the coast, one step at a time was really the only way of handling it.

Otherwise, I'd go insane.

"Taylor!" Lani exclaimed, making my heart leap into my throat. "Look!"

My eyes went wild, trying to spot what new and dangerous foe we were about to meet. I followed the line of her arm until it reached out toward the hotel where there was a large crowd gathered.

"What are they doing?" I asked, pulling off onto the side of the road.

Squinting, I tried to get a better look and recognized almost everyone. Jake and Molly, Dean and Cora. Aiden and Millie, my mom and even Sierra and her surly looking grandfather.

Does he have a weapon?

"They're working," Lani said, her voice becoming hoarse. "On the hotel."

Sure enough, that was exactly what they were all doing. Several people were shoveling up sand and glass, and others were removing downed tree limbs. Millie was painting the numbers onto a new mailbox that had just been installed.

Stepping out of the car, I took Lani's hand and walked up to our friends and family, who greeted us with open arms.

"What are you guys doing here?" I asked, my voice rough from emotion.

"After we got home, I took a drive around the island and saw the damage," Jake explained. "I knew you'd need the help."

"But your own homes..." Lani said, struggling to speak.

"They can wait," Millie answered, taking her hand. "In this town, we take care of our own. And you are one of us now, Lani. You both are." She pulled us into a hug, and tears stung my eyes.

"Okay, well, before my brother loses his shit, let's get back to work," Dean said, giving me a wink.

I silently thanked him, unsure of how long I'd be able to compose myself.

I really didn't want to boohoo in front of the whole damn town.

Lani's arms slid around my waist as everyone went back to work.

"We're going to make it," she said, her head resting against my chest.

"Yeah"—I smiled—"we are."

And, as I looked out at my family and friends, working hard to clean up the town we all loved so much, I knew without a shadow of a doubt that this was where I was supposed to be.

I used to believe, like a good story, love always had an end.

But Lani had shown me that the best stories in life never truly ended.

They just gave way to more.

More dreams, more adventures, and yeah, a lot more love.

EPILOGUE

Leilani

ONE YEAR LATER

"Today is the day!" I said to myself as I took a deep, cleansing breath in and out of my lungs.

Over the past year, I'd found myself saying this sentence quite a lot.

Today is the day I become a wife.

Today is the day we become parents.

But this day?

On this day, we were opening Windows Hotel and Spa.

It'd been a long year, full of amazing highs and a few rocky lows as well. The structure of the hotel had sustained more damage than we'd anticipated—that, or it had been in bad shape to begin with. Either way, we'd had to tear down much of the original building and start over.

It wasn't until the bulldozers had arrived that morning that I realized just how attached I'd become to that stupid old building, and I couldn't stop the tears from falling as they had taken it down piece by piece.

Thankfully, insurance had covered a lot of damage, and we had been able to start anew, bringing back most of what we'd lost. Then, things had begun to roll right along.

Until the day I had woken up with blood on the sheets and had to be rushed to the hospital.

The word *miscarriage* had hung in the air as Taylor and I waited for the tech to find a viable heartbeat for the baby we'd both fallen so hopelessly in love with. When that first little *thump-thump* had filled the room, I hadn't thought I'd ever hear anything sweeter in my whole life.

From that moment on, my activity level had been restricted to desk work, and the pressure for Taylor to finish the hotel had only doubled. He'd worked endlessly, giving fishing tours during the day and putting up drywall at night.

And, somehow, in the middle of all that hard work, he'd still managed to get down on one of those tired knees and ask me to marry him.

Of course I'd said yes.

We had gotten married just days before baby Matthew was born. We'd stood on the beach, barefoot, surrounded by family and friends, as our unborn son kicked his approval deep in my womb. Taylor had cupped my cheek and vowed to be my lifelong partner, promising to always make me laugh and never make me cry.

I'd vowed to be the best wife and mother I could.

It was a promise I held dearly to my heart.

I hadn't come to Ocracoke looking for a family or a home, but that is exactly what I'd found.

"Hey, Aunt Lani?" Lizzie called out, peeking her head into the freshly painted doors of the hotel lobby.

I'd been hiding in here for the last several minutes, trying to calm the last bit of my nerves, but it seemed my smart little niece had found me.

Although, at a whopping eight years old, she wasn't looking so little anymore.

"Yeah, sweetheart," I said. "Over here!"

She found me standing by the large window that over-looked the bay. It was the one major change we'd made to the lobby, knowing it would make a huge visual statement to the guests upon their arrival.

"Hey," she said with a big smile, giving me a hug in the process. "There is a man here to see you."

"Okay." I grinned, loving the yin and yang of this girl.

One minute, she could be lecturing you on quantum physics, and the next, she'd be a perfectly normal kid, complaining about video game levels and how lame it was that she wasn't allowed to be on Snapchat yet.

"Do you know what his name is? Or what he might need? There are a lot of people here today and—"

"Hello, Leilani."

The deep, familiar voice stopped me dead in my tracks.

It'd been a solid year since I heard from the man I called father by name only. The last correspondence we'd had was a formal letter I'd sent him, letting him know I no longer needed his trust fund or the job he'd so benevolently blessed me with.

Since then, I'd heard through the grapevine that his wedding to Becky had been the talk of the company, although no one had actually been invited. And, although Piper was now out on her own, having started an up-and-coming interior design business six months ago, she regularly supplied me with Hart gossip from Hawaii.

Unfortunately, she'd failed to catch this little detail.

It would have been nice to have a heads-up that my father was coming.

"Hi, Dad," I said, feeling suddenly frozen in place.

Lizzie's hands patted my waist, and it was then that I realized she was still here.

"Why don't you go find Taylor and see if he needs any last-minute help with setting up for the ribbon-cutting ceremony?"

She nodded before hopping off toward the door.

Silence settled around the two of us after her departure as my father began to take a slow stroll around the lobby. With his hands neatly tucked behind his back, he checked out every detail—from the beautifully polished floor to the subtle color palette that offset the dark wood tones and vibrant green plants.

"You've done a good job here," he finally announced, giving me an approving nod.

It was the first compliment he'd ever given me.

I would feel proud of myself if I wasn't already.

"Thank you," I answered.

He continued his perusal of the room, ending in front of the large window, his eyes steady on the gentle waves rolling up to the shore.

"Why are you here?" I asked, walking up to stand next to him.

His gaze turned sideways. "I'd like to re-offer your job to you."

I sputtered out something between a laugh and a cough. Matthew had made the same sort of noise this morning, right before he upchucked breast milk all over me.

"What?" I said. "Are you kidding? Dad, I have a family now. Or did you not get the memo briefing from your robot assistant?"

I saw a brief hesitancy in his eyes. *Was that remorse?*

"I know, Leilani. I'm not asking you to move. You can stay here." He swallowed hard before continuing, "I want you to take the role you were supposed to have in our company. Come back. It's where you belong."

"And how does Becky feel about this?" I couldn't resist the jab. Honestly, I couldn't.

"I don't want to leave our family legacy to my wife," he said. "I want to leave it to my daughter."

I turned away, my heart racing.

It was everything I'd wanted…once upon a time.

My father's approval.

The birthright I'd been denied.

All I had to do was say yes.

"No," I answered fiercely.

Turning back around, I met his disappointed gaze.

"No?" he echoed.

"You want a daughter to leave your company to, but ever since I can remember, Dad, all I ever really wanted from you was a father."

"Maybe we can both get what we want?"

I forced a smile, sadness tugging at the corners of my lips, disappointed he was still willing to make a deal when it came to our relationship. "I already have everything I want right here, Dad."

It was getting late, and I had a ribbon to cut. Turning toward the door, I left him standing there, watching the waves tumble in. But, before I left, I offered him one last breadcrumb of hope.

He was my father after all.

"When you decide you want more than an heir and you find yourself wanting a family instead, you know where to find me. I love you, Daddy."

Stepping out into the gorgeous autumn day, I felt a wide grin spread across my face as my husband and infant son came up the walkway.

"You look happy," Taylor said. "Lizzie said someone came to visit you?"

I nodded, giving each of them a kiss on the cheek. "Yeah, but I took care of it."

I'd fill him in on my father's offer later.

And my refusal.

No need to send my overprotective husband on a full-blown manhunt now. Not when we had more important things to do.

"Ready?" he asked, as he handed our son to his mother, who was beaming up at both of us with pride.

He reached down to pick up the largest, most ridiculous pair of scissors I'd ever seen. Looking out at the crowd that had gathered, a crowd filled with our family and friends, I nodded, my excitement building. We stepped up to the podium, excited to start the next big adventures in our lives.

"Let's do this!"

After the tragic death of her husband five years ago, Marin Mendez returns to Ocracoke for closure. Instead, she runs headfirst into Macon Green, a small-town cop with a larger-than-life ego…

The Secrets We Keep… coming February 20th. 2024.

Turn the page for an excerpt…

THE SECRETS WE KEEP
PROLOGUE

It was so damn hot.

I brushed the sweat off my brow, wishing like hell I had chosen to take my lunch break somewhere air-conditioned rather than in the belly of my cruiser.

But as much as I hated the heat, I loved the silence.

Or at least I had enjoyed it—for about five whole minutes.

The waves lapped at the shore as another group of eager tourists disembarked from the ferry. I watched as each car rolled off, their wheels hitting the hot pavement as they made their way onto Highway 12.

They all tried to pretend like they didn't see me, but I knew better.

Everyone always recognized the standard blue and white hues that embodied Ocracoke's patrol cars. When I had been young, the sight of it alone would have made me stop in my tracks.

Of course, in my family, it was never me they had chased after.

But that was a long time ago, and now, I was the one behind the wheel.

The tourists continued their way down the highway, every

one of them driving with extra caution, hoping to avoid my scrutiny.

They had nothing to worry about. I wasn't here for them anyway.

Looking back at the water, I gazed across the bright blue sea toward the other side. I tried to see the mainland, so far out in the distance, away from all these tourists and their minivans.

Away from this island and all its bullshit.

But all I saw was water. It was all I ever saw. Nothing but fucking water.

Letting out a sigh, I took another bite of the turkey and rye I'd bought from a local place down the street and tried to settle my thoughts.

But growing up in a house as tense as mine, I'd never learned the subtle art of relaxation, and on top of that, my mind was all over the place.

I'd known moving back here would be an adjustment.

But lately, it had been like living in my own personal prison.

After I'd graduated from high school, the military had seemed like an obvious choice. It gave me the opportunity to leave Ocracoke and opened my eyes to a world I would have never seen otherwise.

I thought pivoting into the police force would do the same, and it did for a while, but when I was stationed in nearby Charlotte and my chief mentioned a position had opened up in my hometown, I hesitated.

I'd grown up here. I knew what it was like.

But I'd come back anyway.

For a while, it'd been good.

Real good.

But now, here I was, staring out at the ocean, eating a dry sandwich, wondering what the rest of the world was doing, and counting down the hours until my shift was up.

Usually, the busy summer months kept me fairly occupied. But lately, even the tourists had been on their best behavior.

Everyone was thankful for a safe town, but the days were really starting to drag.

So far today, I'd given a couple of warnings to a few kids who had been cruising down the main drag in a golf cart they were clearly not old enough to be in. I'd received a call from a local woman, complaining about a renter's dog and the unwelcome presents it was leaving in her yard.

I'd been back for two years, and every day was pretty much the same.

We had our fair share of hurricanes. But, aside from that, nothing bad ever happened in Ocracoke.

I thought it would be the perfect place for us.

But you know what they say about coming home again…

I watched the last of the tourists head down the highway toward the shops and restaurants and wondered how it would feel to drive down those streets and not know all its dirty little secrets. To get off that ferry and learn about the history and beauty of this place without feeling the burden of keeping it safe.

But I was not a tourist. I was a native, and when I looked around Ocracoke, all I saw were memories and regret.

I opened a bag of chips and started to pull a handful out when, out of the corner of my eye, I saw a familiar car pull into the lot and park.

Well, the word *park* might not be the correct choice. The car had sort of haphazardly scooted into a parking spot, barely making it between the lines, before coming to an abrupt halt.

I watched with a curious gaze as a man I recognized from town got out and started to fiddle with his keys. He looked down as if he'd never seen them before, going through each of them, one by one.

Finally, he picked the one he wanted, holding it out in front of him, inspecting it for much too long.

What the hell is he doing?

He turned back toward his car, and his hand moved toward the door handle. He shoved the key in, a vain attempt to lock it, but it wouldn't budge.

"Wrong key, asshat," I muttered as I watched him try again and fail again.

I grumbled under my breath, knowing it was now time for me to intervene. Setting the remnants of my lunch aside, I let out a groan and pushed the door open.

This guy was a friend of my dad, and while, in most families, that might make this a pleasant exchange, in mine, it just made it fucking awkward.

I'd said I was bored, but this was not what I'd had in mind.

Stepping out of the car, I stretched to my full height.

My mom always said she had no idea where my six-foot-four frame had come from. Both she and my dad were on the shorter side, and I never knew if she was trying to tell me something by that or if she was just making idle conversation.

Like with a lot of things having to do with my parents, I'd chosen not to ask.

I made a point of shutting the car door with a bit of force, hoping the sound would alert him of my presence. I didn't like sneaking up on people if I didn't have to.

It seemed to work. His eyes turned and found mine, and although he tried to hide it, I saw them widen ever so slightly.

"Hey, Raymond," I said, nodding my head in his direction.

"Oh, hey, Macon. Um, Green—I mean, Captain Green."

For the older folks who had been around since I had been a kid, they never knew how to address me. Some still called me by my first name. Others tried to show me respect and called me by my official title. I honestly couldn't give two shits what they called me as long as they didn't end up in the back of my cruiser.

Unfortunately for this guy, he had done just that on

multiple occasions, and I was afraid he was about to get another stamp on that imaginary frequent flyer card he seemed to be working on.

I folded my arms across my broad chest as his eyes tried to avoid mine. "Saw you having a bit of trouble with your keys. Figured I'd come over and see if you needed some help. You haven't been drinking again, have you?"

I'd learned to not beat around the bush with Ray.

"Oh, no, Macon. I'm clean," he assured me. "Been so for a long while."

I gave him an appraising look that told him I wasn't so sure I believed him. "So, what's with the keys?" I asked, and then I pointed toward the car with my right hand. "And the shoddy parking job?"

"Oh, well, you know how it is. Dang car has been giving me trouble for weeks. Couldn't get the thing started, and now, I'm running late."

"Late?"

He motioned toward the ferry.

I nodded, remembering he had been hired as a captain a while back. My dad had been a captain once. I still remembered the look on his face when he'd told me the good news.

"Things are gonna be different for us, Macon. You just wait and see."

He was fired four weeks later.

Things were not different. They never were.

"You sure it's just the keys?" I asked, giving him the chance to be honest.

I knew he'd said he was clean, but I'd rather have him tell me he was drunk now so I could drive him to the local AA meeting than find out about it later and have to take him to the station.

"Just a rough day," he said before adding with a bit of hesitance, "I'm sure you understand."

My jaw ticced. "What is that supposed to mean?"

His face blanched as he took a fearful step back. "Nothing,

Macon. Really. It's just with your wife—ex-wife, I mean," he stammered, as I stared him down. "And the sheriff being on their honeymoon. I thought—"

Thankfully his words were cut short by the sound of static on my radio, followed by a very convenient way out of this conversation for Raymond.

"Unit 2, this is dispatch. Can you please provide your current 20?"

Raymond looked at me and then toward the ferry while my mind was still hovering around that comment, he made about Kristy.

Did everyone know they were on their honeymoon this week?

I looked up at Raymond, noticing the way he looked at me.

Of course, they did.

This fucking town and its fucking gossip.

I let out a frustrated sigh, rubbing a hand over my face. I didn't want to deal with any of this today.

You don't have to stay…

"Better hurry up then. You don't want to be any later than you already are."

He visibly relaxed, his head bobbing up and down in agreement. "Will do!" he said adamantly as he scurried off.

I didn't want to deal with anyone and their bullshit today.

"Oh, and, Ray?" I hollered.

He turned, his eyes wide again.

"Bring that car round my place soon," I said. "I'll take a look at it for you."

He hesitated but nodded before turning back around.

As I grabbed my radio and responded to our dispatcher, I watched Raymond board the ferry, and my eyes drifted back to his car.

Why do I feel like I just made a huge mistake?

PRE-ORDER NOW

ACKNOWLEDGMENTS

This August, I hit the big five. Five years as a published writer. It still blows my mind to even type that sentence. Looking back at everything I've accomplished, I know I couldn't have gotten here if not for the support of everyone around me.

My biggest support system has been and always will be my husband and kids. These three motivate me, inspire me and are my unending source of joy in this world. I love you guys.

Jill Sava — Thank you for everything you do.

Ami Waters – I love you. That's all.

Jovana Shirley—Thank you for another beautifully edited book.

To my beta readers, Katy Nielsen, Carla VanZandt and Jill Sava, thank you for once again being my guinea pigs.

And once again, thanks to Katy Nielsen for proofing. You're an angel.

Berg's Book Reviewers – Thank you guys! You are awesome!

Berg's Bibliophiles – I love you crazy ladies!

Bloggers – Thank you for all that you do!!

READERS—As always, thank you a hundred times over.

ABOUT THE AUTHOR

J.L. Berg is the USA Today bestselling author of the Ready Series, the Lost & Found series, and many more. Originally from California, she now resides in central Virginia with her high school sweetheart, two children, and three dogs. When she's not writing, she enjoys spending time with her family or indulging in her love for Doctor Who. J.L. Berg is represented by Jill Marsal of Marsal Lyon Literary Agency, LLC. For the latest book updates, audio news, and more, be sure to visit her website.